Book Seven
Of
The Commitment Series

B

A BADGER BLISS BOOK

By

KAREN D. BADGER

DEDICATION

I dedicate this book to families everywhere, but especially to my two sons, Heath Louis Badger and Dane Andrew Badger who are the role models for two of the children in this series. These two boys have been the source of my greatest worries and my greatest joys and pride throughout their childhoods. They are largely responsible for my very close friendship with Miss Clairol, I might add! We have had our own share of tailspins over the years, but we always found the strength to pull the nose up before we crashed.

Heater and Dane-o, thank you for your unconditional love and acceptance over the past 30+ years as our lives transitioned into what it is today. I love you with everything that I am, and despite the trials and tribulations of raising children, I would do it all over again.

I love you, my sons.

Mom

ALSO WRITTEN BY KAREN D. BADGER AND AVAILABLE FROM BADGER BLISS BOOKS:

ON A WING AND A PRAYER
YESTERDAY ONCE MORE
THE BLUE FEATHER
ALL MY TOMORROWS
1140 RUE ROYALE

The Billie/Cat Commitment Series:
IN A FAMILY WAY
UNCHAINED MEMORIES
HAPPY CAMPERS
COLLECTIVE IDENTITY
SWEET ANGEL
RELATIVE-LY SPEAKING
TAILSPIN

www.badgerblissbooks.com

Book Seven
Of
The Commitment Series

B

A BADGER BLISS BOOK

By

KAREN D. BADGER

TAILSPIN

Cover design by Karen D. Badger

A Badger Bliss Book
Published by Badger Bliss Books
Georgia, VT 05468

www.badgerblissbooks.com

Print book ISBN 13: 978-1-945761-22-5
Print Book ISBN 10: 1-945761-22-9
Ebook ISBN 13: 978-1-945761-23-2
Ebook ISBN 10: 1-945761-23-7

First Edition, December, 2017

Printed in the United States of America and in the United Kingdom

ACKNOWLEDGMENTS

I am blessed and honored to have a fantastic group of beta readers and editors…Carol Poynor (Chief Eagle Eye), Chris Parsons (our friend from across the pond), my 83-year-old mom, Ellie Atherton (my number one fan), and my loving wife, Barb Sawyer (aka, Bliss), to name a few. You all bring so much to the quality of the story…not to mention the reputation of the author – LOL! Without you all, I would look like a literary idiot! Seriously, though, I appreciate each and every one of you. Thank you for all you do!

I also want to thank my sons and grandkids for providing me with endless fodder to use in this series...and to my childhood friends for helping me to create memories of the adventures we embarked on as children. If our moms only knew...just sayin'!

CHAPTER 1

"Do you see them?" Cat strained to see over the heads of the crowd at the airport. As usual, her short stature put her at a disadvantage.

Billie scanned the area until she caught sight of corn silk yellow hair atop the head of a tall, slender young man. "There they are." She reached for Cat's hand and drew her through the crowd waiting at the gate.

Billie waived excitedly. "Seth…kids! Over here."

A broad grin broke out across boy-man features as Seth noticed his mother. He took his little sister's hand and shuffled her along in front of him while keeping a watchful eye on the young lady who walked by his side. "Come on, Tara, keep up. I don't want to lose you in this crowd."

Tara clamped down on his arm to avoid being separated from her siblings.

Sixteen-year-old Seth, fourteen-year-old Tara, and nine-year-old Skylar were returning from their yearly month-long summer vacation with their great grandmothers, Josephine Wyclyffe and Alexandria Spirakas in Charleston, South Carolina. The family tradition had started three years earlier during an emotional family reunion.

Finally, the distance between the mothers and children closed as warm embraces quelled feelings of yearning and homesickness.

"I missed you so much." Cat embraced each child lovingly. Her voice was choked with emotion.

Seth endured the wet kisses Cat placed on his cheeks. "Sheesh, Ma. You'd think we were gone for a year instead of a month."

"Well, it feels like a year," Cat replied.

Billie was amused by the humorous sight before her. At sixteen, Seth was six-feet tall and bristly-chinned. Billie watched as he bent nearly in half in order to submit himself to the attentions of his very excited, and vertically challenged mother. As for herself, she was accosted by Skylar, who launched into her Mommy's arms the moment she was within reach.

"Mommy, I missed you." Skylar burrowed her face into Billie's neck.

Billie wrapped her arms around the child and held her close. "I missed you too, kitten."

Cat turned her attentions to Tara. "Come here, you."

Fourteen-year old Tara Charland was already promising to be a stunning beauty. As tall as Cat, her slim figure was developing shapely curves that she tried very hard to camouflage under baggy jeans and oversized T-shirts. Short, spiked, red-gold hair provided stark relief against a peaches and cream complexion.

After several death-grip hugs, Cat held her daughter at arm's length. Her smile quickly evaporated. "Tara, what have you done to your hair?!"

Tara grinned ear to ear. "Grandma Jo took me to get it done. Cool, huh?"

"Very cool, Tare," Billie said. She gave Tara a high-five, and leaned in close to a fuming Cat. "She's *your* grandmother." Billie winked at Tara, and acknowledged the silent 'thank you' her daughter sent her way.

Still in Billie's arms, Skylar leaned forward and put her arm around Cat's neck. Cat had no choice but to take the little girl from Billie's arms.

"Oomph! Goodness, Sky-baby, you're such a big girl. Pretty soon you'll be bigger than Mama."

"Ma, you don't have to be very tall to be bigger than you," Seth teased.

"Why you little rugrat," Cat replied. "I ought to—"

"Ought to *what?*" Seth towered over Cat and glared down at her, while he tried to keep a straight face.

Cat put Skylar down and started tickling her son mercilessly. After ten years of being his stepmother, she knew exactly where the sensitive spots were around his middle.

"Okay. Stop. I give." Seth conceded defeat to the much smaller woman.

"Smart man," Billie said. "Now why don't you and your sisters go fetch the luggage before round two begins?"

The kids headed toward the luggage carousel while Billie and Cat waited.

"Billie, did you see her hair? How could you tell her it was cool?" Cat said.

Billie placed her hands on Cat's shoulders. "Look, love, if our daughter wants to look like a punk rocker, then fine. She's just expressing herself. She could be doing a lot worse than spiking her hair and wearing baggy clothes."

Cat looked into Billie's expressive face and remembered the marijuana incident with Tara and her cousin Crystal in the park two years earlier. She silently chided her wife of eight years. *God, Billie, I hate it when you're right.* Outwardly, she shrugged. "Yeah, I guess you're right, but if she keeps this up, I'm buying stock in Miss Clairol." She ran a hand through her own red-toned mane.

Billie laughed. "Count me in!"

Cat rested her head on Billie's arm and looked across the terminal as their children approached them, laden with luggage. All three wore golden tans, their hair lightened by the South Carolina sun.

"Skylar looks healthy, doesn't she?" Cat remarked. "Three years ago I thought for sure we were going to lose her. I'm so happy the low dose chemo rid her body of leukemia."

"She looks *very* healthy, Cat. She's been cancer-free for nearly a year now. I'd say she's won that battle," Billie rested her head atop Cat's.

"I can't believe how tall she's grown in the past month."

"Cat, everyone looks tall to you." Billie grinned unashamedly at her wife.

Cat flashed a crooked smile at Billie. "Now I know where your son gets it. You will pay for that later."

"I'm counting on it," Billie replied.

Cat hip-checked Billie then quickly scooted away before revenge could be administered. She took Skylar's duffel bag and hung it over her shoulder then offered her hand to the little girl. "Let's go find the car and head home," she said.

On the trip home, the kids were full of questions about Steve, Karissa and Missy. Having been gone for a month, they were anxious to get home to spend the rest of their summer vacation with friends.

Cat and Billie sat side by side in the front seat of the family station wagon and sent nostalgic glances toward each other as they listened to the children talk. If felt good to be together again.

***

"Do you think dinner will be edible?" Cat asked.

Jen set the last paper plate on the picnic table and glanced at Billie and Fred, who were diligently tending the burgers and hot dogs on the grill. "Well, unless they charcoal them black there's not much they can do to kill them." Jen chuckled. "At least there'll be salads and chips if we *do* end up calling the morgue."

Cat joined her friend in laughter as they put their heads together to enjoy their private joke.

"I know you guys are talking about us," Billie shouted from across the yard. She turned to Fred. "They think we can't cook. If they only knew we pretend to be lousy at it so we don't have to do it very often." She snickered at her own joke, but stopped when she realized Fred wasn't laughing. "You *can* cook, can't you Fred?"

Fred's eyebrows arched upward. "Nope." He grinned. "And from what I hear, neither can you."

"Can too," Billie countered.

"Can not," Fred replied.

"Can too." Billie shook the spatula at him.

"Not."

"Kids," Billie yelled to the five heads bobbing up and down in the pool. "Tell Fred I can cook."

"Oh, *sure* you can, Mom," Tara said sarcastically. She rolled her eyes at Karissa.

"Well, you can heat up a pretty mean can of soup," Seth added. Stevie nodded his agreement.

"Mommy makes good microwave popcorn," Skylar offered helpfully.

"Madame Microwave! It takes a lot of skill to operate such a complicated piece of equipment. And to think you actually produce mouth-watering dishes at the same time. Well, I'm impressed," Fred said teasingly.

Billie was steaming. Not only had her kids betrayed her (the ungrateful wretches), but she had to endure culinary jokes from someone who couldn't even boil water.

"Oh, yeah? Impress *this*!" Billie shoved Fred into the pool, chef's hat and all.

Everyone in the yard collectively held their breaths as the spray of water from Fred's belly flop settled around them.

Fred rose to his feet in the shallow end of the pool, soaked to the bone. He struggled to wade to the edge of the pool toward Billie. He wore a wide grin on his face. "Okay, you got me. I guess I deserved that."

"Yes you did." Billie reached down to pull him onto the deck.

"And you deserve this!" Fred planted his feet and yanked backward, sending Billie over his head into the pool behind him.

Billie broke through the surface of the water, spitting and sputtering. She took one look at Fred standing in the shallow end of the pool, the limp chef's hat sitting crookedly on his head, water running in rivulets down his face, and burst out laughing.

The two friends fell into each other's arms and laughed heartily as the children splashed them. Their wives stood by, shaking their heads at the childish antics of their spouses.

Suddenly Skylar shouted, "Fire!"

All heads turned to the grill where black smoke was billowing out of every crack. Jen reached it first and threw the cover open as she turned off the gas.

Cat approached her friend and looked at the black lumps that neatly lined the rack. "Call the morgue?" Cat asked.

"Call the morgue," Jen agreed.

Billie and Fred looked at each and once more fell into peals of laughter.

***

Cat sat at her vanity and carefully applied a thin layer of night cream to her face. Billie approached her from behind, placed her chin on Cat's shoulder and wrapped her arms around her. She grinned at her in the mirror. "You really don't need that stuff you know. Your skin is soft and beautiful all by itself." She planted a kiss on her neck.

"It's soft *because* I do this each night, Billie. You ought to try it." Cat dropped a dab of cream on Billie's nose.

Billie snapped her head back. "Hey!" Billie wiped the cream off and sniffed at it. "Smells nice."

Cat looked at Billie in the mirror. "I had a good time at Jen and Fred's this afternoon. It was really nice of them to host a picnic to welcome the kids home."

Billie grinned. "Yeah, it was fun, wasn't it?"

"They're good friends, Billie. We're lucky to have them."

"The best," Billie agreed.

"They'd have to be. Not everyone would put up with your cooking."

Billie clutched at her heart. "Ouch! I'm wounded."

"C'mere and let me kiss the boo-boo," Cat said.

Billie eagerly approached her still sitting wife and dropped to her knees.

Cat grabbed the sides of Billie's robe and pulled them open, exposing generous, creamy white breasts. Eyes wide, she visually feasted on the sight before her. "Now where did you say you were wounded?"

Billie pointed to her right nipple. "Right here."

"Oh, really?" Cat took the erect nipple into her mouth, causing Billie to gasp. "Oh, I can see by your reaction that it really does hurt. Maybe I should kiss it some more?"

"Yeah, that's it. More kisses," Billie replied, short of breath.

Cat feasted hungrily for several more minutes then stopped to look at Billie once more. "Are you hurt anywhere else, my love?"

"Let me see. Oh, yeah, right here. I'm hurt over here too." Billie pointed to her left nipple.

Cat was more than happy to administer additional first aid as Billie moaned in mock agony. Several moments later, Cat stopped and rose to her feet. She took Billie's hand, led her to the bed and pushed her down onto in the middle of it.

"Billie, I think I need to do a thorough examination. You know—just to be safe. Is that all right with you?"

"You're the doctor, Cat, but before you start, tell me, will this be a very expensive house call?"

"Oh, yes, very expensive I'm afraid. I'm not sure you can afford it."

"Well, maybe we can work out some alternative method of payment."

Cat rubbed her chin and walked back and forth at the foot of the bed. "Hmm, let me think." After a little more pacing, she stopped and faced Billie. "I'll tell you what. I'll take partial payment tonight, and then we can barter for the rest of the bill. You know—you do something for me—I do something for you. Get the idea?"

Billie rose to her elbows. "You mean, like taking it out in trade?" Her eyebrows danced wickedly on her forehead.

"Exactly!"

"You're on, Doc," Billie threw herself flat on the bed, her arms and legs spread wide. "Go for it!"

Cat dropped all pretense, dove on top of Billie and began the most thorough and lengthy examination in the history of medicine.

CHAPTER 2

Billie answered her intercom. "Yes, Deb?"

"Billie, your next appointment is here," Deb replied.

"Send them in." Billie stood and straightened her blazer as Deb opened the door and ushered two attractive women inside. Billie walked around her desk to greet the ladies and extended her hand. "Billie Charland," she said.

"Billie," the taller of the two women said. "My name is Shannon Nash, and this is my wife, Julie."

Billie turned to Julie and offered her hand. "Julie." She addressed Shannon once more. "It's common for lesbian couples to refer to each other as wife, married or not. Are you..."

"Yes," Shannon supplied. "Thanks to you, we can proudly say that we are legally married. That's the primary reason we came to you. Anyone who can pioneer the movement for gay and lesbian marriage should be able to help us with our problem."

Billie directed Julie and Shannon to the two chairs opposite her desk. "Have a seat." While she waited for her new clients to settle in, she looked them over carefully. Shannon appeared to be the dominant partner. She was tall and slim with short dark hair. Julie was of slighter build and a bit more feminine than Shannon, with shoulder length blond hair.

Billie sat behind her desk and picked up a pen and notepad. "Now, what exactly can I help you with?"

"Well, I have a seven year old daughter, Kaleigh, from a previous marriage, and now that Shan and I are married, and I've taken her last name, Shannon would like to adopt her," Julie explained.

"I see," Billie said. "That shouldn't be too difficult, given there is no other parent to contend with. May I ask how Kaleigh's father feels about this?"

"I have no idea how he feels," Julie replied.

Billie frowned. "Are you not in touch with him?"

"No," Julie replied.

"Where is he?" Billie asked.

"Quite frankly, we don't know," Julie replied. "He disappeared when Kaleigh was just a baby."

"You have no idea at all where he is?" Billie asked.

"He's a deadbeat asshole," Shannon piped in.

Billie looked at Shannon who sat rigidly in the chair next to her wife. Billie raised one eyebrow. "Would you mind explaining that statement?"

Billie watched Shannon visibly struggle to calm her temper.

Shannon took a deep breath and smiled when Julie placed her hand over hers. She closed her eyes for several long moments. Finally, she opened them and looked directly at Billie.

"Billie, Julie and I have known her ex since high school," Shannon explained. "He was captain of the football team, and the most arrogant son of a bitch you'd ever want to meet. He managed to woo Jules here, and she agreed to marry him right after graduation, even though she knew her heart lay elsewhere."

Billie watched the women carefully as Shannon relayed her story. Julie's eyes never left her wife's face. Adoration was clearly apparent in her eyes.

"Jules settled into the role of housewife while I went out of state to college," Shannon continued. "We stayed in touch during my first semester, but pretty soon, we drifted apart. When I came home during the Christmas break, she was several months pregnant with Kaleigh. I tried to see her, but Gary—that's her ex—threw me out of the house and threatened to harm Julie if I came back. I learned later that he had a habit of beating her whenever the mood struck him. It wasn't until I came home on break during my sophomore year that I learned he had deserted her when Kaleigh was just four months old."

"Let me interrupt for a moment," Billie said. She turned to Julie. "So, considering you had to divorce him before marrying Shannon, you must have been able to find him at some point."

"Actually, no," Julie replied. "He's been missing for seven years. He just disappeared. No one has heard from him since he left. Not even his parents. I petitioned the courts to have him declared legally dead, and the court granted a divorce based on his desertion."

Billie rose to her feet and walked to the picture window that overlooked the busy mall below. She turned around, leaned her backside against the windowsill, and braced her hands on either side of her hips. "You said that Kaleigh is seven years old?" she asked.

"Seven and a half, actually," Julie replied.

"And Gary's been gone for exactly how long?"

"Seven years and two months. Almost to the day," Julie said.

"When did you file for divorce?" Billie asked, confused about the timing of the whole thing.

Shannon rose to her feet and approached Billie. "Look, let me sum things up for you. Gary disappeared when Kaleigh was four months old. I transferred to a college closer to home so I could be near Julie and Kaleigh. Julie and the baby lived with her mother for the next two years while I finished school. When I graduated, I found a decent job that allowed Julie and me to live together. Kaleigh was almost two and a half by then. We've been together ever since."

Shannon stood behind Julie to finish her story.

"Since we had no idea where Gary was, Julie couldn't divorce him. We researched the laws and discovered that after seven years of desertion, she could be granted a non-contested divorce in a matter of weeks, so we waited out the seven years. Four and a half years after we moved in together, we went to court and the divorce was granted. That was two months ago. Last month, we were legally married. Now, here we are, wanting desperately to make our family complete with my adoption of Kaleigh."

Shannon stopped talking abruptly when she finished her last comment. After a few moments of silence, Billie pushed herself off the windowsill and sat down behind her desk. She propped her elbows on the desk, made a teepee with her fingers, and rested her chin on her fingertips. "If the courts granted you a divorce based on seven years of desertion, why didn't you ask for an adoption decree at the same time?" she asked.

"We did," replied Julie. "The problem is that when Gary's parents found out about it, they filed for custody of Kaleigh in Gary's name. Billie, we've been a family for the past four years. I can't let them take my baby away."

Billie narrowed her eyes at the two ladies. "And exactly what basis did they use for claiming Kaleigh would be better off with them?" Billie asked, already knowing the answer.

Julie looked Billie straight in the eyes. "Because we are lesbians."

"Okay." Billie slapped her hands down on the desk and rose to her feet. She leaned over her desk, and addressed both ladies. "You've got yourself a lawyer. See Deb on the way out to review payment plans and to sign the retainer. You'll also need to fill out complaint forms detailing the exact nature of your problem, including any information you can think of that will help me research the case. Deb will provide you with a standard package of forms. Fill them out and send them in as soon as possible. As soon as I've made some progress, I'll call you and we'll set up a meeting to review the details. Sound okay to you?" she asked.

Shannon helped Julie to her feet and wrapped her left arm around Julie's shoulder. She shook Billie's hand firmly. "Sounds great."

***

Billie was mentally exhausted. She stepped into the kitchen to find Cat at the stove, busily preparing dinner. Scenes like this brought such warmth to Billie's soul, knowing that she enjoyed a wonderfully warm and normal family life with the woman and children she loved with all her heart.

"Hey love," Billie said as the screen door creaked behind her.

A smiled crossed Cat's face as Billie approached her. "Hi, baby!" Cat rose to her tip toes to place a kiss on Billie's lips.

Billie dropped her briefcase to the floor and wrapped her arms around Cat. "Come here, love."

Cat rubbed her hands up and down Billie's back. "Rough day?"

"Busy one." Billie looked over Cat's shoulder at the pan simmering on the stove. "That smells good. Whatcha cooking?"

Cat looked into Billie's face. "Don't tell me that after ten years together, you still can't tell what I'm cooking?"

Billie had the decency to look ashamed. "I'm sorry, sweetheart. I guess I just don't pay as much attention as I should. Forgive me?" Billie placed a kiss on Cat's nose.

Cat smiled. "You're lucky I know you love me, otherwise I might think you've been taking me for granted."

Billie's face went ashen at Cat's comment. She furrowed her brow and looked seriously at her wife. "You don't really mean that, do you Cat? Do I take you for granted? You'd tell me if I did, wouldn't you?"

Cat frowned and cupped the side of Billie's cheek. "Billie, are you all right?" she asked.

"Do I take you for granted, Cat?" Billie pulled her closer within the circle of her arms.

"No you don't. Baby, what's this all about?" Cat pushed a stray lock of hair out of Billie's face and tucked it behind her ear.

Billie took a deep breath and sighed. She lowered her forehead to Cat's. "I took on a couple of new clients today who risk losing their daughter to ex in-laws in a custody battle. It reminded me to be grateful for everything that we have. If I've taken you or the kids for granted—at any time…" Billie paused to swallow through a throat constricted with emotion.

"Sweetheart, you have not taken us for granted. We love you, and we know how much you love us. Okay?" Cat took Billie's face between her hands.

Billie smiled through teary eyes and nodded her head. "Okay."

"Good." Cat released herself from Billie's embrace to tend to the simmering pan on the stove.

Billie looked over Cat's shoulder and peered into the pan. "Chicken with mushrooms and wild rice in wine sauce, right?"

"Correct!" Cat lifted a spoonful of savory rice to Billie's lips.

"Oh, God, Cat. That's wonderful!"

"Thank you, sweetie," Cat replied. "Now, tell me about these new clients of yours while you set the table."

"Well..." Billie began.

"Ma, what's for dinner?" Tara demanded as she burst into the kitchen and allowed the screen door to slam behind her.

Both mothers turned toward their daughter.

"Tara, turn your butt around, go back out that door, and come back in without letting it slam," Billie scolded.

"Mom!" Tara exclaimed impatiently. She looked back and forth between Billie and Cat.

"You heard your mother, Tara," Cat added. "Honey, you've got to learn not to slam the door."

"Christ Almighty!" Tara headed out the door and back in again. She closed the door in such exaggerated gentle movements that even the hinges didn't squeak. She put her hands on baggy denim clad hips and said sarcastically, "Is that better?"

"The door—yes. Your language—no," Cat replied. "I don't want to hear that kind of talk come out of your mouth again. Do you understand?" Billie leaned back against the stove and watched the exchange.

"Well?" Cat stared down the rebellious teenager.

Tara stared back in a determined effort to show her mothers who was in control.

Cat held her own during the confrontation. She stood up straight with her arms crossed in front of her. Cat suddenly wondered where her little girl had gone. Here before her was a young lady, intent on making a statement. From the top of her spiked red hair to the tips of her Nike clad toes, she stood rigid and determined. Cat realized that with her severely baggy jeans, oversized T-shirt and leather necklaces, that her daughter was the picture of a streetwise rebellious youth.

Frustrated nearly to the point of anger, Cat broke the gaze and looked down. She rubbed her forehead. "Tara, go to your room."

"But I'm hungry!" Tara objected.

"I'll call you when dinner is ready. After dinner, you'll go back to your room."

"No way!" Tara exclaimed. "Karissa and I are going to the mall after dinner."

"Correction, Karissa is going to the mall after dinner. You are going to your room," Cat answered.

"But, Ma!" Tara whined.

"Go!" Cat's gaze met her daughter's eyes as she pointed toward the living room.

A hateful sneer crossed Tara's face and she angrily stomped through the kitchen.

Cat counted to ten and turned to face Billie again. "That child..."

Billie pulled Cat in close. "Cat, honey, she's just feeling her way around, trying to find out who she is," Billie said. "She reminds me a lot of myself at that age."

Cat looked at her wife. "You had red spiked hair?" she teased.

Billie shrugged one shoulder. "Something like that. She'll be fine Cat. Just give her some space. You'll see."

"Billie, we can't let her run wild. There's so much out there that can hurt her. Drugs, violence, sex. Oh, my God, sex! Billie, I don't even want to think about that," Cat agonized.

"You know, she's old enough to understand the consequences of careless sex. It might be a good idea to talk to her before she makes a mistake out of ignorance," Billie suggested.

"Are you volunteering?" Cat asked hopefully.

Billie looked at Cat and grinned. "You know, I should say no. After all, I had to tell Seth on my own because some cute little redhead chickened out, but I won't do that to you. Why don't we talk to her together?"

"Okay." Cat kissed her on the nose and felt relief flooding through her.

Billie smiled broadly at the bright eyes that stared back at her. "You are so damned cute!"

Cat slapped Billie's arm lightly. "You're just saying that to stay on my good side. After all, without me, you'd have to eat your own cooking!"

"Busted!" Billie replied.

***

"Hey neighbors!" Jen came through the kitchen door to see Billie and Cat loading the dishwasher with dinner dishes.

"Hi, Jen," Billie and Cat replied together.

Jen stopped and looked at her friends. "You two never cease to amaze me," she commented. "Do you guys do *everything* together? Heck, I can hardly get Fred to put his dishes in the sink, never mind help load them into the dishwasher!"

Billie approached Jen and patted her cheek with an open palm. "I keep trying to tell you, Jen, you need to find yourself a woman."

"That thought *has* crossed my mind," Jen replied, half seriously. "Got anyone in mind?"

"Jen, if I thought you were even a tiny bit serious about that..." Billie mused.

"Stop it, you two," Cat scolded. "All you've got do is teach Fred a few lessons about housekeeping."

"Uhh, Cat? Have you ever heard the saying, 'you can lead a horse to water'?" Jen asked through raised eyebrows.

"What you need to do is give him a scare. You know, make him realize he's taking you for granted," Billie suggested. She glanced at Cat and remembered their earlier conversation.

"I guess I've just made things way too easy on him over the years. I guess because I'm a stay-at-home mom I feel it's my responsibility to take care of everyone," Jen reasoned. "After all, I *don't* work outside the home," she added.

"Whoa. Wait just a minute there," Cat exclaimed. "Just because you're a stay-at-home Mom doesn't mean you don't work hard. Jen, your house is spotless. Your laundry is always done. Your kids always have a parent to come home to after school. Honey, you work damned hard. You might not have an outside income, but the wealth you bring to your home and family is immeasurable. Fred is blind if he doesn't see that. What would he do without you? What would any of them do?" The indignant anger came through in Cat's voice.

Jen stood there for several moments, brow furrowed, as she absorbed her friend's words. She took a deep breath, and nodded her head. "Maybe you're right, Cat," she said. "I guess I need to work on showing him just how much he *does* need me." Jen's eyebrows dancing evilly up and down.

"Oh, oh. I'm not sure I like the sound of that," Billie said. "Jen, what's going through that wicked mind of yours?" she asked.

Jen chuckled. "You'll see. In time, you'll see," she replied.

Billie looked at Cat with a 'now look what you've done!' expression on her face.

Cat smiled nervously.

Jen turned around when she reached the door. "Oh, by the way, I actually came over to invite the two of you to the movies Friday night. Our treat," she said.

Cat and Billie looked at each other and simultaneously nodded. "Sure. I think we're free," replied Billie.

"Cool. The movie starts at nine p.m. Maybe we can go out for dinner first," Jen suggested.

"Sounds great, Jen. We'll pick you and Fred up at...let's say, six o'clock. Does that sound okay?" Cat asked.

"Six o'clock it is. I'll see you later, 'kay?" Jen waved over her shoulder and headed out the door.

Billie turned to Cat and placed her hands on her hips. She lowered her chin to her chest and looked out through hooded eyes at her wife.

Cat felt uncomfortable under Billie's scrutiny. "What? Billie, all I did was let her know she had a voice. She doesn't deserve to feel inferior. She works very hard at home."

Billie visually relaxed her stance and opened her arms. Cat entered them willingly. "I know, sweetheart. I know. Maybe Fred *does* need to learn a lesson," she said. After a short pause, she added, "I just hope Jen doesn't go overboard."

"Jen? Overboard? She wouldn't do that, would she?" Cat asked seriously.

Billie raised one eyebrow at her wife. "What do *you* think?" she replied.

Cat gulped. "I think Fred's in trouble."

CHAPTER 3

"Billie? It's Shannon Nash on line two. I tried setting up an appointment with her to come in later in the week, but she insisted on talking to you first," Deb said across the office intercom.

Now what could that mean? Billie thought to herself. "All right, Deb. Thanks." Billie picked up the phone and pressed the number two on the keypad. "This is Billie," she said into the receiver.

"Billie. Hi. Shannon Nash. Look, Billie, it doesn't look like I can break away from my meetings during the day. Would it be possible to meet one evening this week? Maybe Julie and I can take you and your wife out for dinner and discuss the case. I'm really sorry to inconvenience you like this," she explained.

Billie thought it over for a moment. She had learned a few years earlier from a domestic violence case in which the wife finally died from the abuse, not to let herself become personally involved with her clients. It was against her better judgment, but something about this woman, and about this case, compelled her to accept. "All right. I guess that would be okay. Which night would be best for you?" Billie asked.

"Friday," Shannon replied.

"Friday..." Billie pondered. *Did we have something planned? Damn, I wish I could remember.* "I think Friday is okay," she commented. "Let's go ahead and schedule it, and I'll check with Cat to see if we already have plans. If we do, I'll get back to you," Billie said.

"Cat?" Shannon inquired.

"Oh, I'm sorry. Cat. Short for Caitlain. My lovely wife of eight years," Billie explained.

"Cute. I like it. I'm looking forward to meeting her. What do you say to dinner at Trader Duke's at six p.m.?" Shannon suggested.

"Sounds fine to me. We'll see you then."

Billie hung up the phone and turned back to the legal brief spread across her desk. *Okay, what are the facts here,* she said to herself. *Let's see, one absent father, gone for more than seven years. Two legally married women, one the biological mother of the child. Two sets of grandparents, one set supportive, one set combative. The problem isn't with the father. He's given up his rights through desertion. The problem is the in-laws. No, no, the problem is homophobia. That's the real issue here.* "Shit," Billie said out loud.

Just then, the intercom rang.

"Yes, Deb?" Billie held down the speaker button.

"Billie, it's your daughter on line one. She sounds upset," Deb replied.

"Thanks, Deb." A lump of fear settled in the pit of her stomach. She picked up the phone. "Tara? Sky?"

"Mom, this is Tara. Mom, we can't find Sky," Tara said breathlessly.

"What do you mean, you can't find Sky?" A tinge of panic edged her voice.

"We can't find her. We've looked everywhere," She said in a voice choked with emotion.

Billie realized Tara was beginning to panic. She inhaled deeply and forced herself to calm down. "Okay. Tara, honey, tell me what happened. When did you see her last?" Billie was barely able to control her stomach, which was about to commit nervous mutiny.

"I don't know. 'Rissa came over about ten o'clock, and we went to my room to listen to my new CD. Sky and Missy were in the backyard playing in the tree house. When it was time to fix lunch, I yelled for her to come in, but she was gone," Tara explained.

Billie looked at her watch. Three p.m. "So she's been missing for three or four hours?" Billie asked. "Where did you look for her?"

"We looked everywhere, Mom. I called Jen, but she wasn't home. I even called Seth at work, but his boss said he was too busy to come to the phone. Mom, I'm really scared," Tara finished.

"All right. Tara, honey, I'm on my way home. Did you call Mama yet?" Billie asked.

"Yeah, but she's in surgery right now," Tara replied.

"Sweetheart, don't leave the house in case she comes home before I get there, okay? I'm on my way. Bye." Billie jumped to her feet and headed out the door.

"Reschedule my afternoon, Deb," Billie said as she flew by the secretary's desk.

"Is everything all right?" Deb asked her harried employer.

"Missing kid," she exclaimed as she shoved her arms into her blazer.

"Is there anything I can do to help?" Deb offered.

"Not right now. I'll call you if anything changes for tomorrow," Billie replied.

"Good luck," Deb called to Billie's back as she hurried out the door.

***

By the time Billie arrived home, Missy's mother was pacing frantically back and forth across their kitchen. The moment Billie entered the house she was all over her.

"Billie. God, I'm glad you're here. The girls are gone," she said frantically, grabbing Billie's biceps.

Billie took the woman by the shoulders. "Frannie, I know. Tara called me. That's why I'm here. Look, when did you see Missy last?" she asked.

"Early this morning. She asked to come over here to play with Skylar. If I had known she didn't have adult supervision,

I wouldn't have allowed it." Frannie sent a semi-hostile look across the room to Tara and Karissa who were sitting at the kitchen table with tears running down their faces. Tara winced visibly under the attack.

Billie's anger with this woman rose nearly out of control. She took a step back and placed her hands on her hips. "Frannie, I think Skylar and Missy deserve some of the blame here. Skylar knows better than to run off on her sister without telling her where she's going. Now, I don't know what's happened here, but making Tara and Karissa feel like shit is not going to solve the problem. You got that?" she asked sharply.

Frannie looked like she had been slapped. Eyes wide and blinking furiously, she looked back and forth between Billie and the two girls at the table. Indignation won out as she stomped her way to the kitchen door. She stopped and turned back toward Billie. "I'm going home to call the police." She yanked the door open and left.

Billie sneered as she watched the woman retreat. She made a conscious effort to compose herself and then turned to a devastated Tara and opened her arms. Tara immediately ran to her mother. As tough and independent as the teenager liked to think she was, she was still a vulnerable little girl and still longed for the safety and security of her mother's arms.

Tara buried her face in Billie's chest and cried. "Mom, the police aren't going to arrest me for not watching her close enough, are they?"

Billie kissed the top of Tara's head and then laid her cheek there. "No sweetheart, they aren't. Like I said, this is as much your sister's responsibility as it is yours. I know you love Sky-Bird and that you would never intentionally do anything to harm her." Billie tilted Tara's chin up. "I'm sure she's fine, Tare, but right now, I need to call Mom then we need to wait for the police to come. With their help, I'm sure we'll find her," Billie said encouragingly.

Billie released Tara and reached for the phone on the kitchen wall. She stopped to give a crying Karissa an encouraging hug and a kiss on the head. Tara and Karissa sat side-by-side, holding hands as they watched Billie dial the phone.

"Hello? This is Billie Charland. I need to reach Caitlain Charland. It's kind of an emergency," Billie said into the phone.

Tara and Karissa listened carefully to Billie's side of the conversation.

"Oh. All right then. Thank you, Goodbye." Billie hung up the phone and turned to the girls. "She's already left for home. I guess we'll just sit tight and wait for her."

***

Cat maneuvered the car around the corner of her street and immediately noticed flashing blue lights. It took a few moments to register that they were in front of her house.

"Oh, my God!" Cat pressed her foot suddenly onto the accelerator, causing the car to lurch forward. Just barely in control of the vehicle, Cat came to screeching halt within inches of Billie's car. She jumped out of the car and ran toward the house. "Billie! Billie, where are you? What's happened?"

Billie and Frannie were inside the kitchen, being interviewed by one of the police officers when Cat burst in. "What the hell is happening here?" Her eyes were wild with fear.

Billie broke away from the conversation and reached her hand out to Cat, who soon found herself tucked into Billie's side. "Officer Sullivan, this is my wife, Caitlain. Cat, Skylar is missing," Billie said to Cat as she shook the officer's hand.

Cat looked bewildered, "Missing?"

"Yes, missing," replied Frannie. "And it's *your* daughter's fault." She pointed at Tara.

Billie glared at Frannie while Officer Sullivan intervened. "Ma'am, we don't know whose fault it is. There's no sense making accusations at this stage of the investigation."

"Investigation?" Cat was confused. "Billie, what is he talking about? Damn it! Will someone tell me what's going on here?" she shouted.

"Cat, please calm down. Look, Tara called me at work this afternoon, about three o'clock. The last she knew, Sky and Missy were playing in the tree house. When Tara called her in for lunch, they were gone. She and Karissa spent most of the afternoon searching the house and neighborhood for the girls before she called me. Frannie immediately chose to blame Tara for the whole thing," Billie explained.

"Well, *look* at her," Frannie exclaimed. "Spiked hair, baggy clothes. What's next, tattoos and body piercing? She looks like a hoodlum. How can you trust her to babysit Skylar all day?" she ranted.

Billie rose to her full height and glared at Frannie. Officer Sullivan quickly intervened. "Ah, Ma'am, I think it's best that you go home. I'll be over to interview you when I'm finished here," he said.

Still tucked into Billie's side, Cat reached out her hand to Tara. Once again, Tara quickly took refuge in the circle of love she had been raised within. Cat held the child as her shoulders shook violently with sobs. "Shhh, it's all right Tara. We'll find her. Honey, it isn't your fault," she whispered into the girl's ear as she held her close and placed tiny kisses on the side of her face.

Tara nodded her head and visibly calmed down. "I'm sorry, Mama. I should have watched her closer," Tara apologized.

"Well, we all know how determined your sister is. What's important right now is that we find her. We can talk about blame and responsibility later," Cat said as much to the police officer as to her daughter.

"Cat! Billie!" exclaimed the blonde spitfire as she crashed through the kitchen door. Her grand entrance drew the attention of everyone in the room. "I just got home. The girls left a message on my answering machine about Skylar and Missy. I tried calling to see what was happening, but the line was busy. Look, I've already made a few phone calls. The neighborhood is organizing a search party. Don't worry, we'll find them." Jen said all of this in the short amount of time it took to make it across the kitchen.

"Officer Sullivan, this is our neighbor, Jen Swenson," Billie said.

Jen shook hands with the police officer. "Officer," she said. "What can I do to help?"

"Looks like you're already doing it. Where is the neighborhood group meeting? I'd like to organize the search pattern," he said.

Jen looked at her watch. "In the elementary school cafeteria, in about an hour."

"Okay then. I need to interview Missy's mother, then I'll meet you at the school." Officer Sullivan placed a callused finger under Tara's chin and lifted her face. "Don't worry, Tara. We'll find your little sister, okay?"

Tara nodded tearfully and forced a weak smile onto her face. "Thanks," she said shyly as she watched him leave.

Jen looked at Tara and at her own daughter still sitting at the kitchen table. "Tara, why don't you come to the school with Karissa and me? She looks pretty shaken up about this too, and I think it would do you both some good to lean on each other. Whaddaya say?"

Tara nodded and took the hand Jen held out to her while Karissa took the other. Jen looked at her friends over the teenagers' heads. "Don't worry, we'll find her." Then, with a reassuring nod, she and the girls left.

Cat buried her face in Billie's chest.

She inhaled deeply, and was surprised to feel a shudder run through Billie. She looked into Billie's face and saw unshed tears threatening to spill from beautiful blue eyes. She placed a delicate kiss between Billie's breasts and looked at her again. "We'll find our baby, love. We will. Come on. Let's go to the school."

Billie kissed her tenderly. "I need to call Seth first. He doesn't know what's going on here."

***

"All right. Can I have it quiet in here, please?" Officer Sullivan's voice rang loud from the front of the school cafeteria. He looked over the crowd of approximately one hundred people. "Thank you all for coming. I believe you all know the two children who are missing?" He noted several head-nods from the crowd. "Good. Now, I'd like to begin by searching a square area fanning out about a mile beyond the Charland house on all four sides. If this is a matter of two children wandering too far away from home, we'll probably find them within that area. I'll need you to break into groups of five or so, and then see Jen Swenson at the control booth over there to receive your assigned area. You'll need to move slowly through the search areas, and please search thoroughly. Look over, under and around everything. Heaven forbid something terrible has happened to these children, but be prepared to handle whatever you might find. Any questions?"

A voice came from the middle of the crowd. "When should we check in?"

"Good question. You should each choose a runner for your group. If you find something, send the runner directly back here to the control center where the Charlands and I can be reached by radio. If nothing is found within the next two hours, all of you should return for further instructions. At that point, we will have an alternate search area ready. Any other questions?"

The question Officer Sullivan saw on everyone's face but was left unasked was: *What if the children are found dead?* "All right then. Let's keep our fingers crossed that Skylar and Missy will be found safe and sound. Good luck to you all."

Billie stood next to Officer Sullivan with her arms wrapped around Cat. Officer Sullivan turned to them and placed a hand on Billie's shoulder. "Don't lose hope. We'll find them. I'll check in with you in about an hour."

Cat nodded slightly. Billie just stared straight ahead.

Seth stoically approached his mothers. "Mom, are you ready to go?"

Billie managed a slight smile for her son and nodded.

Seth's gaze moved back and forth between the women. "I know she's okay. I can feel it. I told you once before that we wouldn't let her fly away, and we didn't." Seth smiled broadly. "Now let's go find the little rugrat so I can strangle her for worrying us!"

Billie smiled at Seth's attempt to lighten the mood. Seth had a special connection to his sister through the blood they shared. If he felt in his heart that she was okay, then they at least had hope. Billie located Tara, Karissa and Steve in the crowd and directed their search team toward the door.

***

Officer Sullivan called a temporary halt to the search to allow the volunteers to get some sleep and nutrition before starting again at 5 a.m. the next morning.

Having gone directly from work to the school, Seth volunteered to drive Tara, Steve, and Karissa home. Billie and Cat rode home together.

"They're dead, or kidnapped. I just know it!" Cat cried.

"Cat, don't say that. She's our baby. Please don't say that."

"Billie, it's midnight. The whole neighborhood has been looking for them for seven hours." Cat's fear was evident in her voice. "She's been through so much already. My poor Sky-baby." Cat covered her face with her hands and cried uncontrollably as Billie tried her best to maneuver the car through the streets despite the veil of tears that ran down her cheeks. She pulled into the driveway, shut off the motor and pulled Cat into her arms.

"Cat, please don't lose hope. Please. Sky needs us to be strong."

For several long moments, the two women sat in the driveway, locked in an embrace of communal sadness. Finally, Billie held Cat at arm's length and spoke gently to her. "We have to be strong. We have to believe, okay?" She brushed Cat's hair out of her face and tucked it behind her ear. "Let's go inside. We need to eat and sleep to be fresh for tomorrow morning."

Cat sniffed and nodded and climbed out of the car. She wrapped her arm around Billie's waist and they walked together into the house.

Billie walked into the kitchen and threw the car keys onto the table. The sound of the keys hitting the table reverberated through the silent house like an echo through a canyon. Irritated, Cat turned to chastise her wife for the unnecessary gesture, when suddenly they heard a sound from the living room.

"Mama?"

Cat and Billie's gazes met as they were froze.

"Mommy?"

Cat and Billie were shocked into action. "*Sky*?" they exclaimed together. They rushed into the living room and found Skylar sitting on the couch, rubbing her eyes. Missy lay sleeping beside her.

Billie crossed the distance between the kitchen and couch in four long strides. Skylar soon found herself wrapped in the arms of two weeping women.

Cat gave up any pretense of stemming the flow of tears. "Sky, honey, where were you?"

"Skylar Jean Charland, I don't know whether to scold you or hug you. You had us worried to death!" Billie said through her own tears.

"Billie, call Frannie. You know she's as worried as we were." Cat glanced at Missy, who was just beginning to stir.

Billie picked up the portable phone and dialed their neighbor's number. "Hello, Frannie? Frannie, this is Billie. No! No, Frannie, it's all right. Frannie, listen to me. Missy is here. Yes, she's here with Sky. Hello? Hello?"

Billie pulled the phone away from her ear and looked at Cat. "I expect we'll see her in about five seconds." Just then, the front door burst open and Frannie rushed in. Billie grinned. "I stand corrected!" Billie and Cat watched Frannie run to her daughter and scoop her into her arms.

After several moments of teary welcomes, the women sat the two nine-year-olds side by side on the couch. Cat paced back and forth in front of them for several moments before she stopped and faced them with her hands on her hips. "What were you thinking?" she asked. "We were out of our minds with worry about you. Do you have any idea how much trouble the entire neighborhood went through looking for you two?"

Billie stood by the fireplace mantel, this time not coming to her youngest child's rescue. This was one tongue lashing Skylar needed to hear.

The two girls sat on the couch with their chins on their chests as Cat continued.

"Skylar, your sister is sick with guilt over this. She thinks this is her fault! For crying out loud girls. Didn't you even *think* about how worried we would all be?"

The girls started to cry. Cat continued to pace, too angry to say any more. Silence prevailed throughout the room while Cat paced and Billie and Frannie lent their support through the extended silence. Finally, Cat stopped. "Well? What do you have to say for yourselves?"

"We wanted to go to the park for a picnic," Skylar said in a weak, pathetic voice.

"A picnic? You wanted to have a picnic? You could have done that in the backyard," Cat reasoned.

"But that wouldn't be as much fun," Skylar explained.

"So you just left the yard without telling your sister, and you went to the park?"

"Uh-huh," Skylar said softly. "We put some food in a bag and rode our bikes."

"You rode your bikes out of the neighborhood all by yourselves?" Cat asked. "You know you're not allowed to do that without an adult or Seth and Tara with you. That wasn't very smart, Skylar. What if you got lost—or worst yet—hit by a car?"

"I'm sorry, Mama."

Cat looked at the little girl beside Skylar. "Missy, what do you have to say for yourself?"

"I'm sorry too."

"When did you get back home?" Cat asked.

"We left the park early, but it took a long time to find our way home," Skylar admitted.

Cat threw her hands up into the air. "You got lost on your way home? Jesus Chr…"

Billie stepped forward and put her hands on Cat's shoulders. "Let me take it from here," she said.

Cat went to stand by Frannie and they both crossed their arms and glared at their daughters.

Billie stood in front of the girls. "Look at me," she said.

Both girls turned sad, tear-filled eyes toward Billie.

"Do you know why you came home to empty houses?"

"We were scared when no one was home at Missy's and at our house. We came here to wait for someone to come home," Skylark said.

"Yes, but do you know *why* there was no one home?"

"No," the girls said in unison.

"Because everybody was out looking for *you*. The whole neighborhood was looking for you."

The girls lowered their chins to their chests.

"Skylar, Missy, you both have people who love you very much, and who would be heartbroken if anything bad happened to you. What you did today was very irresponsible and dangerous."

Before Billie could say anything more, the kitchen door swung open, admitting Seth and Tara. They walked through the kitchen and into the living room and stopped in their tracks when they saw their younger sister, safe and sound.

Tara immediately pounced on the younger girl. She sat atop of her and pinned her to the couch. "Don't you *ever* do that to me again, do you understand?" Tara shouted into her face. Tears streamed down her cheeks.

Fearing bodily harm, Billie intervened and pulled Tara from the younger girl. She set her back onto her feet, enveloped the teenager in her arms, and held her close as she released pent up fear and emotions.

"I'm sorry, Tare," Skylar said in a tiny voice.

A much calmer Tara turned in Billie's arms and looked at her sister. "S'okay. Just don't do it again."

"I won't. I promise," Skylar said.

Seth grinned at his mothers. "See, I told you she was fine!"

Cat crossed the room and embraced her son. "Yes, you did, honey."

"All right—all three of you—time to hit the sheets. It's been a rough day," Billie ordered as the children headed for the stairs.

"Ah, Tara?" Frannie said.

Tara stopped her ascent up the stairs and turned to face their neighbor. "Yeah?" she replied.

"Look, what I said earlier…I didn't mean it. I was scared and I was looking for someone to blame. I'm sorry. I hope you can forgive me."

Tara nodded and smiled. "Good night," she said to the three women and resumed her climb.

Frannie extended the apology to Cat and Billie, gathered up Missy, and headed home.

After seeing Frannie out, Cat returned to the living room and found Billie leaning against the mantel, her shoulders shaking as sobs racked her body. She wrapped her arms around Billie and laid her head between her shoulder blades. "I love you," she whispered.

Billie turned around and folded Cat within the circle of her arms. "I love you too," she replied. "We should give Officer Sullivan and Jen a call, then go to bed ourselves. I'm exhausted."

Cat waited patiently as Billie made the calls.

Billie smiled as she hung up the phone after calling Jen.

"What's that grin for?" Cat asked.

"Jen. She really is a good friend, isn't she? She started crying as soon as I told her Sky was okay." Billie yawned loudly when she finished her sentence.

"Come on, you. Time for bed," Cat said.

Arm in arm, they walked toward the stairs. Their children were home and their family was intact once more. Life was good.

CHAPTER 4

"Seth! Dude, you'd better get up or you'll be late for work." Billie called to her son as she prepared to leave for work as well. Cat had already left, having shifted her summer hours to start and end earlier in the day so one of them was home with the children in the early morning and the other, later in the afternoon.

Seth ambled sleepily down the stairs and stumbled to the kitchen table. "I'm beat!" he exclaimed. "Thanks to Skylar, I didn't get enough sleep last night."

"Don't be too quick to blame it totally on your sister, big guy. You know you normally stay up until eleven or twelve on work nights," Billie commented. "Last night was no exception."

"Yeah, I guess," Seth mumbled. "But I don't usually spend seven hours scouring the neighborhood before going to bed either."

"Now *that* I can understand," Billie replied. She wrapped her arms around her son and placed a kiss on his head. "Thanks for not giving up on her, Scout. You were a big help last night. I'm proud of both you and Tara for pitching in to look for your sister."

Seth grinned and nodded.

Billie reached for a travel mug from the cupboard, and poured herself a coffee to go. "You must have been really busy at work yesterday." She looked over her shoulder at Seth.

Seth frowned. "No, not really. Why do you say that?"

"Hmmm. When Skylar turned up missing, Tara called looking for you and your boss told her you were too busy to come to the phone. Now why would he say something like that?"

Seth shrugged his shoulders. "Beats me," he replied. He really didn't want to tell his mother he had been reprimanded at work for the number of phone calls he had been receiving from girls.

"Oh well. Damn, I'm going to be late for my nine o'clock meeting if I don't get moving," Billie exclaimed. She kissed Seth on the cheek. "I guess I'll see you tonight, sweetie."

"Okay, Mom. Have a good day."

Seth rose from his seat at the table and pulled open the refrigerator door. He stood there for several minutes with the door wide open until he finally settled on the orange juice, which he retrieved and drank directly from the carton before putting it back. Next, he grabbed the milk, closed the refrigerator door and set the carton on the table before going to the pantry to decide on which cereal he wanted for breakfast. Just then, his cell phone rang.

"Hello?" Seth answered in his man-boy voice.

"Hey, Seth. Steve here. Are your moms gone yet?"

"Yeah, finally!"

"Cool! Are you ready for Friday night?" Steve asked.

"I...I suppose so."

"You're not going to chicken out on us, are you, Seth?" Steve warned.

"No, I guess not," Seth replied after a short pause. "You know, our parents are going to kill us."

"*If* we get caught. Are you forgetting they're supposed to go out together Friday night?"

"Yeah, I remember. Did Timmy get the stuff?" Seth asked.

"His older brother is getting it for him. We're supposed to meet him in the graveyard on Friday around seven."

"Okay. Look, man, I'm gonna be late for work. I gotta go. I'll talk to you later, all right?" Seth said.

"Sounds good! Catcha later!" Steve answered and then hung up.

Seth ended the call and stared at his phone for long moments. His conscience was getting the best of him. *You are such a mama's boy!* A voice nagged at him. Furrowing his brow, he shook the offending intruder off and nodded his head. "We'll see about that," he said out loud. "We'll just see."

***

"Tare? Tare, wake up." Skylar shook her sister awake.

"Go away!" Tara swat at the hands that were prodding her into awareness.

"Come on, Tara. It's almost ten o'clock. It's Wednesday. We always go to the mall on Wednesdays," Skylar whined.

Tara rolled over and looked at her little sister. "You are a real pain in the ass, you know that?"

"I'm telling Mama you said ass," Sky replied.

"Well, so did you," Tara pointed out then rolled over and pulled the covers over her head once more.

"Yeah, but you said it first!"

Tara sat up quickly, threw her covers off and grabbed the front of Skylar's shirt. She pulled their faces close together. "So what?" she challenged. "Ass! There, I said it again. Ass, ass, ass, ass, ass!" Tara released her sister and flung herself back down onto the bed. "Ahh! Why did God make little kids anyway?" she shouted.

Undaunted, Skylar continued to beg. "Come on, Tara. I wanna go to the mall."

Tara continued to ignore her.

"I bet 'Rissa's up and ready to go," Skylar said.

Tara threw her hands up. "All right! I'll get up. You're gonna nag me all morning if I don't, aren't you?"

"Yep," Sky replied.

"Ugh. I hate mornings." Tara hung her legs over the side of the bed. She looked at Skylar. "Go make yourself useful and call 'Rissa. Tell her we'll be ready in about twenty minutes."

Happy to do her idol's bidding, Skylar scampered off to the living room to make the call while Tara dragged herself out of bed. She walked over to the full-length mirror on her closet door, and took in her appearance. She shook her head side to side. *Why do I have to be so ugly? Look at me! My hair sucks, my skin sucks, my body sucks! Christ! I even have boobs! I hate them! Why couldn't I be a guy? They've got it made!*

Tara chose from her usual preference of baggy jeans and T-shirt and carried her clothes to the bathroom where she planned to put them on after taking her shower. She stood up after using the toilet, and glanced into the bowl. Her eyes widened with surprise and disgust. "Shit!" she exclaimed. "Shit! Shit! Shit! This is just what I need!" She dreaded this day, and hoped it would never come. At fourteen, she was well behind most of her friends, and just assumed that it would never happen.

Skylar ran into the room. "Tare, 'Rissa will be over in about ten minutes." Skylar followed her sister's gaze into the bowl. "Ahhhhh," she screamed. "Tara, you're bleeding! Call Mama, quick before you die!"

Why are little kids so dumb? Tara wondered. She shook her head. "Sky. Sky, will you calm down? I'm not going to die!"

"But there's blood in there!" Skylar pointed to the bowl.

"Yeah. Lucky me. Now I'm gonna have to walk around all day feeling like I'm wearing a diaper." She rummaged through the supplies under the bathroom sink. "Where are they?" she asked out loud.

"Where are what?" Skylar asked.

"The pads."

"You mean like the pads of paper we use for school?"

Tara stopped in her tracks and stared at her sister in disbelief before returning to her search. After long unsuccessful moments, she gave up and paged Cat at work. "Ma? This is Tara," she spoke into the phone when Cat returned the page.

"Hi, honey. Is everything all right? Your sister didn't run off again, did she?" Cat asked.

"No, she's right here. Ma, I've got a problem. I need some help finding..." Tara began.

"What is it sweetheart? Are you okay?"

"I'm fine. Ma, I need some pads," Tara explained.

Several seconds of silence passed before Cat responded. "Pads? As in sanitary napkins?"

"Yes," Tara answered. She was humiliated beyond belief.

"You started your period?" Cat asked excitedly.

"Say it a little louder, Ma. I don't think they heard you in the ER," Tara exclaimed.

"Oh, my God! My little girl is growing up," Cat gushed.

"Ma…Ma, the pads?" Tara asked impatiently.

"Of course. There's a box under the sink in my bathroom. Help yourself, honey."

"Thanks," Tara said, in a hurry to get off the phone before her mother embarrassed her even more. "Look, Ma, 'Rissa and I are taking Sky to..." Tara started.

"Do you feel all right, honey? Do you want me to come home?" Cat asked. "I mean, do you have cramps or anything? Maybe you should take a couple of Tylenol before they set in," she recommended.

"Ma, I'm fine—really. All I need is a pad."

"Well, maybe you'll be one of the lucky ones and not have cramps," Cat continued.

"Ma, I gotta go. 'Rissa is waiting for us to go to the mall."

"Okay. Well then, have a good day, and take care of your sister, okay? Oh, and Tara, now that you're becoming a young lady, Mom and I need to have a talk with you some time soon, all right?"

Oh groan!!! Tara agonized internally. "Okay, Ma. I'll see you when you get home. Bye!"

Tara quickly hung up the phone before Cat could say anything else then ran into her mothers' bathroom to get what she needed. On her way back to the common bathroom, her phone rang once more.

"Hello?" Tara said into the phone.

"Hi, sweetheart, it's Mom," Billie replied. "Mama just called. I understand you have some news for me?"

"Mom! Christ! Has she called the TV and radio stations about it too? I started my period. It's no big deal!"

Billie chuckled. "She *is* just a bit enthusiastic about it, isn't she?"

"Mom, this is humiliating. I really hate this," she whined.

Well, get used to it, sweetling. You've got about forty or so years to put up with it."

"Well *that* sure makes me feel better!" Tara exclaimed. She could hear Billie chuckling on the other end of the line.

"Did Mama tell you to take some Tylenol for the cramps?"

"Yes, Mom, she did, but I feel fine."

"Well take some anyway. Sometimes the cramps don't start right away."

"Mom, Mama said something about a talk. Do we have to?"

"Yeah, we do. Honey, you need to know how to be smart and safe. I promise we'll make it short, okay?"

"Oh, all right. Look, 'Rissa and I are taking the runt to the mall, so I gotta jump in the shower. I'll see you when you get home, okay?"

"Okay sweetheart, and by the way—congratulations!"

"For what? Becoming a routine blood donor? If I wanted to do that, I'd visit the Red Cross." Tara laughed at her own joke. "Bye, Mom," she said then hung up the phone.

***

"Jen? What are you cooking for dinner?" Fred asked from his recliner.

"Nothing," Jen replied.

Fred's head snapped around. "What do you mean nothing? Did you order pizza?"

"Nope."

"Take out?"

"No. I'm on strike," Jen explained.

Fred rose from his chair and walked toward the kitchen. He leaned against the door frame separating the kitchen from the living room and crossed his arms. "You're joking, right?"

"No, I'm not."

"Jen, do you feel all right? It's not like you to act this way."

"Well, Fred, just how am I supposed to act? Am I supposed to fix your meals, wash your clothes, clean your house and see to your every need? Is *that* how I'm supposed to act?"

"Well...yeah," he replied. "Isn't that how you've always acted?"

Jen nodded. "I suppose it is, but you know what—I'm tired of taking care of everyone and not being appreciated for it."

"What do you mean? We appreciate you," Fred replied.

"Maybe in your own way you do, but more than ever, I feel like I'm being taken for granted. I mean, look at your reaction just a few moments ago when I said I wasn't cooking dinner. You almost became unhinged. Honey, life has fallen into a mundane pattern of you going to work every day and me staying home and being the good little housewife. It's *expected* that I will take care of everyone and never complain. I'm tired of it. Fred, I want to get a job."

Fred raised his eyebrows. "A job?" he asked incredulously.

"Yes, a job."

"And just what kind of job do you think you can get?" he asked.

Indignation kicked in. Jen placed her hands on her hips and looked her husband square in the face. "You say that as if I have no skills at all. Are you forgetting that I *did* go to college? Are you forgetting that I have a degree in elementary education? Look, Fred. I've already checked with the school, and they are willing to hire me on as a full-time, paid, teacher's aide. After I re-certify, I could even be promoted to teacher as soon as there's an opening," she explained.

Panic began to set in. "Jen, be reasonable about this. Who will take care of us if you go to work?" Fred asked.

"We all will, Fred. Don't you see? Steve and Karissa are both in high school. They don't need me to be home for them after school any more. We could all pitch in to keep the house clean, do the laundry and make the meals. Fred, with today's economy, most households *require* two incomes. A two income family is more the norm in today's society than not—especially when there are no small kids to stay home for."

"But Jen, you don't *have* to work. I make enough to support all of us," Fred tried to reason.

Jen approached her husband and took his face between her hands. She kissed him gently. "Honey, this isn't about your ability to support us. You've done a wonderful job at that. This is about me feeling fulfilled, about feeling like I'm independent. Can't you understand that?"

"But...but..." he stammered.

"Look, Fred, put yourself in my shoes. Your wife works all day, pays all the bills, takes care of everyone financially, while you stay home, clean, cook and then sit around doing nothing for the rest of the day while the kids are at school and all your friends are at work. Your wife comes home at night. You wait on her hand and foot, cook her meals, do her dishes and iron her clothes for work the next day. Now consider doing that day after day for nearly twenty years. Think about it Fred. Do you think you'd be ready for a change?" Jen asked.

Fred's brow furrowed with thought. "Has it really been that bad, Jen?"

Jen smiled. "No. It's hasn't been bad at all. But the kids are both teenagers now. They don't need a full time nanny. It's time they start learning how to take care of themselves. I want to feel more productive, Fred. I'm going to accept the position at the school."

Fred held her gaze for several moments. Finally, he nodded and said, "Okay. I'll support you in this. Yeah. We can give it a trial run. It's going to be very different, but I can see how much this means to you."

"A *trial* run?" Jen said hotly. "Fred, there's something you don't understand. This is *my* decision—not yours. There is nothing trial about it. I really appreciate your willingness to be supportive Fred, but don't patronize me by pretending to go along with it, thinking you'll make the final decision on how permanent this becomes."

"Well *excuse* me, Miss Career Woman!" Fred retorted sarcastically. "Don't let me stand in your way!"

"Look Fred, I know this upsets you, but you'll see in time that it's a good thing. It's something I really need to do for myself."

"All right. All right, Jen. I'll do what I can to support you." Fred tried hard to make peace with his wife. He grinned ear to ear and squinted mischievously. "Well, I think I'm going to need some cooking lessons if you expect me to help with dinner from now on. Maybe I can even get one up on Billie at our next cookout."

Jen said, nodded her head. "Good plan, Fred. Good plan."

***

Jen let herself into her neighbor's kitchen. "Well ladies, congratulations are in order. I've got a job!"

Cat put down the spoon she had been using to stir a pot of beef stew and turned to hug her friend. "Jen, that's wonderful news!"

"So did Fred shit a brick when you told him?" Billie asked. She set the last plate on the table then joined the group hug.

"Enough to build a small house," Jen replied. "He wasn't too happy about it at first, but once I made him realize he had no choice in the matter, he changed his mind, and he's now being quite supportive."

"Very cool!" Cat added. "So, fill us in. What's the job, and when do you start?"

"Teacher's aide at the elementary school. I start the first day of the fall semester. That's about six weeks away. I am so excited I could burst!" Jen helped herself to a taste of the stew. "Wow, this is good!"

"So, how did this all come about?" Billie asked.

"I refused to cook dinner last night. I told him I was on strike," she explained.

"You didn't!" Cat replied.

"I did! It's amazing just how fragile the male ego is. We had a long talk about *wanting* to work, versus *having* to work, and about me feeling more like an unappreciated maid and caretaker than anything else. When he put himself in my shoes, he finally realized how I felt. Anyway, things are about to change in the Swenson household. I'm not so sure the kids are going to like it, but it's time they started to learn how to take care of themselves."

"Change. It's funny how people resist it," Billie commented. "Some change is inevitable. Change isn't always bad. Sometimes it signals growth."

"I think people just become too comfortable with routines. Change adds a level of discomfort that isn't always pleasant to deal with," Cat explained.

"You might be right, but like Billie said, some change is inevitable. Learning to adapt is sometimes smarter than fighting it," Jen added.

"Okay, enough with this psychological crap," Cat exclaimed. "Speaking of change, have you heard that we have a *new* lady living in this house?"

Jen looked back and forth between her friends as her mind imagined all sorts of things. "Don't tell me you two have gone kinky on me. Tell me you're not a threesome!" she begged.

"No! No, I mean, we have a newly *christened* lady living here...Tara," Cat explained.

"She's gonna kill you for telling," Billie warned.

"Tara?" Jen questioned. Seconds later, the light bulb came on. "Oh! I get it. Karissa started almost a year ago. Time to have 'the talk'," she winced.

"Yeah, I know," Cat complained. "My biggest fear is that Tara knows more about it than we do," she added, chuckling.

"Tara knows more about what?" Tara walked in on the conversation, followed closely by Karissa.

"Hey sweetie," Jen said. "Your moms were just telling me your big news."

"Ma!" Tara cried. "Please tell me you didn't," she begged, throwing her hands out to the sides.

Cat looked at her guiltily. Billie looked at Cat. Jen looked at the floor.

"Ahh!" She stomped through the kitchen on her way to her room.

Karissa just shrugged her shoulders and followed her friend.

CHAPTER 5

Cat picked up the ringing phone. "Hello?"

"Hi, love. Could I ask you to pick up the dry cleaning on the way home? I know it's out of your way, but it looks like I'll be running a bit late tonight," Billie asked.

"You haven't forgotten about dinner tonight have you, Billie?"

"No, I haven't. Actually, what I'm planning to wear is in that load of dry cleaning," she explained. "If you pick it up for me, it will save a little time."

"Okay. I can do that. What time do you expect to be home?"

"I should be there no later than five."

"All right. I'll see you then. I love you, sweetie."

"Love you too, Cat. See you soon."

***

"Tara. Tara, honey, come up here please," Cat yelled down the cellar stairs.

Tara scampered up the stairs, followed directly by Karissa. "Yeah?"

"Okay, sweetie, here's the number for the restaurant we'll be going to, and the number to my beeper. If anything goes wrong, don't hesitate to use them, okay?"

"Mom, you're just going out for dinner and a movie. We'll be fine," Tara complained. "Geesh, you'd think I was still a kid or something."

"Honey, you never know what could happen. I'll feel better knowing you can reach us in an emergency," Cat explained. She turned around in a circle. "How do I look?"

Cat wore a pair of form-fitting, high-waisted blue jeans, black dingo boots and a lightweight black sweater that was open at the neck and came just below her denim waistline.

"You look very cool, Mom," Tara commented, "But the jeans need to be baggier." She turned to Karissa. "Let's go back downstairs before Sky eats all the popcorn."

Cat raised her eyebrows at the retreating teenagers just as Billie came down the stairs wearing a blue pinstriped business suit.

"Aren't you going to get dressed for dinner?" she asked Cat. "We're running out of time."

"You're going dressed like that?" Cat asked incredulously.

"Well, of course. I always dress like this for business," Billie explained. "Come on, you'll make us late. We're meeting them at six."

Cat placed her hands on her hips and furrowed her brow. "Business? Billie, who do you think we're having dinner with?"

"Shannon and Julie Nash. I told you about them, remember? They're the ones with the seven year old daughter and the custody battle. We're meeting them at Trader Dukes at six to discuss their case." Billie saw the confusion on Cat's face. "Cat, I told you about this Tuesday night."

Cat shook her head. "Billie, we were out searching for our daughter all evening and half the night on Tuesday. You did *not* tell me about this. Don't you think I would remember something like that?"

"You'd better hurry and change your clothes. We're going to be late," Billie replied.

"Billie, we can't meet your clients tonight. We made a date with Jen and Fred for dinner and a movie."

Billie furrowed her brow. "Shit! Cat, I forgot all about it when I agreed to this business meeting."

Cat took Billie's face between her hands. "Honey, I'm sure the fiasco we went through with Skylar on Tuesday night caused a momentary lapse of memory. That's completely understandable."

Billie placed her hands on her hips. "Now what? I can't cancel the meeting on such short notice. Hell, they're probably on their way to the restaurant already."

Cat sighed deeply. "Do we both have to go to the meeting?"

Billie chewed on her bottom lip. "I suppose not, however, I *did* say we'd both be there."

Cat knew how important Billie's job was to her. Billie was in heaven when she was totally absorbed in a case. Cat loved to see the look of intense concentration and devotion on her face whenever she was caught up in research on the Internet at home. Billie truly loved her job, and Cat knew how important her image was to her clients. The decision was easy. She would call Jen and Fred, and reschedule their date.

"Hello, Jen?" Cat said into the receiver. "Jen, we have a conflict, and I'm afraid we'll have to reschedule our date for tonight. No. No, everyone is fine. It's just a business conflict with a couple of Billie's clients. I'm really sorry to drop this on you at the last minute," Cat apologized. "Okay, Jen. Our apologies to Fred too. All right. Let's make plans for next Friday. Okay. We'll talk to you later. Love ya! Bye." Cat saw the look of regret on Billie's face as she hung up the phone.

Billie took Cat by the shoulders. "Cat, I'm sorry about this. I thought for sure I told you. Obviously I didn't. I'll apologize directly to Jen tomorrow."

"I guess I'd better put something on that's a little more formal, huh?" Cat asked.

Nodding gratefully, Billie replied, "Yeah, I guess so." She kissed Cat lightly on the nose then leaned her forehead against the smaller woman's. "Thank you, Cat."

"You're welcome. I'd better hurry. We're going to be late."

***

"Seth...Steve. Over here."

Seth and Steve made their way stealthily toward their friend's voice coming from behind the gravestone.

"Timmy, why in hell did we have to meet in a graveyard, of all places?" Seth asked.

"Because no one would ever think to look for us here."

"You aren't afraid, are ya, Seth?" Steve teased.

Seth shot a dirty look at his friend. "Knock it off, all right? It just seems kind of weird, that's all," he said.

"Did you get the stuff?" Steve asked Timmy.

"Yeah, it's right here," Timmy bent over to retrieve a bag propped against the stone. The sound of glass clanging against glass reverberated through the dark night as Timmy lifted the bag.

"Cool. Give it over." Steve reached for the bag.

Timmy pulled the bag out of reach. "Hey, not so fast. Let's find a spot to sit where we can't be seen from the road."

The three friends moved silently between the gravestones, being careful to tuck themselves out of sight when the headlights of cars driving by illuminated portions of the area with their headlights. Finally, they made their way to the top of a long stairway that led to the lower levels of the cemetery.

"This looks like a good place." Timmy sat on the top step. "It's pretty far from the road. The only way someone will see us is if they drive right through the graveyard."

"Okay. Let's have some." Steve sat down next to Timmy.

Timmy and Steve both looked at Seth. "Well? Are you going to join us?" Timmy asked.

Seth looked at his friends warily and shifted from one foot to the other. He really didn't want to be there at that moment, but he feared he'd look like a scared baby in front of his friends. He shrugged his shoulders and sat down next to Steve and watched while Timmy pulled three bottles out of the bag. Soon, all three boys sat there, each cradling a bottle of cheap Irish whiskey.

Timmy unscrewed the cap from his bottle and held it to his nose. "Phew! Man, that smells really strong." He brought the bottle to his lips and allowed a small sip to enter his mouth. Seth watched Timmy's eyes grow wide. Timmy immediately began to cough and his face turned beet red before he finally regained control. He looked at his friend and presented them with a pained smile. "Wow! That's good stuff. What are you waiting for? Drink up," he said.

Steve and Seth looked doubtfully at the red hue on their friend's face, and slowly removed the caps from their own bottles. Steve grinned nervously, took a drink, and immediately duplicated Timmy's coughing fit from a few minutes earlier. "Timmy's right. This stuff is good," Steve said in a raspy voice.

Following suit, Seth reluctantly drank from his own bottle and tried with all his might not to choke as the burning liquid ran down his throat. Seconds later, it hit his stomach like a blowtorch. Seth's eyes flew open as the inferno raged inside his gut. "Oh, yeah, great stuff." Seth thanked God that he wasn't Pinocchio.

Seth rose to his feet and paced back and forth, while trying to maintain his tough guy image as the intoxicating liquid started to turn his legs to jelly. Moments later, the fire had cooled as he rejoined the others on the steps. A goofy grin spread across his face as he turned to look at his friends.

Before long, the three boys held half-empty bottles in their hands and giggled like school girls while they nudged each other's shoulders.

Seth's head bobbed side to side and he struggled to control his reflexes. *Why are Stevie and Timmy so far away?* He sat shoulder to shoulder with his friends and tried hard to concentrate on them when they talked. The ringing in his ears made it difficult for him to understand what they were saying. At one point, he hit himself in the nose while brushing an errant lock of hair from in front of his eyes. "Hey, guys, I can't feel my face. I'm nub. Ha! I said nub. I mean I'm numb."

"Cool, man." Timmy's eyes were nearly closed into small slits as he took another long swig from his bottle.

"Hey, Stevie, where ya going?" Seth said when Steve rose unsteadily to his feet.

"I gotta take a leak, dude." Stevie stumbled into the nearby bushes.

"Watch out. You might get poison ivy on your dick, man." Timmy laughed at his own humor.

"Eat shit and die, Timmy." Steve ventured deeper into the bushes.

While Steve was gone, Timmy turned to Seth. "This is really a rush, man. Wouldn't it be cool to be wasted like this in a boat? I mean...you have a hard enough time standing up in a boat when yer straight, never mind drunk."

"I'm not drunk." Seth jumped to his feet and nearly fell down the stairs from total lack of balance. Seth caught himself on the railing and stood tall with his chest puffed and weaving side to side. "See. I'm perfekly fine." Seth lost his balance once more and landed clumsily on the step beside Timmy.

Moments later, Stevie rejoined his friends on the steps. "Did someone say something about a boat?" he asked. His face was a mere fraction of an inch from Seth's.

"Geesh, Steve. Your breath smells like dead fish. Get outta my face." Seth pushed his friend away with just enough force to send Steve sliding down the stairs. His butt hit the edge of each step as he slid. When he reached the bottom, he sat there, whiskey bottle still intact, and looked up at his friends at the top. "Whoa!" he said. "That was way cool."

Seth and Timmy looked at each other and burst out laughing. They wobbled to their feet and made their way down the stairs, taking two at a time at breakneck speed and nearly falling over in the process. When they reached the bottom, they helped Steve to his feet. To their surprise, there was a rapidly growing bloodstain on the back of Steve's trousers.

"Whoa, dude," Timmy exclaimed. "You're bleeding, man."

"Where?" Stevie tried desperately to look behind him.

"On your butt." Seth tried very hard to hold in a laugh.

"On my butt? Wunnerful," Steve said. "Funny. It doesn't hurt."

"We could have my mom look at it for you. You might need stitches," Seth offered.

"No way, man. Your mom is *not* looking at my butt. How would you like *my* mom to look at *your* butt?" he asked.

Seth looked at his friend like he had been slapped in the face. "That's cold, Steve. Way cold. I get your point, dude."

"What are we gonna do about it?" Timmy took his final drink and threw the bottle into the bushes.

"I gotta either take you home or to the hospital, man," Seth said to Steve.

"Home. I'm not letting some cute nurse chick look at my butt either," Steve explained.

"Okay. Now if I can just remember where I parked my car..." Seth mused.

***

"May I help you ladies?" inquired the hostess.

"Yes. We're meeting someone here for dinner. The name is Nash? Shannon Nash?" Billie supplied.

The hostess looked at her reservation book. "Nash. Yes, follow me," she instructed.

Billie led Cat through the maze of tables with a hand on her back, as they followed the hostess to an alcove near the back of the room. Shannon and Julie Nash were waiting for them. Shannon immediately rose to her feet as Billie and Cat approached. She extended her hand to Billie. "Billie," she said.

Billie took her hand and nodded to the woman seated at the table. "Shannon, Julie," she said. She wrapped her arm around Cat's shoulder and stepped behind her. "Cat, I'd like you to meet Shannon and Julie Nash. Ladies, this beautiful creature here is my wife, Caitlain. Cat, for short."

Cat smiled broadly and extended her hand to the ladies.

Shannon took her hand first. "Shannon Nash. It's so nice to meet you. When Billie said you were beautiful, that was quite an understatement!"

Billie narrowed her eyes.

Cat beamed, her face flushed with embarrassment. "Stop it. You're making me blush!" She turned her attention to the woman still seated at the table and extended her hand once more. "You must be Julie."

Julie smiled. "That would be me. Have a seat. It's so nice to meet you."

Before Billie could reach it, Shannon held out the chair for Cat and gently pushed it under her as she settled herself in. Cat looked up and smiled broadly. "Thank you," she quipped lightly.

Shannon bowed at the waist. "My pleasure," she said before walking around the table to sit next to Julie.

Billie narrowed her eyes once more and sat in the last available chair next to Cat.

As soon as Billie was seated, the waiter approached the table and took their drink order. He left them with menus to peruse while he retrieved their beverages.

"Billie, I'd like to apologize again for inconveniencing you like this. I have been extremely busy at work lately and I just couldn't break away to meet with you at the office. I hope you'll accept this dinner as our way of thanking you for being so flexible," Shannon said.

Billie nodded. "As a rule, I don't meet personally with clients. I learned that lesson several years ago. However, I have a particular yen for cases like yours. I detest prejudice, pure and simple, especially when it's homophobic in nature. For that reason, I decided to bend the rules a bit."

"Well, we certainly do appreciate it, don't we, honey," Shannon replied, looking at Julie, who just nodded.

Cat looked back and forth between the women. Somewhere in the back of her mind, it bothered her that Julie seemed so passive compared to Shannon. She decided to find something out about the two ladies.

"Shannon," Cat said. "You mentioned being very busy at work. What kind of work do you do?"

Shannon put her menu down and smiled brightly at Cat. "I'm a marketing executive for a national advertising firm. I work out of a local office in the downtown area."

"I see," Cat replied. "How about you, Julie? What keeps you busy all day?"

Julie laughed. "I'm a domestic engineer, better known as a housewife. Our daughter Kaleigh keeps me hopping," she replied.

Cat liked Julie. She could see the sparkle in her eye as she talked.

"Billie told me a little something about your case. How old is your daughter?" she asked Julie.

"Kaleigh is seven, going on twenty," Julie answered. "I never would have imagined that one child could be such a handful!"

"You should try three!" Cat replied.

"Three?" Julie exclaimed. "Gosh, I'd be losing my mind! How old are they?"

"Well, Seth is sixteen, Tara is fourteen and Skylar is nine," Cat answered.

Shannon immediately interrupted the conversation. "Sixteen? No way! You can't possibly be old enough to have a sixteen year old child."

"Actually, Billie is Seth's biological mother and the two girls are mine, although you'd never know it by the way they act. Tara is so much like Billie, it isn't funny," Cat chuckled.

Billie took Cat's hand and kissed the back of it. "And Seth is exactly like you, my love," she said. She looked sideways at Shannon.

Cat smiled back and nodded in agreement.

"So what keeps *you* busy, Cat?" Julie asked.

"She's a doctor," Billie said proudly.

"Actually, I'm an anesthesiologist," Cat replied.

"Wow, I'm impressed," Julie said. "How do you have time for a job like that, *plus* three kids?"

It was Cat's turn to reach for Billie's hand. "Well," she said, "Billie and I pretty much share the workload evenly, and the kids are pretty good about picking up after themselves. Oh, and we have a wonderful support system in our neighbor, Jen, who has saved our butts on several occasions. I don't know what we'd do without her," Cat explained.

"It sounds like you have a wonderful life," Julie said wistfully.

"It's more than wonderful," Cat replied.

"Well, with your help, Billie, maybe our lives will improve as well," Shannon remarked.

"There is always a loser in a case like this, Shannon," Billie replied. "I really hate fighting cases based on emotional issues. Legally, this is an open and shut case. The law is clearly on your side. Emotionally, it will cause deep wounds. The child may lose a set of grandparents, who probably love her very much," Billie replied, leading the rest of the evening's conversation toward the legal case at hand.

***

"Did you hear that?" Jen asked.

"Hear what?" Fred replied around a mouthful of medium-rare steak.

"I just heard my name. Someone just said something about a neighbor named Jen. Didn't you hear it?"

"Ah, no, I didn't."

Jen strained her neck to look in the direction she thought she heard the voice come from. "I *know* I heard it!" she exclaimed as she finally spotted the table in the alcove. There at the table, she saw four women. The two with their backs to her looked vaguely familiar. They looked very much like they were engaged in lively conversation, laughing, and smiling.

The woman with short dark hair almost appeared to be flirting with one of the women, while the blonde at her side smiled and chatted amicably. Suddenly, the two women with their backs to Jen turned to look at each other.

"Oh. My. God," Jen exclaimed in a hoarse voice. "That's Billie and Cat over there."

"Where?" Fred asked.

"Over there." She pointed, trying hard not to be noticed by the two women. "So that's why they broke our date?" she rasped. "It doesn't look like a business meeting to me. It looks like Billie and Cat have bigger fish to fry than us, Fred." Hurt filled Jen's voice.

Fred patted Jen's hand. "Jen, don't jump to conclusions," he said. He looked at the women just as all four laughed suddenly. "Hmmm. I have to admit that the little gathering at the other table really doesn't look like a business meeting."

"So much for best friends," Jen said sadly. "I want to go home."

Fred looked at his wife incredulously. "But Jen, we just got here. They just barely delivered our meals."

"We'll ask for doggy bags. Fred, I really don't want them to see us."

"For crying out loud! Oh, all right," he said after seeing the hurt expression on Jen's face. "I guess it would be kind of awkward if they saw us."

Jen touched the side of Fred's face. "Thanks, hon," she said as she called the waiter over.

***

"Billie! Did you see that?" Cat exclaimed.

"See what?" Billie maneuvered the car through the dark city streets.

"Up there, in the cemetery," Cat replied. "I thought I saw something."

"Cat, who in their right mind would be in the cemetery at 10:00 p.m.? You must be seeing things."

Cat turned back around in her seat and folded her hands in her lap. "Maybe," she mumbled.

"So, what did you think of Shannon and Julie?" Billie asked.

"I really liked Julie. She's kind of quiet though."

"With Shannon around, I'm surprised she gets a word in edgewise," Billie remarked.

Cat looked at Billie. "I sense you don't like Shannon very much." she said.

Billie grinned sheepishly at Cat and chuckled to herself. "It's not that I don't like her. It's...well, it's the fact that she was openly flirting with you that I didn't appreciate," she explained.

Cat was flabbergasted. "She was not!"

"Oh, yes she was. *When Billie said you were beautiful, that was quite an understatement!*" Billie mocked. *"You can't possibly be old enough to have a sixteen year old child!"*

"Why, Billie Charland, I do declare you're jealous!" Cat said in her best Grandma Alex voice.

"Yer damned right I am, darlin'," Billie replied as Josephine Wyclyffe, causing a round of laughter that lasted the rest of the way home.

CHAPTER 6

Cat and Billie entered the kitchen to the sounds of the TV blaring loudly from the family room in the basement.

"I'll get it," Billie said.

"All right. While you do that, I'll check on Skylar." Cat detoured into the living room on her way to the second story bedrooms.

Billie descended the basement steps quietly, intending to sneak up on Tara to scare her from behind. She looked around when she reached the bottom stair. The back of the couch faced the cellar stairs, illuminated in stark relief by the only light source in the room—the TV. She saw no apparent sign of life. The room was seemingly empty. "Tara?" she said.

Two heads popped up quickly from behind the couch, followed by lanky bodies scurrying into a seated position.

"Mom!" Tara exclaimed nervously. "You're home early!"

"Apparently, not early enough!" Billie replied. "Wanna introduce me to your friend?" She crossed her arms and struck a pose that clearly indicated her agitated state.

Tara looked back and forth between her mother and her companion. "Ah, Mom, this is Kevin. Kevin, my mom," Tara said haltingly.

"Kevin," Billie reached out to shake the youngster's hand just a little too firmly. "Nice to meet you, now, I think it might be a good idea if you said goodnight to Tara."

Kevin winced as his hand was squeezed between Billie's fingers. He looked at Billie towering over him. "Ah, yeah. Right. Goodnight. Good idea." He turned to Tara. "I guess I'll see you later."

"I'll walk you to the door," Billie offered.

"Mom, you don't have to do that," Tara protested.

"Oh, yes I do. You wait right here, sweetheart, okay?" Billie replied in a saccharine voice.

Tara frowned. When Billie used that tone of voice, it usually meant she was in big trouble. A worried expression masked Tara's face as she watched Billie, followed by Kevin, ascend the stairs. Kevin looked back at Tara with an expression of sheer terror on his face. Tara winced once more.

Cat entered the kitchen at the same time Billie did.

"Sky is sound asleep, love, oh, and Seth isn't home yet," she proclaimed. She stopped short when she noticed the young man following closely behind Billie. Her eyes opened wide and then narrowed into slits. She placed her hands on her hips. "And who is this?" she asked sternly.

Billie took Kevin's arm and pushed him ahead of her, toward Cat. "This," she said with emphasis, "is Kevin. It seems he was keeping our daughter company while we were out. Kevin, this is Cat—Tara's *other* mother," Billie said.

A confused expression crossed Kevin's face. He shook Cat's hand. "Nice to meet you."

Before Cat could say anything to the frightened young man, Billie took his arm once more and guided him toward the door. "Kevin was just leaving," she said. Billie pulled the door open and stepped aside for Kevin to exit. "Goodnight, Kevin," she said firmly.

"G...Goodnight," he said and made a hasty retreat out the door. He broke into a dead run down the driveway as soon as his feet hit pavement.

Billie closed the door and turned back to Cat. "Looks like we need to have that talk with Tara," she said. "I just hope it isn't too late."

***

Tara sat on the couch in the family room. "For crying out loud, we didn't do anything!" Tara exclaimed. She looked at both mothers, who stood before her, anger radiating from their body language.

"Tara, when I came into this room, the two of you were flat-out horizontal on the couch. Christ, I couldn't even see you until you scrambled to sit up!" Billie shouted.

"But we didn't do anything! Just a little kissing," she explained.

"You don't need to lie down to kiss, Tara," Billie responded angrily.

"Wait. Wait a minute," Cat tried to calm Billie down. "Look, if you said you didn't do anything, I guess we have to believe you."

Her comment drew an incredulous look from Billie. She turned back to Tara.

"Tara, do you understand what *could* have happened? Do you understand that allowing yourself to get into the position Mom found you in could lead to things you are not prepared to handle?" Cat asked while Billie paced behind her.

"Gee Ma; even *I* know you can't get pregnant by kissing. Geesh! I *did* have sex education in school. I *do* know how babies are made," Tara said sarcastically.

Billie looked to Cat with an expression on her face that clearly communicated her desire to strangle their oldest daughter.

Cat placed a restraining hand on Billie's arm to calm her. "Tara, we really can do without the sarcasm," Cat scolded. "Look, you're fourteen years old. You're a smart girl. We all know you can't get pregnant by kissing, but you can get pregnant by allowing the heat of the moment to carry you away, allowing yourself to do something you'll regret later."

"Ma, I had no intentions of having sex with Kevin," Tara said in a raised voice.

Billie stopped pacing and stood behind Cat's shoulder. "But did Kevin have intentions of having sex with you?" she asked sternly.

Tara looked at both of her mothers. "I...I don't know," she admitted. "Yes. No. Maybe. Heck, I don't know. I wouldn't have let him anyway," Tara vowed.

Billie looked at Cat for silent approval for what she was about to say to their daughter.

Cat nodded her head slightly in affirmation and began to pace back and forth in front of the fireplace.

Billie sat beside Tara and took the girl's hand in her own. Tara refused to look her in the face. Billie placed her fingers under Tara's chin and forcibly turned her head so that their eyes met. "Tara," Billie began. "Honey, you do know that if Kevin wanted to have his way with you, he might have succeeded, just because he's bigger and stronger than you. He could have used force to take what he wanted."

Billie silenced Tara's emerging protest with two fingers against the teenager's lips.

"I'm not saying he *would* have done that, but he *could* have. Baby, most teenage boys are testosterone bombs waiting to explode. It's foolish to tempt fate by teasing them like that," she explained.

"I wasn't teasing him," Tara said. "How can you even suggest such a thing?"

"Tara, you were lying on the couch with him, kissing him and allowing him to run his hands over your body. All the while, you had no intention of putting out. Like it or not, that's teasing. You're lucky we came home when we did, or things might have gotten out of control."

Billie paused and looked at her daughter while Tara studied her hands in her lap intently. Billie looked at Cat when Cat stopped pacing and stood directly in front of them.

Cat sat on the coffee table, facing Tara. "Tara, honey, look at me," she urged the teenager. When Tara finally met her gaze, she smiled. "Sweetheart, you know I love all of you with all my heart. We both do. You know that, right?" she asked.

Tara nodded.

"Well," Cat's voice choked with emotion when she began to speak again. "Honey, do you understand how your sister was conceived?" she asked.

Tara shrugged. "Obviously, there was a guy involved."

Cat nodded. "Yes, there was, but not in the way you think. You were only five, so I don't know how much you remember. Honey, your sister was conceived through rape," she explained.

Tara's eyes grew wide. "By that man who beat you up?" she asked.

"Yes," Cat replied. "He was bigger than me, and stronger than me, and he took what he wanted. He threatened to hurt you and your brother if I fought him."

Tears filled Tara's eyes and Cat took Tara into her arms. The dam holding back Tara's tears burst, allowing them to flow freely down her cheeks.

Billie sat on the other side of Tara and rubbed her back. She placed a gentle kiss on her cheek.

Cat held Tara at arm's length. "Honey, I don't want you to think for one moment that I didn't want your sister. The moment I realized she was growing inside of me, I fell in love with her. Her conception is the only thing that kept me sane after what that man did to me. Tara, you'll be a woman soon enough. You'll fall in love, get married and have children of your own some day, but please don't rush it, and please don't put yourself at risk for having it forced on you. Do you understand, sweetheart?" she asked gently.

Tara closed her eyes and squeezed the tears from between her lids. She nodded and looked at her mothers. "I understand. I'm…I'm kind of tired. Can I go to bed?"

"Of course, love." Cat hugged her daughter once more. "I hope you have sweet dreams."

Tara hugged both mothers then bid them goodnight.

***

Cat sat on the edge of their bed and stared at the floor.

Billie glanced at her from the corner of her eye. "Cat?"

"I'm sorry, love, I didn't hear you. What did you say?" Cat replied.

Billie was brushing her teeth, within Cat's view, with the bathroom door wide open. She spit the rest of the toothpaste into the sink and quickly rinsed her mouth and brush then shut off the water. "Cat, are you all right?"

Cat nodded in a distracted sort of way. "Yes, I'm fine. I just can't stop worrying about Tara."

Billie sat on the bed next to her and draped her arm around Cat's shoulder. Cat immediately rested her head against Billie's cheek. "Honey, I know you are. I'm worried too, but I think we got the point across to her tonight."

"Billie, it's the *way* we had to do it that I'm upset about. It just seemed like such a hard topic to broach, you know?"

Billie looked into Cat's eyes. She never grew tired of looking at those beautiful green orbs. Each glance reminded her of how much she loved this woman. She smiled and nodded. "I know what you mean. To be honest with you Cat, I don't know if she would have really understood it until now," Billie reasoned.

Cat rubbed her face with both hands. "You may be right, Billie, but being a teenager is hard enough without having to learn something like that," Cat explained.

"Cat, I think you did a really good job of explaining to her that even though Sky wasn't conceived in love, she *was* born in love...and she is certainly being raised in a loving environment." Billie squeezed her shoulder slightly. "She'll be all right. I'll talk to her about it tomorrow if you think it will help," Billie offered.

Cat looked at Billie and smiled. She caressed the side of Billie's face. "Billie, have I ever told you what a good Mom you are?"

"Thank you, sweetheart." Billie lowered her face to capture Cat's mouth with her own. "And so are you," she added after a heartfelt kiss.

Once more, blue eyes met green as a spark of desire jumped between them. Without breaking the gaze, Cat gently brushed the erect nipple that stood out so prominently through Billie's nightshirt.

Billie gasped.

Cat smiled. "You liked that didn't you, my love?" Cat slid to her knees on the floor in front of Billie and pushed Billie's nightshirt up.

Billie braced herself and spread her legs to allow Cat closer access. She dropped her head back and moaned as Cat inhaled one erect bud into her mouth. Spurred on by Billie's reaction, Cat placed one hand flat on Billie's breastbone, and pushed slightly until Billie lay back on the bed, her legs hanging off the end and feet securely planted on the floor.

Cat ran both palms across Billie's abdomen and grasped the waistband of Billie's panties. A moment later, the panties were discarded. "Shirt next."

Billie briefly sat and helped Cat pull the T-shirt over her head. That, too, was discarded.

Cat felt a flood of desire invade her abdomen as she took in the beauty of the woman before her. Tears unexpectedly filled her eyes. "How did I get so lucky?" she asked softly.

Billie lifted her head from the bed and looked at Cat kneeling before her. She sat up and took Cat's face between her palms. "Sweetheart, you're crying. What's wrong?"

"Nothing is wrong. In fact, everything is oh, so right. I love you, Billie. I have never been happier in my life."

"Then, why the tears?"

"I…I don't know. I guess I'm just overwhelmed by what I feel for you…for us…for our life together."

Billie smiled and wiped the tear that had fallen to Cat's cheek. "So this is happiness leaking from your eyes."

Cat nodded.

Billie pulled Cat's face toward her and kissed her tenderly. "I love you, Cat. You've completely owned me since the day you walked into my aerobics class ten years ago. No matter how crazy our lives become, I look forward to spending every minute of it with you."

Cat looked directly into Billie's eyes. "I want you," she said.

Billie kissed her again. Soon the intensity of the kiss increased to the point that a deep growl grew from the depths of Cat's chest. Cat rose to her feet and one more placed her palm on Billie's chest. She pushed her back onto the bed and lay direct on top of her, breast to breast.

Billie wrapped her arms around Cat and with her feet, pushed them both toward the headboard. She grasped Cat's T-shirt. "Off with this."

Cat made short work of her T-shirt and panties and melted into the circle of Billie's arms. She explored Billie's neck and chest with her tongue, encouraged by the moans emitting from Billie's throat.

Cat realized she had the upper hand. She abruptly rose to her knees and knelt between Billie's legs. Slowly, the leaned forward and placed feather-light kisses from Billie's neck to her navel as her hands explored her body.

Cat paused and was nearly overcome by the look of near orgasmic pleasure on Billie's face. "You are so beautiful," Cat whispered. Cat's hand sought out Billie's pleasure point.

Billie's bottom rose completely off the bed as the intensity of the erotic assault increased.

Billie pushed herself closer to Cat. "Now, Cat. Please. I need you."

Cat complied and deeply penetrated Billie.

Billie's head pressed deep into the pillow and she released a long guttural moan from the depths of her throat.

Cat realized that Billie was very near the precipice and increased her ministrations. Soon, both women fell into a rhythm and before long Cat could feel Billie's body tighten around her hand.

"Let it go, love. I want all you have to give," Cat whispered.

Cat was overcome with emotion as she watched euphoric desire flush across Billie's breasts, shoulders and neck.

Billie soon found herself suspended in a place between reality and dreams as she clung to the edge of desire—so close, yet clinging on for dear life—wanting desperately to sustain the moment for as long as possible. Soon, the choice was no longer hers. Her body gave in. Waves of passion carried her away and deposited her safely into the arms of her beloved.

Several moments later, blue eyes met green and a silent message of love passed between them. Billie was captivated by the creature within whose arms she lay. She couldn't get enough of this beautiful woman with hair the color of autumn leaves. She blinked and allowed a few captive tears their freedom.

"Sweetheart, what's wrong? Did I hurt you?" Cat asked softly.

Billie caressed the side of Cat's face. "Cat, that was the most beautiful thing I have ever experienced. Thank you so much for choosing to love me."

Cat smiled and placed a delicate kiss on Billie's lips. "It wasn't a choice, my love."

Billie smiled and tried desperately to stifle a yawn.

Cat pulled down the sheet and motioned for Billie to climb in. "Come here."

"But, Cat, what about you?"

Cat placed two fingers on Billie's lips. "There will be time for that later. You're tired. Come."

Billie gave in and snuggled against Cat. Cat pulled the blankets over both of them and wrapped her arms around Billie. Within moments, Billie was fast asleep.

CHAPTER 7

Brrrrrrring! Brrrrrrring!

"What the hell?" Billie shot upright in bed.

Cat immediately followed suit. "Oh, my God! What time is it?" She reached for the clock on the bedside table.

Billie fumbled with the receiver in the dark. "Who could be calling at this hour?"

"No one calls in the middle of the night unless it's bad news," Cat said. She sat rigidly beside Billie and clutched the blankets to her chest while she listened to Billie's end of the conversation.

"Hello?" Billie said into the receiver.

"I just thought you'd like to know that we're on our way to the hospital."

Billie's head snapped up. "Jen?"

"We're bringing Stevie to the hospital for stitches," Jen began again.

"Jen? Jen, what happened?" Billie asked.

"Your son happened, that's what!"

"Whoa, wait a minute. What are you talking about?" Billie demanded.

"Billie, what is it?" Cat asked urgently.

Billie covered the receiver with her hand. "Cat, go check on the kids...please."

Cat quickly scurried off the bed, grabbed her robe to cover her nakedness and she ran toward the door.

"Stevie just got home. Apparently, Seth got him drunk tonight then pushed him down a set of stairs," Jen explained, bitterly. "He has a gash three inches long on his backside!"

Billie ran her hand through her hair. "Jen, you must be mistaken. Seth wouldn't do something like that."

"Oh, yeah? Go check his room. I'd venture to guess he isn't home yet," Jen said sarcastically.

Billie looked beyond the bedroom door into the hallway. Fear gripped her insides as Cat ran back into the room.

"Billie, Seth isn't in his room. My, God, it's after three. Where is he?"

Billie closed her eyes and composed herself. "Jen, I have to go," she said into the receiver. She did not want to admit to her friend that her son indeed was not yet home.

"He isn't there, is he?" Jen insisted.

"I'll talk to you in the morning Jen," Billie replied.

"Yeah, well, maybe that's not a good idea, Billie. Maybe our families need a break from each other for a while," Jen remarked.

"Maybe we do." Anger fueled Billie's response. "Goodbye, Jen."

Billie put the phone on the nightstand and faced Cat. "Cat, that was Jen. She claims that Seth got Stevie drunk tonight, then pushed him down a set of stairs. They're bringing Stevie to the hospital for stitches right now."

Cat folded her arms across her chest and started pacing. After crossing the room several times she stopped to look at Billie. "He wouldn't do that, would he?"

"I don't know, Cat. I hope not. But if he's in the same condition as Stevie, I'm more concerned about him driving his car drunk. I'll kick his ass from here to kingdom come and back if he is!"

Cat nodded her head in silent agreement.

"Look, I can't just sit here and wait for him to come home. I'm going to look for him." Billie grabbed a pair of running shorts and a T-shirt and slipped them on.

"I'm going with you," Cat insisted. "I'll wake Tara and let her know what's going on. She'll need to keep an eye on Sky if we're not back before they get up."

***

The tips of Cat's fingers were raw as she chewed at her nails. She and Billie drove all around the vicinity, looking for their errant son. It was now nearly five o'clock and the sun was making its way over the horizon. Billie was a nervous wreck as all sorts of horrible scenarios ran through her mind, including the possibility that he had been in a drunken accident and was now lying dead by the side of the road.

Deciding to return home to call the police, they were met by the sight of Seth's car in the driveway.

Cat let out a muffled cry of relief.

Billie reacted with anger. She brought the car to an abrupt halt, just inches behind Seth's car. She threw the door open and quickly emerged, slamming the door behind her. In three long strides, she reached Seth's door. Unfortunately for him, he was passed out across the front seat.

"Billie! Billie!" Cat quickly made her way around the front of the car, just in time to see Billie pull Seth out of the car by two handfuls of his shirt.

Still in a drunken stupor, Seth offered no resistance. Billie dragged him out of the car and roughly laid him over the trunk on his back. Without releasing the hold she had on his shirt, Billie leaned in very close, the expression on her face clearly indicating her anger. Cat stood by, desperately wanting to intervene, but restrained herself.

For long moments, Billie held eye contact with her son, who realized, despite his inebriated state, how much trouble he was in.

"Mom..." he began.

"Don't you 'Mom' me!" she spat into his face. "You are so in trouble, young man!" she hissed. "Hand them over." She held out her hand.

Seth looked at her blankly.

"Now!" she nearly shouted.

Seth's brow crinkled and he looked at Cat…clearly confused.

"Your car keys, Seth. Hand them over," Cat said.

Seth looked back and forth between his mothers. His eyes opened wide as realization crossed his face. "No, way!"

"Yes, way!" Billie returned. "Put them here." She held her hand close to his face.

"But Mom!" he whined.

Billie grabbed his shirtfront again and pulled him closer. "Look Seth, you violated the number one rule...no drinking and driving. For Christ's sake, Seth, you're only sixteen years old. God damn it! You could have killed yourself and Stevie too."

Billie abruptly released him and walked away to compose herself. She turned back to her son, who was busy adjusting the front of his shirt, and again held out her hand for the keys. Seth begrudgingly gave them to her. "For the foreseeable future, you drive only to work and back. At all other times, the car is mine. Is that understood?" Billie said sternly.

Seth refused to answer. He stood there with his hands on his hips and his gaze on his shoes.

Billie knew she wouldn't get a response from the young man. "Now, don't think for one moment that this is over. You and I are going to have a long talk once you've had a chance to sleep this off. I want an explanation, including where you got the alcohol, and just how Stevie ended up needing stitches."

Seth looked up suddenly. "Steve needs stitches?"

Billie just nodded.

Seth leaned against his car, still somewhat intoxicated. It was obvious to Billie that he was struggling with the news that his best friend needed medical attention.

Cat approached Seth and rubbed his back. "Go on up to bed. We'll talk about this later, okay? I'm sure Stevie will be fine."

Seth looked at his mother through moist eyes. He nodded slightly and headed for the house, purposely avoiding Billie's gaze. Billie and Cat stood there and watched their son shakily negotiate the steps. When he was safely inside the house, Cat turned to Billie and raised her eyebrows.

Billie immediately became defensive. "Now don't tell me I was too hard on him, Cat. He could have killed himself or someone else. This is one mistake he will pay for dearly with his freedom."

Cat stepped into Billie's personal space and raised herself on tiptoe. She placed a gentle kiss on Billie's lips. "Actually, I agree with you," she said. "Now, we have about two hours before Sky gets up. What do you say we try to get some sleep now that all three of the kids are home, safe and sound?"

***

Billie leaned against the wall. She held the receiver to her ear and she listened to it ring three times before being answered.

"Hello?" a masculine voice responded.

"Fred? Fred, this is Billie. Is Jen home?" she asked

"Yeah, but I don't think she wants to talk to you," Fred replied.

"Fred, this is bullshit and you know it. We can't let our friendship go to hell over something our kids have done. Now let me talk to her," Billie demanded.

"Billie, let me have the phone," Cat insisted after listening to Billie's end of the conversation.

Billie reluctantly handed the receiver to Cat.

"Fred, honey, this is Cat. How is Stevie this morning?"

Billie silently berated herself for not asking about Stevie's health before asking after Jen.

"Stevie will be fine," Fred replied. "He has a gash in his backside that required about a dozen stitches. He'll be sore for a while, but it's nothing debilitating."

"Good. Give him our best, okay? Look Fred, Seth is still in bed, so we haven't had a chance to hear his side of the story. Has Stevie said anything about what happened last night?"

"I'm afraid Stevie wasn't making a lot sense himself last night. He was pretty much incoherent. He said something about the graveyard, and whiskey, and then something about a boat. I don't know. I'm sure it was the alcohol talking," Fred explained.

"Graveyard?" Cat asked. She looked at Billie with raised eyebrows. "I knew I saw something last night!"

"You saw them?" Fred asked.

"Coming home from dinner last night around ten, Billie and I passed the graveyard, and I was sure I saw some movement in there. If we had known it was the boys, we would have stopped."

"Well, its water under the bridge at this point. Look, Jen and I think the boys need some time apart. We need to send the message that this kind of behavior is unacceptable," Fred stated.

"I agree that this behavior is unacceptable, but keeping the boys apart isn't necessarily the answer Fred," Cat replied.

"Look Cat, we've made our decision. I've got to run," he replied haltingly.

"Fred, please let me talk to Jen," Cat pleaded.

"Good bye, Cat."

Cat stared in disbelief at the receiver in her hand. "He hung up on me! I can't believe he hung up on me!"

"I'm going over there. Something else is going on here that they're not telling us about. We've had spats before over the kids and they haven't led to this kind of hostility. Heck, remember that disastrous camping trip several years ago?" Billie asked. "The kids fought like cats and dogs nearly the whole time."

"Billie, maybe we should let them cool off for a while. I can understand them being angry with Seth if they think he's caused Stevie harm. Anyway, we need to hear Seth's side of the story before we confront the Swensons."

"Did I hear Stevie's name?" came a husky voice from the doorway.

Billie and Cat turned to look at the source of the question and saw a bedraggled Seth half standing, half leaning against the kitchen door frame.

Billie's eyes narrowed at her son, who winced under the scrutiny. "I think you have some explaining to do," she said.

Seth walked across the kitchen, dragging his feet along the way, and dropped heavily into a chair. He propped his elbows on the table and lowered his head into his hands. "Where would you like me to start?"

"Try from the beginning." Cat sat in a chair opposite Seth. Billie paced the floor behind her son.

Seth sat back in his chair and folded his hands on the table in front of him. He hesitated and picked at the imaginary dirt from beneath his nails, all the while, avoiding his mother's gaze.

"Well?" Cat prompted.

"I didn't want to do it, but I was afraid I would look like a wuss if I didn't," Seth said. "It wasn't my fault."

Billie walked around the table and stood behind Cat. She leaned in to address her son. "I don't want to hear about fault, Seth. You are most definitely at fault. You chose to drink. You chose to drive. I'm sure no one twisted your arm."

Seth lowered his chin to his chest.

Billie resumed pacing, this time, behind Cat.

Cat touched Seth's hand. "Seth, where did you get the alcohol?"

"You know my friend, Timmy Rabidoux? Well, his older brother got it for us," he confessed.

"What's his name, Seth?" Billie asked in mid-stride.

"Randy."

Billie continued to pace. Silence prevailed except for the sound of footsteps crossing back and forth. Long moments later, Seth broke the unbearable silence.

"So, is Stevie all right?" he asked.

"Yes he is, no thanks to you. He needed a dozen stitches," Billie ran her hands through her hair. "Seth, what were you thinking?" She placed her hands on the table and leaned toward her son. "What in God's name were you thinking? You are only sixteen. You could have been killed. You could have killed Stevie as well."

Seth hung his head once more. "I know," he replied softly.

Billie pushed herself away from the table and crossed her arms over her chest. "I am so angry with you right now."

Cat approached Billie and took her hands in hers. "Billie, honey, come sit and let Seth explain his side of the story, okay?"

Billie's gaze met Cat's. The tenderness in Cat's eyes had an immediate effect on her anger. She took a deep breath and silently chided herself for violating the primary rule of her trade…innocent until proven guilty. She realized that she wasn't giving Seth an opportunity to defend himself. She closed her eyes for a moment to regain her composure then pulled out a seat at the table.

"Okay," Billie said to her son. "Explain yourself."

Seth cleared his throat and looked from Billie to Cat, and back again. "Timmy suggested to Steve and me that we have a guy's night out and drink a little whiskey. He said his brother could get us the stuff. I really didn't want to do it. I warned them that our parents would kill us if they found out, but they teased me and called me a mama's boy, so I went along with them," he started to explain.

"They called you a mama's boy?" Cat asked.

Seth just nodded. "Yeah. It's kind of tough living in a house full of girls. Top it off with two moms, and…well, you get my point. I get teased some times, but I try to ignore it."

Billie frowned. "Who is teasing you, Seth?" she asked in her best 'I'm gonna kick their asses' voice.

Seth threw his hands up. "Gee, Mom, are you gonna fight all my battles for me? It's bad enough that I get teased. I don't need you beating their Dads up too," Seth exclaimed.

A tiny smile crossed Cat's face as she watched her son back Billie off. Billie was taken aback by Seth's directness.

She sat back in her seat, with her eyebrows raised high on her forehead.

"So go on," Cat urged. "How did you end up in the graveyard, and how was Stevie hurt?"

Seth leaned his forearms on the table. "We went to the graveyard because Timmy said it was one place no one would look for us. Steve cut his butt when he slid down the stairs onto a broken bottle."

"So you didn't push him?" Billie asked.

Seth's eyes flew open. "Push him? Why would I push my best friend down the stairs?" he asked unbelievably.

"That's what Jen told us last night when she called," Billie replied.

"Where would she get that idea?" Seth asked.

"She must have gotten it from Stevie," Billie said. "Or at least, that's what she understood Stevie to say."

Seth stood up and pushed his chair back. He held his hands out to the sides and tried desperately to defend himself. "I did *not* push Steve down the stairs. If he's telling his mom a lie to shift the blame to me, I'm gonna pound him!" Seth headed toward the door.

"Get back here, Seth. You're not going anywhere," Billie commanded.

Seth stopped at the door and turned to look at his mother. "Mom, I can't let him accuse me like that. I didn't do it!" he stated adamantly.

Cat rose from her chair and approached her son. She cupped the side of his face with her palm. "We believe you, Seth, but the fact is, Jen and Fred want to put a little distance between our families for now."

Seth narrowed his eyes. "Are you saying I'm not allowed over there anymore?"

Cat nodded.

"Seth, come back here and sit down. We're not finished with this discussion," Billie said.

With the trio once again seated around the table, Billie cleared her throat and delivered the punishment. "As I said last night, your driving privileges are suspended except to go to work. In addition, you will have an eight o'clock curfew for the next two weeks."

"How am I gonna get to school?" Seth asked.

"If you don't have your car back by the time school starts, you'll take the bus," Billie replied.

"Oh man! I'm gonna look like a real loser to the guys," he complained.

Billie tapped her forefinger on her son's chest. "Anyone who breaks the law and does something as dangerous and stupid as drinking and driving is acting like a loser. I would have *never* put you in that category, Seth. You are a very good kid who made a very bad decision. I don't want to see that happen again. Understood?"

"Don't worry. It won't," Seth replied sadly.

Cat circled the table and wrapped her arms around her son and then kissed him on the head. "Go get your shower. I'll whip you up some pancakes for breakfast before you go to work. Okay?" she offered.

Seth nodded and rose to his feet. He stopped at the doorway to the living room and turned to look at his mothers. "I'm really sorry about this," he said. "It won't happen again."

After watching her son go, Cat turned to Billie. "First Skylar and her disappearing act, then Tara and her horizontal mambo, and now, Seth. I think it's a conspiracy!" she exclaimed.

Billie circled the table and folded Cat within her arms. "I'm going to get on line and add 'Miss Clairol' to our stock portfolio. I have a feeling it's going to do well this year," she joked.

CHAPTER 8

Billie stretched her long legs out on the couch and rested her head upon the overstuffed arm. Her right knee was bent and pressed into the back of the couch. Cat lay on her side between Billie's legs. Her long golden red hair was spread across Billie's breasts and her left arm was squeezed between the couch and the warm body beneath her. She sighed contentedly and enjoyed the feel of Billie's free hand running up and down her back. 'An Affair to Remember' was playing softly on the television across the room.

Cat pointed to the TV. "I love this part. Watch his face when he realizes she's paralyzed. See? Right there. He sees the portrait he painted of her on her wall. Remember the salesman sold it to her when she came into the gallery in her wheelchair?" Cat looked at the amused expression on Billie's face. "Billie! I can't believe you've never seen this movie."

"I never had the patience to sit through one of these old shows. Or maybe I just never had anyone I wanted to watch them with." Billie traced the end of her finger along the side of Cat's face.

Cat smiled. "Have I told you yet today that I love you?"

"Once or twice, I think. But I never tire of hearing it." Billie cupped Cat's face in her palm.

Cat inhaled deeply and leaned into Billie's touch. She closed her eyes for the briefest of moments. "Listen," she said.

Billie stopped and concentrated on her environment and frowned. "I don't hear anything," she said.

"Exactly. God, Billie. I had forgotten how quiet the house can be," Cat remarked.

Billie lazily played with Cat's hair. "Well it won't be for long. Seth should be home from work in a few hours."

"It was nice of Mom and Dad to take the girls for the night," Cat said. "I think Tara is still a little preoccupied with the talk we had with her last night. I hope Mom can get her to open up and talk to her about it. God knows she won't talk to me. Besides, she was at loose ends this afternoon without Karissa," she added. "Time with Mom and Dad will do her some good I think."

"I know what you mean. Missy is spending the weekend with her Dad, so Sky is on her own as well," Billie replied. "Sometimes I wish there were fewer years between Tara and Sky. Tara's at the age where Skylar is just a pain in the ass to her. Poor Sky adores her sister, but Tara doesn't have time for her. I feel really bad for the little rugrat sometimes."

"You know that's perfectly normal," Cat replied. "Drew was kind of an afterthought, so she was a little younger than the rest of us. I was the next oldest, so I got stuck playing with her all the time. I love her to death now, but I can remember how angry I was when Mom made me take her everywhere with me."

"Maybe being any only child gives me a different perspective," Billie observed. "I would have loved having a little sister to tag along with me."

Cat rolled onto her stomach and braced her hands on the couch on both sides of Billie. She lowered her face to Billie's and stopped a hair's breath away from her lips. "I'll bet you were a beautiful child," she breathed into Billie's mouth.

Billie took Cat's face between her palms and kissed her passionately.

Brrrrrring! Brrrrrring!

Cat pulled her mouth from Billie's and looked at the phone. "Damn!" she whispered.

"Let it ring," Billie urged.

"Billie, I can't. What if it's one of the kids?"

Billie pressed the back of her head into the arm of the couch. "Grrr. I guess you're right," she admitted.

Cat climbed off the now heated wife and went to answer the phone.

"Hello."

"Hi. Is Billie home?" a female voice replied.

"Yes, she is. May I ask whose calling?"

"Shannon Nash."

"Just a moment, Shannon." Cat handed the phone to Billie. Her eyebrows perched high on her forehead.

Billie covered the receiver with her hand and frowned. "What is she doing calling me at home on a Saturday?"

Cat shrugged.

Billie brought the receiver to her ear. "Shannon, this is Billie. Is there a problem?"

"Hi Billie," Shannon chirped cheerily. "No problem at all. I just wanted to call to thank you for last night's dinner. Julie and I had a really good time. We both thought Cat was just a doll. In fact, Julie and I enjoyed your company so much that we would like you to join us for an afternoon on the lake. We have a pontoon party boat with lots of room for both of you and your kids. What do you say?" she asked hopefully.

Billie was taken aback by Shannon's unexpected invitation. It wasn't often that clients wanted to socialize. "Ah, let me run that by Cat. Could you hold on for a minute?"

"Sure... take all the time you need," Shannon replied.

Billie covered the receiver once more. "They want us to join them for an afternoon on the lake. Can you believe it?"

Cat narrowed her eyes. "Do you really think we should? You don't usually like to socialize with clients."

"You're right, but they won't be clients for very long. Their case is basically open and shut," Billie explained. "So, what to do you think? A boat ride *does* sound nice."

"I thought you didn't like Shannon," Cat commented.

"I don't dislike her, Cat. I just don't appreciate her being nicey-nicey with my wife. I'll just keep an eye on her, and if I don't like what I see, I'll throw her overboard. How's that?" Billie replied with a lopsided grin.

The childlike look of excitement on Billie's face was something Cat couldn't resist. "You know, you're awfully cute when you smile like that. If you really want to go, then let's."

"Cool!" Billie returned the receiver to her ear. "Shannon, it sounds like a date, but it'll be just Cat and I. Seth is working, and the girls are doing an over-nighter with their grandparents. Yeah, it *is* too bad. You're right—Skylar is pretty close to Kaleigh's age. I'm sure between the four of us, we can think of ways to entertain her. As long as there is no paper dolls involved, I'm in!" Billie laughed. "I guess we'll see you in about twenty minutes then. Okay. Bye," Billie said after giving Shannon their address.

Billie turned to Cat. "They'll be here to pick us up in about twenty minutes."

"I guess we'd better change our clothes. I wouldn't want Shannon and Julie catching us still in our nightshirts in the middle of the afternoon," she chuckled.

Billie drew Cat into an embrace. "It's not every day we get to laze around and not get dressed. I was kind of enjoying it."

"So was I, love. So was I, but I don't think going bra-less is proper attire for boating."

"You may be right...not unless there's a wet T-shirt contest involved."

Cat snickered. "Those killer breasts of yours would be sure to win. They should be registered as lethal weapons."

Billie took Cat's hand and led her toward the stairs to the bedrooms. "If we had more time, I'd show you lethal."

"Promises, promises," Cat joked.

***

"How do I look?" Cat asked as she turned around in circles.

Billie ogled her wife dressed in shorts, tank tops, deck shoes and baseball cap. She stepped into Cat's personal space and nuzzled her neck. "Good enough to eat," she replied.

Cat caught Billie's face between her hands. "I don't think so, Big Guy. You *had* your chance. You passed it up for an afternoon on the lake, remember? You'd better have some good bait if you want fish for dinner tonight," she added with a wide grin on her face.

Billie's eye widened. "That was really, really bad, Cat!"

Cat raised her arms out to the sides. "Hey, I never said I was a comedian."

The sound of a car horn reached their ears.

"They're here," Billie said. "Let's go."

"Wait. Let me grab the sunscreen." Cat rummaged through the medicine cabinet in the bathroom. "Here it is. I guess we're all set."

Billie stepped onto the porch just as Shannon rang the doorbell. She extended her hand in greeting. "Great timing."

"Are you all set for a day on the water?" Shannon asked.

"You bet. Thanks for the invitation," Billie replied.

"Our pleasure." Shannon offered her arm to Cat, who took it willingly.

Billie looked questioningly at Cat.

As they approached the car parked at the curb, Julie climbed out, followed by a little girl with blonde ringlets who glued herself to Julie's side.

Cat was immediately smitten with the little tyke. She released Shannon's arm and bent over to address the little girl. "You must be Kaleigh."

Kaleigh smiled shyly and half buried her face in Julie's shirt.

Julie tried to shake her daughter loose, and urged her to be more social. "Kaleigh, sweetie, this is Miss Cat, and that is Miss Billie," she said. "She's pretty shy until she gets to know you, then she'll talk your ears off," Julie added.

Shannon held the car door open for Cat. "What do you say we head for the lake?"

Before stepping into the car, Cat noticed another vehicle approaching them from down the street. "Billie, isn't that Jen?"

"Yes, it is," Billie replied.

Billie and Cat waved cheerfully as Jen's car approached. They were sorely disappointed as they watched a deep frown cross Jen's features and her car speed up as she drove past them.

Billie and Cat looked at each other sadly. Billie shook her head back and forth, and Cat wiped tears from the corners of her eyes. In the back seat of Shannon's car, they held hands and communicated their sorrow to each other silently as they conversed with Shannon and Julie on the way to the lake.

***

Shannon's car came to a full stop in front of Billie and Cat's house. "Julie, Shannon, thank you for a wonderful afternoon. We really enjoyed ourselves," Cat said.

Shannon quickly climbed out of the driver's seat and opened Cat's door for her. You are entirely welcome, Cat. It's just too bad Billie got a little wet."

Billie exited through the door on the opposite side of the car in time to see Shannon gallantly open Cat's door. Billie had to consciously remind herself that Shannon was probably just being a gracious host. "A *little* wet?" Billie said incredulously. "Try soaked to the bone."

"Kaleigh didn't mean to knock you overboard. She just gets a little rambunctious sometimes and doesn't know her own strength." Julie tried hard not to laugh through her explanation.

"I've told her a million times not to run across the deck of the boat, but you know kids. They've got a knack for acting first and thinking later," Shannon chimed in. "Isn't that right, Kaleigh?" she added.

Billie looked over the roof of the car at Cat. "Don't we know it!" they said in unison, causing both to laugh at their timing.

"Well, we hope it didn't spoil the afternoon for you," Julie said apologetically.

Billie smiled. "Not at all. After all, what's a little water among friends?"

"I'm glad you feel that way," Shannon observed. "So... considering Kaleigh and Skylar didn't get a chance to meet today, how about a cookout at our place tomorrow?"

Billie experienced an odd feeling of being invaded, and of being rushed into a relationship she wasn't sure she wanted. However, she didn't want to disappoint Cat, who had thoroughly enjoyed Julie's company that afternoon.

"I think we're free. Cat?" Billie deferred.

"Yes, I don't think we have anything else planned."

"I guess that's a yes," Billie said, "however, let's have the cookout here so Seth can join us when he gets off work."

"Sounds good to me," Shannon replied. "Why don't we give you a call tomorrow morning and set up a time and figure out a menu?"

Cat turned to Billie. "Maybe Jen and Fred would be willing to join us as well."

Billie's thoughts flew immediately to the nagging sensation that had been plaguing the back of her mind since Jen's dismissal of them earlier that day. "We can certainly offer, Cat, but don't get your hopes up."

Cat nodded her head repeatedly. "I know, but like you said, we can certainly offer." She looked at Shannon and Julie. "You don't mind, do you? Jed and Fred...and their kids, Stevie and Karissa are our closest friends."

"No, please. The more the merrier," Shannon replied.

"Good. Then we'll hear from you tomorrow morning?" Cat reiterated.

"Tomorrow morning," Shannon repeated. "Well I guess we'd better get the little one home. It's nearly time for dinner."

Julie waived to them over the top of the car. "See you tomorrow."

Cat wrapped her arms around Billie's waist as they watched Shannon and Julie drive away. "Did we just commit our entire weekend to your clients?"

Billie enveloped Cat in an embrace. "Looks that way, doesn't it?"

"I hope we're not making a mistake," Cat said softly.

"That thought has crossed my mind as well, but somehow, I don't think so. You know, maybe it's time to develop new friendships. It could be that Jen and Fred are becoming tired of us. Who knows what's motivating Jen's behavior of late," Billie mused.

Cat looked at Billie. "I'm worried about her, Billie. Something besides the situation with Seth and Stevie has got to be wrong. For the life of me, I can't figure it out."

"Well, maybe we need to give her some space. Hopefully, she'll come around soon. If not, then we'll confront her directly. If the friendship is truly lost, then we'll have nothing left to lose by trying," Billie reasoned.

Tears welled in Cat's eyes. "I hope the friendship isn't lost. I truly love Jen. I love her like she is one of my sisters—maybe even more—in a different way."

Billie nodded. "I know, baby. I know. I don't want to lose her either. We'll work it out somehow." Billie squeezed Cat gently and took her hand to lead her toward the house.

***

"Hello, Fred? Hi, this is Cat. Is Jen right there?" Cat paced the living room, her cell phone held tightly in her nervous white-knuckled grasp.

"Cat, Jen can't come to the phone right now. She isn't feeling well," Fred explained.

"Isn't feeling well? Is there something I can do?" Cat's medical training immediately came to the forefront.

"No. It's just a little upset stomach. She'll be fine," he explained.

"Can I come to see her?" Cat suggested.

"Cat..." Fred said haltingly. "Cat, she really doesn't want to see you right now. Neither of you."

"Damn it, Fred! Billie and I have no idea why she—no...why *both* of you are so upset with us. How can we defend ourselves? How can we make amends when we don't even know what we did wrong? This isn't fair."

"I'm sorry, Cat, but now isn't the time to discuss it. Look, I've got to go," he said stoically.

"Fine. Have it your way, but know that this isn't over. You'll have to talk to us sooner or later. Goodbye," she said firmly. Cat disconnected the call before Fred could voice a response.

"Ahhh!" Cat began to pace the room. "That man!" She stopped in front of Billie. "You know, most of the time Fred is carefree and quite easy to manipulate, but all of the sudden, he's so stubborn and obstinate."

"He's defending what's his, Cat. I'd do the same. The tamest animal will turn wild in defense of its family. I sure wish I understood what's behind it, but I can't say that I blame him," Billie observed.

During Cat's rampage Seth had emerged from his room upstairs. He stepped into the living room just as Cat let out her last frustrated scream. "What's up?" he asked.

Billie and Cat turned toward the stairs at the sound of their son's voice. "Hey Scout," Billie said. "We were just discussing how Jen and Fred seem to be angry with us all of the sudden and we really don't understand why."

"Yeah, I know what you mean." Seth dropped heavily onto the couch. "Steve stopped into the store today to talk to me against his parents' wishes. Oh, by the way, he's gonna be fine. His butt is a little sore, but he's okay."

Cat sat on the coffee table in front of her son. Billie joined him on the sofa. "So, what did Stevie have to say?" Cat prompted.

Seth looked back and forth between his mothers. "Well for starters, they're pretty upset with me. They think I pushed him down the stairs on purpose. Steve was too drunk to remember any of it to tell them what really happened, and they're also mad at me for driving him home drunk," Seth admitted.

"I can't say that I blame them," Billie interrupted. "You're paying for that with the loss of your car. We were none too pleased about it either."

Seth had the decency to look ashamed. "Anyway, Steve said something about you and Mom having 'better fish to fry'," he said to Cat. "That made absolutely no sense to me."

Cat sat up straight and looked at Billie. A frown crossed her face. "Better fish to fry? What the hell...I mean, what on earth does she mean by that?"

"I have no clue," replied Billie. "Did Steve say anything else, Seth?"

"Only that his Mom wasn't feeling too good today and he had to get back home to help his dad rake the yard," Seth answered. He looked back and forth between his bewildered mothers. "I'm hungry. Is there anything to eat?"

Cat snapped out of her daze and smiled broadly at her son. "Just like a kid," she joked. "The whole world could be coming to an end, and all they think about is eating. Come on, rugrat. Let's raid the cupboard and see what I can whip up for dinner." She rose to her feet and extended her hand to her son.

Seth quickly rose to his feet and scooped Cat into his arms. She wiggled, giggled and screeched as he carried her into the kitchen. Billie chuckled and followed in their wake.

CHAPTER 9

Julie crossed the yard carrying a bag full of picnic goodies. "Hey, there. Are we too early?"

Billie looked up from behind the grill where she was squatting to turn the propane gas on. "Hi, Julie. Your timing is perfect." Billie looked toward the driveway where Shannon was opening the trunk of the car.

Julie held the bag up. "Where would you like this?"

"You can put it on the picnic table over there," Billie instructed. "Is there anything that needs to be refrigerated?"

"Not in here. The salads are in the cooler. I think Shan is trying to get it out of the trunk right now."

Billie noticed that Shannon was indeed struggling to get something out of the trunk, and ran to help her. "Can I give you a hand with that?" she asked.

Billie watched as the distress which was evident on Shannon's face quickly dissolved into relief. "Phew! You sure can. Julie has a habit of packing the cooler *after* it's already in the trunk. This thing weighs a ton," Shannon exclaimed.

Together, they hefted the cooler out of the small trunk and placed it on the ground behind the car.

"What have you got in this thing?" Billie asked.

Shannon chuckled and opened the lid. Inside, neatly packed, were several cans of soda, beer, a bottle of wine, macaroni salad, potato salad, fruit salad, and an assortment of condiments...all on ice. "Julie believes in coming prepared."

"I'll say," Billie replied. "I guess we'll have plenty of food even if I *do* murder the burgers on the grill!"

Shannon grinned. "You too, huh? Julie says my cooking is the best remedy for obesity. No one would dare eat it. She won't let me anywhere *near* the grill."

"The last time I grilled, Cat called the morgue to take the burgers and dogs away. She and our friend Jen...ah...ah... well, anyway, it was pretty funny," Billie said haltingly. A wave of sadness washed over her at the mention of Jen's name.

Shannon placed a hand on Billie's arm. "Are you all right?" she asked.

Billie shrugged it off. "Yeah, I'm fine." Changing the subject abruptly, she shoved her hands into the back pockets of her cut-offs and looked around distractedly. "Maybe I should give Cat a hand. She's in the house making hamburger patties."

"Thanks for the offer sweetie, but I'm finished," Cat said. She approached the ladies carrying a large plate of jumbo burgers ready for the grill. "Hi, there, Shannon," she quipped before addressing Billie. "Have you started the grill?"

Billie's hands flew out of her pockets and into the air. "Damn! No, I was sidetracked. I'll do it right now," she said apologetically and headed in the direction of the grill.

"My fault. She was giving me a hand." Shannon hefted the cooler and walked beside Cat toward the picnic table. "So where are the kids?" she asked Cat.

"They should be on their way home right now," Cat replied. "At least the girls are. Seth is working. He should be home in a couple of hours. We'll have to save him some of these burgers or we'll never hear the end of it," she chuckled. Cat looked around. "Where's Kaleigh?"

"Asleep in the back seat of the car. She was so wound up after our day on the boat yesterday it took hours for her to settle down. I don't think she finally crashed until about eleven o'clock last night," Shannon answered.

Cat and Shannon migrated toward the table where Julie was laying out place settings for eight. "Well, I hate to break it to you, but she's bound to go home again today all wound up," Cat remarked.

"Who's that?" Julie asked.

Shannon dropped the cooler heavily on the bench and embraced her wife. "Our daughter, dear heart. Cat was just remarking that yesterday's frenzy will probably be worse tonight," She placed a kiss on Julie's nose.

"Heaven help us!" Julie exclaimed.

"If it's any consolation, we'll have a wound up rugrat on our hands as well. Speaking of which, I believe they're home," Cat observed as sounds of children's voices came from the driveway.

"Mama!" shrieked a high-pitched voice. Skylar ran across the yard and into Cat's arms, nearly knocking her to the ground.

"Goodness, Sky Baby! One of these times you're going to find us both in a heap when you do that," Cat exclaimed.

"Sky Bird!" Billie shouted from the grill area. "How's my girl?"

"Mommy!" Skylar threw herself into Billie's arms, only to be hoisted up and swung around in a circle.

"Did you have a good time with Grandma and Grandpa?" Billie asked the child

Skylar nodded vigorously.

"Where's your sister?" Billie added.

"She went to the house. She said she hates being cursed, whatever *that* means," Skylar complained.

Billie grinned at Shannon and Julie. A knowing looked passed between them, indicating they knew *exactly* what that meant.

"I gotta pee," Skylar whispered loud enough for the neighbors to hear. She wiggled out of Billie's arms and scurried into the house.

A scuttle from across the yard drew their attention back to the driveway once more.

"Mom! What happened?" Cat asked worriedly. She saw her mother hobbling toward her on a pair of crutches. Her father followed close behind, hovering like a mother hen.

"Kitten, maybe she'll listen to you. She wouldn't let me bring a wheelchair home from the hospital," Doc said.

"For Heaven's sake, Doc. I'm not an invalid, you know," Ida complained.

"Mom, what happened?" Cat asked again.

"She twisted her ankle stepping off the porch last night," Doc explained.

Billie took charge of the situation and led Ida to the closest lawn chair. "You know, Mom, you didn't have to keep the girls last night. Had we known about this, we would have come after them," Billie said.

"Nonsense," Ida replied. "It's just a sprain. I'll be fine. I'll not let something so trivial get in the way of spending time with my grandchildren," she said stubbornly while Cat examined her ankle.

Doc looked at Billie. "Now you know where Cat gets it."

"What is that supposed to mean?" Cat asked Doc pointedly.

"You know what it means. Your stubbornness, that's what," he said sternly.

"Well, now that you're here, you're staying for the cookout, and I won't take no for an answer," Cat said.

"See what I mean?" Doc said to Billie.

Billie grinned.

"No dear, you have company. We wouldn't dream of intruding," Ida said coyly.

A look of sheer enjoyment passed between Shannon and Julie as they watched the interaction between Cat and Ida.

Ida's remark reminded Cat that they did indeed have guests. Bolting upright, she exclaimed, "Where are my manners? Shannon, Julie, these are my parents, Ida and Doc O'Grady. Mom and Dad, this is Shannon and Julie Nash."

After introductions were over, Ida looked around the yard. "Where are Jen and Fred, dear?"

Billie and Cat exchanged a nervous look. "They won't be joining us today, Mom. I'm afraid Jen isn't feeling well. She has some sort of stomach bug," Cat explained.

A voice came from behind the group of people. "So, what's for eats?"

All eyes turned to see a spike-haired Tara standing there with hands on her hips, baggy jeans spilling down over her shoes and an oversized T-shirt hanging loosely on her shoulders.

Shannon looked at Tara then back to Julie. Billie swore she saw an expression cross Shannon's features that covertly hid a knowing thought. She also noticed the same expression cross Julie's face in response.

Cat held her hand out to her daughter. "Tara, come over here and meet our guests."

Tara sauntered over to stand next to Cat and waited to be introduced.

"Ladies, our daughter, Tara. Tara, this is Shannon and Julie Nash," Cat said.

Tara reached her hand toward their guests and greeted them one at a time. "Nice to meet you," she said politely, then, impatiently, she turned to her mother. "When do we eat? I'm starved."

"The grill is heating now. We'll throw the burgers on in a few minutes," Cat answered.

Tara gave Cat a knowing look. "You aren't gonna let Mom cook, are you?" Her comment sent Shannon and Julie into fits of laughter.

"I heard that," Billie called from across the yard where she was busily scraping the grill.

Doc strolled toward Billie. "Don't worry, daughter, I'll give you a hand."

A look of relief crossed Tara's face. "Thank you Grandpa," she whispered under her breath.

"Why don't you run into the house and get the chips and deviled eggs for me, love?" Cat suggested to her daughter.

Shannon and Julie watched Tara walk toward the house. "She's a lovely girl," Julie commented.

"I like her look," Shannon added. "She looks like she's very confident in herself."

"At that age, they *all* think they're invincible," Cat replied. "She used to have beautiful, long golden blond hair until a couple of weeks ago when she came home from a month with our grandmothers in South Carolina. Thanks to Grandma Jo, her hair is now classified as a dangerous weapon."

"Your daughters look a lot like you, Cat," Julie observed. "I can imagine you looked exactly like your little one when you were that age."

"I suppose Seth looks just like Billie?" Shannon asked.

"In a way. He's tall like his mom, and he has finely chiseled good looks...kind of how you'd think Billie would look if she were a man, but that's where the resemblance ends. He's quite blonde, and his personality is more like mine than Billie's," Cat explained. "On the other hand, even though Tara looks like me, she is all fire and brimstone like Billie. Sky is pretty much a mixture of us both," she added.

Julie laughed. "Sky sounds a lot like Kaleigh. As you saw yesterday, when she first meets you, she's calm, shy and reserved...a lot like myself, but when she's wound up, she's all Shannon."

"Hey, I resemble that remark," Shannon joked. "You know, I should go check on her. She'll be pretty upset if she sleeps through the cookout." On that note, Shannon headed across the yard toward the driveway to collect her daughter.

Cat looked over to the array of lawn chairs where her mother was fanning herself with her hat. "Hey, Mom, how about a glass of lemonade?" Cat suggested. She watched as Ida enthusiastically nodded her approval. She turned back to Julie. "How about you?"

"Sounds wonderful," Julie replied.

"Okay. If you don't mind giving me a hand, we'll go fetch enough for everyone," Cat said.

"I'm at your service. Lead the way," Julie followed Cat to the house, passing Shannon along the way. Shannon was carrying a still sleepy Kaleigh. "Lemonade?" she asked her wife as they passed.

"Sounds great," Shannon shot back as she made her way toward the lawn chairs to introduce Kaleigh to Ida.

On their way up the porch steps, Cat and Julie were nearly bowled over by Tara, whose arms were laden with bags of chips, and by Skylar, who was in a hurry to see who the little girl was she saw Shannon carry across the yard.

Julie grinned at Cat. "I'm not used to such traffic!"

***

The cookout was a wonderful success. The afternoon was spent visiting, playing lawn games and enjoying good food. Even the burgers were good, thanks to Doc's careful monitoring of Billie's cooking. Skylar and Kaleigh spent nearly the entire day playing with Skylar's dolls in the tree house. When Seth arrived home two hours into the festivities, Shannon and Julie fawned over his tall good looks. Not one to shirk off compliments, he hung around and made himself as charming as possible, even going so far as to play catch with his sister... something he normally had no time for. Little did he know, Shannon and Julie were more interested in Tara's athletic abilities as she smoothly fielded Seth's throws than they were in his.

By late afternoon, it was obvious that Ida's foot was swelling and quite uncomfortable. Finally, after much scolding, Ida listened to her husband and daughter and allowed herself to be taken home. By early evening, the ladies cleared away the dishes, put away the leftover food and retired to the lawn chairs in front of a blazing campfire Billie had started in the cinder block fireplace. The kids all went their separate ways...Tara to the office to e-mail school friends, Seth to the family room to play video games, and Skylar and Kaleigh to Skylar's room to play paper dolls, leaving the four adults to a peaceful evening in front of the fire.

As dusk settled in around them, Shannon opened the bottle of wine they had brought and poured drinks for everyone. An easy camaraderie fell over the ladies as though they had known each other for years. It was this easiness that prompted Shannon to ask her question.

"So how long has Tara known she's gay?"

Wine spewed from Cat's mouth straight into the fireplace, sending the red-haired woman into a coughing fit. Billie patted her back repeatedly while her airway recovered

"What did you say?" Cat demanded.

Shannon looked back and forth between Cat and Billie, and then at Julie, an ashen hue covering her features. "Ah, I'm sorry. I thought you knew."

Cat was speechless. She looked at Billie, searching for any evidence that she agreed with Shannon. "Billie?" she asked.

Billie looked at Cat, thoroughly confused. She had no idea how to answer Cat's questions. She turned to Shannon. "What makes you think Tara is gay?" she asked.

"I'm surprised you don't know. Julie and I saw it almost immediately," Shannon said. "Her boyish look, the spiked hair, baggy clothes, athletic ability. Even her handshake was firm," she explained. "Cat, does she have a special girlfriend? Does she have a boyfriend?" Shannon asked.

"Yes on both counts," Billie replied in Tara's defense. "Karissa is her best friend, and I would assume Kevin is a boyfriend, considering the position I caught them in two nights ago," she added.

"What is Karissa like?" Julie asked.

"Karissa? Well, I guess she's a normal fourteen-year-old. She's a pretty girl. She looks like her Mom. Curly blond hair and blue eyes. I wouldn't say she's overly feminine, but she's certainly not butch either," Cat answered.

"Does she seem to compliment Tara?" Shannon questioned.

Billie didn't like where the questions were going. "Wait just a minute. Are you suggesting that Tara and Karissa are a 'couple'?"

Shannon did her best to diffuse the situation. "No, not at all. It's just been my experience that even as teenagers, butch girls tend to hang out with feminine girls. That is, unless they're really hard-core butch, then they usually form gangs...not a group of kids you want your daughter associating with, by the way," she explained. "Look, I'm not saying that Karissa is gay. Hell, I'm not even sure Tara is gay, especially after your comment about this boy...Kevin, was it?" she said to Billie. "It's just that my gaydar is pretty accurate, and I felt it around Tara."

Cat remained silent throughout this exchange, but shook her head back and forth.

Julie touched Cat's hand. "Cat, why does the possibility of Tara being gay upset you so?" she asked sincerely.

Cat looked at Julie. "Julie, when did you realize you were gay?" she answered with a question of her own.

"In hindsight, I guess I always knew. In reality, not until after Kaleigh was born and Shannon came back into my life."

"Shannon?" Cat asked, leaving the implied question unasked.

"I knew pretty early on...probably around Tara's age," she answered.

"And did you act on it?" Cat continued to question.

"No. It wasn't until I was in college that I had my first same sex experience," Shannon supplied.

"Billie didn't act on it either until after her divorce," Cat volunteered. "I myself, on the other hand, came out pretty young. I was raised in a house under a blanket of unconditional love. My parents made it clear from my earliest memories that there was nothing we could ever do to jeopardize their love. Coming out to my family was very easy for me. Coming out to the world was not."

Cat took a deep breath to control her shaky voice before she continued. "I was about Tara's age when I realized my orientation, and I came out immediately. Life was wonderful at home, but an absolute nightmare at school. I worry that the same situation might happen today. I don't want my daughter to feel the pain and humiliation I did. I don't want my daughter to become another Matthew Shepard." Cat finished the last sentence through a broken, tear-filled voice.

Billie immediately rose from her chair and knelt in front of Cat. She gathered Cat into her arms. "Shh, it's okay Cat. We don't know what the truth is at this point. Tara will decide that for herself. All we can do is be supportive. Tara won't become another Matthew Shepard. We won't let that happen."

Julie reached for Shannon's hand and squeezed it tightly, indicating with a nod that it was probably time to leave. As they rose to their feet, Cat sat back in her chair, once again composed.

"I'm sorry," she apologized. "Please don't feel that you have to leave."

Billie led Shannon into the house to retrieve her daughter as Julie walked over to Cat and hugged her. "It's getting late, Cat. We've got to get Kaleigh home to bed. Look, don't fret over what we said about Tara. For all we know, she's a straight girl who is just trying to act tough. Believe me, we're no experts. Okay?"

Cat nodded. "Truth is, Julie, that thought *has* crossed my mind. I guess it was a shock to hear it voiced by someone else."

"Just because we think it, doesn't make it true, Cat. Remember that. Like Billie said, Tara will decide for herself," Julie said.

Cat embraced her new friend. "Thanks, Julie."

"You're welcome. Now we really need to get going. If Kaleigh is as wound up as I think she is, it will take the next couple of hours to settle her down and get her to bed." Julie laughed. "Thanks so much for having us over. We really had a good time."

"Thanks for coming. We'll have to do this again," Cat walked Julie through the yard toward her car where Shannon and Kaleigh were waiting.

After saying goodbye to their new friends, Billie and Cat turned to each other and searched familiar eyes for reactions to the day's events.

Cat was the first to speak. "The truth, Billie. Has it ever crossed your mind that Tara might be gay?"

"Has it crossed yours?" Billie replied as they both nodded their heads.

CHAPTER 10

Beep...beep...beep.

Billie glanced at the clock. Five a.m. She silenced the alarm and then rolled back into the warm indentation vacated by her body just moments before.

Cat stirred when the alarm so rudely interrupted her sleep. "Why?" she asked sleepily.

"Why, what?" Billie replied without opening her eyes.

"The alarm goes off at five every morning. Why does it seem earlier than normal on Mondays?"

Billie rolled over and opened her eyes to see green orbs just barely peeking out behind partially closed lids. Her heart flip-flopped in her chest at the sight of woman beside her. If she had only moments to live, she would want to spend them just like this... lying side by side with Cat, nose to nose, breathing the same air and sharing the same heartbeat.

Billie smiled. "Monday morning comes early because the weekend is much too short."

Cat nodded. "I agree." She placed a delicate kiss on Billie's lips. "Did you sleep well?"

"Not bad," Billie traced the tip of one finger along the side of Cat's face. "It took a while to drift off, especially after that conversation with Shannon and Julie last night, but once I was asleep, I was out for the night."

Cat took Billie's hand from her face and brought it to her lips. She kissed the palm. A broad smile spread across Billie's face. "I know what you mean," Cat said. "I must have laid here for nearly an hour before falling asleep."

"Have you got a busy day ahead of you?" Billie asked.

"Two surgeries this morning and one in early afternoon. I'm hoping to be home by four o'clock or so," she replied. "How about you?"

"We have the preliminary court hearing on Shannon and Julie's case this morning, and I've got a ton of paperwork to catch up on, although, I *could* bring that home," Billie replied. She propped herself up on her elbow. "Maybe we can take the crew out to dinner tonight if I can get home at roughly the same time you do. How does that sound?"

"A night off from cooking? It sounds great!" Cat exclaimed.

"All right. It's a date," Billie quipped. "I'd better get my butt in gear and get to the office early. Maybe I can get a jump on the paperwork." Billie got out of bed and reached a hand toward Cat. "Wanna join me for a shower?"

Cat smiled and stretched lazily. "Wash my back?" she asked wickedly.

Billie knelt on the bed and slowly crawled toward Cat until she was straddling her. She lowered her face toward Cat and lightly brushed Cat's earlobe with her lips. "I'll wash anything you'd like."

Cat's eyes flew open and she suddenly placed her hands on Billie's chest and pushed. Not expecting the move, Billie was easily thrown off balance onto her back on the bed. Cat quickly jumped up and tore off her nightshirt. "Last one in is a rotten egg!"

"Cat, you are going pay for that!" Billie threatened light-heartedly as she scrambled into a sitting position and watched Cat run into the adjoining bathroom.

Cat stepped into the doorway and shook her naked butt at Billie. "Promises, promises!" she teased. Cat shrieked when Billie jumped off the bed and chased her back into the bathroom.

***

As it turned out, Cat did not make it home early that evening, as a bus load of high school kids was involved in a near head-on collision with a trailer truck, filling the Emergency room and creating a need for the OR and surgical staffs to remain beyond their scheduled shifts. Luckily, there were no fatalities from the accident, but several young people required emergency surgery, thus resulting in a very long workday for Cat. Unfortunately, Monday's events set the pace for the remainder of the week. Between Billie and Cat's late hours and unexpected caseloads, they barely saw each other. It seemed that just as one of them managed to get home early, the other had to work late. By the end of the week, they had each spent a significant amount of time with the children, but very little with each other. When they crawled into bed together in the evening, they barely had time to cuddle and exchange loving words before exhaustion took over and passed them into the world of unconsciousness.

By the time Friday rolled around, they were missing each other terribly.

Billie looked at Cat over her shoulder as she threw her legs over the side of the bed to get up. "Cat, regardless of what happens at work today, I am leaving at noon. We haven't spent more than ten waking minutes together all week. I miss you."

Cat smiled into the pouty face of her tall lover. "Me too, love. As of late yesterday, I didn't have any surgeries scheduled for this afternoon, so if my luck holds out, I'll be home early too."

Billie smiled crookedly back at Cat. "Good. I'm looking forward to spending time with you. I also want to get to the bottom of whatever is ailing Jen. Do you realize she hasn't spoken to us in over a week? And she's refusing to return our phone calls. I don't like it, Cat. Something is up and I intend to find out what it is."

Cat rolled to her side and cuddled Billie's pillow. "I feel bad for the kids. They miss Stevie and Karissa. I don't think it's fair for Jen and Fred to punish the kids like that," she added. "If her gripe is with us, then she needs to let us know and leave the kids out of it."

"You're right, Cat," Billie called from the bathroom. "We'll give her a call this afternoon when we get home, okay?"

"Sounds good." Cat crawled out of bed and went into their closet to retrieve a clean pair of scrubs, which she threw on the bed before stripping off her nightshirt and heading toward the bathroom to shower.

Billie was leaving the bathroom just as she entered. "Will you be joining me?" Cat asked hopefully.

Billie smiled and placed a kiss on Cat's lips. "Just as soon as I turn on the coffee maker. I'll be right back."

Cat leaned her cheek against the bathroom door and sighed in contemplation. She loved Billie with all her heart, and heaven knows, she still had the power to make her knees weak, but lately, something was missing. She didn't know what it was, but she felt like their lives had become so distracted. Life seemed so hectic lately that they rarely had time to concentrate on just them.

She couldn't believe how much their lives had been thrown into an upheaval of late by the kids. Ever since they returned from their one-month stay with the grandmothers in South Carolina, all hell had broken loose. Between Seth coming home drunk...to having 'the talk' with Tara after her encounter with Kevin in the family room...to the possibility that Tara might be gay...and Skylar and Missy disappearing, sending the whole neighborhood out on a search and rescue mission, she was sure she'd lose her mind. Then there was Jen and Fred. For some reason, Jen had suddenly broken all ties with them. Cat was at a loss as to what had caused it...and Jen wasn't talking.

Cat felt like her life was out of control. It was in this state that Billie found her when she returned from making coffee.

"Cat, are you all right?" Billie asked. She approached Cat and stroked her hair.

Cat looked into Billie's eyes and sighed, not saying a word.

"That was an awfully big sigh, my love," Billie observed. "Wanna talk about it?"

Cat shook her head and allowed herself to be enveloped in Billie's arms. Wrapped in her cocoon of love, with her own arms firmly encircling Billie's waist, she listened to Billie humming softly to her.

Finally, Billie planted a firm kiss on the top of Cat's head. "Are you all right, Cat?" she repeated tenderly.

Cat nodded. "Thank you for loving me, Billie."

"That is oh, so easy to do, my love," Billie replied and kissed her once more. "We'd better get into the shower if we're going to make it to work on time."

"Okay," Cat whispered back. She reluctantly released her hold on Billie and followed her into the bathroom.

***

As planned, both ladies were home relatively early that afternoon. Billie made it home first, and was lounging on the couch watching the local news when Cat arrived. Cat threw her keys on the kitchen table and dragged herself into the living room where she dropped heavily onto the couch beside Billie. She kicked off her shoes and burrowed into Billie's embrace. A sigh of contentment escaped her lips.

"It feels so good to be home," Cat exclaimed.

Billie held Cat close. "Yes it does."

"Where are the kids?"

"Sky went to the beach with Missy and her mom. Seth is working, and it appears that Tara has a new friend. She's gone to the mall with a girl named Kelly," Billie replied.

"Kelly? Was she here with Tara?" Cat asked.

"No. Tara was on the phone with her when I got home. They're meeting at the mall."

"Oh," Cat said distractedly.

Billie noticed the faraway look in Cat's eyes, but decided not to question it. If she guessed correctly, the same thoughts crossed her mind earlier when Tara announced she was meeting this new girl at the mall. She decided to push the anxious feelings aside for the time being.

"How was your morning, love?" Billie asked.

"Okay," Cat replied before falling silent once more.

Billie was uneasy with Cat's detached behavior. "Hey, why don't we give Jen a call and see if she'll talk to us today," she suggested.

Cat sat up and looked at Billie. "All right."

Billie pulled her cell phone from her pocket and looked intently at Cat. She traced the side of Cat's face with her fingertips. "Are you feeling okay, kitten?"

Cat locked eyes with Billie. "I'm okay, love," she replied. "Just a little distracted. I'm worried about Tara and Jen," she explained.

Billie nodded and squeezed Cat's knee. "I know. Me too, but worrying won't solve anything. Like Shannon said, Tara's sexuality will be her own choice. We can only be there to offer advice and support," she mused. "As for Jen...hopefully she'll talk to us today, then, just maybe, we'll finally find out what we did to offend her."

"Let's give her a call," Cat suggested.

Billie punched Jen's number into the phone. Moments later, a male voice greeted Billie cheerfully.

"Speak to me!" the voice said.

"Fred?" Billie asked, a little taken aback by the unusual greeting.

"No, this is Steve. Sorry, I thought you were my girlfriend. Do you want my dad?" he returned.

"No, actually, I'd like to speak to your Mom, Steve. This is Billie."

"Mom's not home," Steve said quickly. "She's at the grocery store. Hey, is Seth home?"

"Seth is working. He should be home in a few hours. So, your mom is grocery shopping?" Billie repeated.

"Yeah, she just left about 10 minutes ago," he replied. "Hey, I've got another call coming in. It might be Melissa. Can I let you go?" he asked urgently.

"Sure Steve. Tell your Mom I called, okay?" she requested.

"All right, Billie. Later!" he said before hanging up.

Billie hung up the phone and slipped it into her pocket. "She's shopping," Billie explained. "We just missed her."

Cat rose to her feet. "No we haven't. Let's go. We'll intercept her at the store."

"What? Cat, are you serious?" Billie asked.

"I sure am. Look, you wanted to put an end to this, right? Well, she isn't returning our calls. She snubs us when she drives by. She's keeping our kids apart. I don't know about you, but I getting tired of it. She owes us an explanation, and I intend to get it—even in the grocery store," Cat extended her hand to Billie. "Are you coming with me?"

Billie grinned ear to ear. When Cat was determined, there was no stopping her. She reached for Cat's hand and rose to her feet. "Lead the way."

Moments later, they pulled into the parking lot of the town's largest supermarket.

"Look, there's Jen's car," Cat said. She pointed to the vehicle parked two spaces away from theirs.

"Are you sure you want to do this, Cat?" Billie asked.

"The alternative is to let things continue as they are, Billie."

Billie nodded. "You're right. Let's go."

Billie grabbed a shopping cart and pushed it in front of them as they walked across the parking lot,

Cat looked at her with eyebrows arched into her hairline.

"Hey, we might as well get a few groceries while we're here," Billie reasoned.

Cat shook her head from side to side and led the way into the store.

"What?" Billie said innocently while following Cat into the store.

Cat and Billie scanned each aisle as they passed through the store, looking for any sign of their friend.

"She's gotta be here somewhere," Cat said. "Her car is in the parking lot."

Billie pointed excitedly. "Look! There she is. In the frozen food aisle."

Jen was lazily browsing the aisle, when she became aware of something rapidly approaching her. She looked up and immediately recognized the determined look on Cat's face.

"Shit!" Jen said under her breath and she turned her cart around to quickly walk away.

"Jen! Jen!" Cat called out loudly to Jen's retreating back. "Wait! We need to talk to you."

"Leave me alone, Cat," Jen replied over her shoulder.

Jen increased her pace down the aisle, only be intercepted by Billie coming toward her from the other end. She realized she had been ambushed, and was now was trapped between them.

Jen looked back and forth between Cat and Billie. "Do you two always tag team the underdog?" she spat out vehemently.

"Jen, we didn't tag team you. We just need to talk," Cat explained. Cat placed her hand on Jen's arm, only to have it shaken off.

Jen tried once more to get past them. "There's nothing to talk about," Jen said.

Billie stepped in front of her cart to stop her. "Well, we think there is."

"Billie, please let me by. Don't make me call for the store manager," Jen warned.

Billie raised her eyebrows. "What's wrong with you Jen? What have we done to warrant such treatment?"

Jen narrowed her eyes and tried to pass once more. Again, Billie blocked her way.

She looked around frantically and spotted a store worker stocking shelves at the other end of the aisle. She waived to the young man. "Excuse me," she shouted. "Could you please fetch the store manager for me? I seem to have a problem here." The young man immediately jumped to his feet and went in search of the manager.

Billie placed one hand on her hip and ran the other through her hair. "Jen, why did you have to do that? We only wanted to talk. Cat, come on. Let's go. This is useless." She extended her hand to Cat who took it willingly.

Together Cat and Billie exited the store and walked toward their car. Little did they know, Jen nearly followed them, stopping at the large glass windows at the front of the store to watch then walk across the parking lot. Upon reaching the car, they opened the doors and climbed in.

Billie was seething with anger. "Damn her! Why does she have to be so stubborn?"

Cat sat in the passenger seat, staring straight ahead and remained silent for long moments.

Billie took several deep breaths to get her own emotions under control. Finally, she reached to turn the key in the ignition.

Cat's hand suddenly flew over and covered Billie's. "No, Billie," she said. "This isn't over yet. We came here to find the truth, and we're not leaving until we have it." Before Billie could stop her, she reached for her door handle and was out of the car in seconds and heading toward Jen's car.

Billie rolled down her window. "Cat what are you doing?"

"She has to come out of there sooner or later, Billie. I told you I'm not leaving until she talks to us." Cat leaned against Jen's car and crossed her arm in front of her.

"Jesus Christ! You're going to get us arrested, Cat."

"I'm not moving until she talks to us."

Billie threw her door open and joined Cat by Jen's car. "I hope you know what you're doing."

Cat scanned the front of the store just as Jen exited, pushing her cart before her. "Here she comes," Cat said. Cat pushed herself off Jen's car and stood erect, her body language making it clear to Jen that she meant business.

Jen stopped in mid-step when as she spotted Cat. Then, with determination, she continued toward her car, intending to put an end to the woman's harassment once and for all.

Jen stopped behind her car, opened the trunk and proceeded to place her groceries inside. Billie stepped forward to help her while Cat stood there with her hands on her hips. Once the groceries were loaded, Jen turned to them and reached up to adjust the unruly yellow ringlets that covered her head. "Okay," she said. "Let's get this over with. What do you want from me?"

"We want to know why you're so angry with us, Jen. We want to know what we could have possibly done that would cause you to throw away our friendship. We want to know why you think it's necessary to punish the kids by keeping them apart," Cat began before she reached the point of mute frustration.

Billie watched the play of emotions fly across Cat's face as she stated her demands. Jen's reactions were equally as interesting, as she wore her heart on her sleeve. It became obvious to Billie at that moment that this was just as hard on Jen as it was on Cat and herself.

"You really don't know, do you?" Jen said incredulously.

Cat raised her arms out to the sides. "Know what?" she shouted.

"Well, it sure didn't look like a business meeting to me. You were having way too much fun for business," Jen started.

"What the hell are you talking about?" Cat asked.

Jen crossed her arms. "Hello? I was there. Two Fridays ago. Trader Dukes at dinner time? I saw you laughing and joking with those women. Remember? You broke our date. If you didn't want a night out with Fred and me, you could have said so instead of pulling that bullshit on us." Jen started to pace. "Of course I can't blame you. Why would you want to be friends with me? Look at me! I'm fat! My face is breaking out!"

Suddenly, the dam broke and Jen started to cry. Billie immediately wrapped Jen in her arms and looked frantically at Cat who was also pacing back and forth, one hand on her hip and the other hand worrying her bangs while she desperately tried to understand what Jen was telling them.

Finally, it all began to make sense. Cat looked at her friend wrapped in her wife's arms and it suddenly became clear.

Cat fought tears as she approached Billie and Jen and added her arms to the fray as she joined them in a group hug.

After regaining some semblance of control over her emotions, Cat broke from the group and encouraged Jen to lean against the car. Billie joined her as Cat faced them both.

"Jen, believe it or not, we *were* in a business meeting that night at Trader Dukes. Those two women you saw us with were Billie's clients. They couldn't make a daytime meeting so they invited us to dinner. Somehow, our signals got crossed and Billie agreed to the dinner meeting, not remembering that we had already accepted your dinner and movie invitation," Cat explained.

"It's true, Jen. My screw-up, I'm afraid," Billie confessed.

Cat approached Jen and cupped the side of her face in her palm. "Jen, we would never blow you guys off. We love you, don't you know that?" Cat stated, making Jen cry even harder.

Cat opened her arms to Jen, who went into them willingly. After several long moments of soft whimpering, Cat held Jen at arms' length and smiled broadly. "So when are you due?" she asked.

Jen's eyes flew open, as did Billie's. "Due?" Jen asked breathlessly. "What do you mean?"

Cat frowned. "Jen," she said excitedly, "You've been ill for a while now. You're an emotional wreck. You said you were putting on weight. Your face is breaking out. Honey, all those things to me indicate that you're probably pregnant."

Jen shook her head side to side. "No, I can't be. I had a tubal ligation years ago. It can't be," she said in disbelief.

Once again, Cat held Jen's face between her hands. "Sweetheart, tubal ligations have been known to fail. They aren't foolproof."

Jen continued to shake her head. "No. It can't be," she said again.

Billie was bubbling with joy on the inside, but unsure about expressing it, considering her friend was in denial about the possibility. On the outside, her logical self took over. "Well, there's one way to be sure," she said. "I'll be right back." Billie headed across the parking lot and back into the store.

While Billie was gone, Cat once again took her friend into her arms. "Sweetie, we missed you so much," she said though her tears.

Jen wrapped her arms tightly around Cat. "I'm sorry I've been such a bitch," she said. "I thought you replaced Fred and me with your new friends."

Cat was dumbfounded. "Jen, how could we ever replace you? Don't you know you hold a special place in our hearts? Honey, that night at Trader Dukes...why didn't you come over to the table? We would love to have shared you with Shannon and Julie," she asked.

Jen wiped the tears from her face and sniffed loudly. "We didn't want to interfere, Cat."

Cat shook her head side to side. "What am I going to do with you?" she joked.

Billie approached the ladies carrying a bag."Okay, let's go home. We've got some work to do,"

"Work?" Jen said.

Billie reached into the bag and pulled out a box. "Home pregnancy test."

A crooked smile crossed Cat's features as a look of trepidation crossed Jen's.

"Billie, I'm going to drive Jen's car home for her. I think her emotional state is a little too fragile right now to handle it," Cat said.

"Okay. I'll meet you at Jen's."

***

Billie, Jen and Cat lined up side by side and bent over the bathroom sink while they waited impatiently for the results. Finally, they came.

"But...but...but the tubal," Jen said. Her voice trailed off in disbelief as she looked at the plus sign on the dipstick.

Billie and Cat looked across Jen's back at each other and smiled. Tears welled in their eyes.

Jen stood erect and looked back and forth between her friends, her eyes wide with something close to fear. "I...I...I'm pregnant!" she exclaimed. "How can that be?"

"How? Jen, this is your third child. Don't tell me you don't know how it happened," Billie joked.

"No! I mean, yeah, I know *how,* but...but...you know...how?" she asked again. "This can't be happening," she added. One hand flew to her forehead while the other grasped the edge of the sink.

Cat noticed the pale hue to her friend's face. "Jen, are you all right? Maybe you should lie down for a while," she said.

"No. I'm okay. I'm just a little light-headed," Jen explained.

"Have you eaten today?" Billie asked.

"A few crackers this morning," Jen replied. "It was all I could keep down."

"Okay, time to eat," Cat said. She took Jen's hand and led her to a chair at the kitchen table.

Jen sat there staring straight ahead while Cat busied herself throwing lunch together. Billie sat across the table from Jen and covered her friend's hands with her own. "Jen, honey, how do you feel about this?" she asked.

Jen broke out of her daze and looked at her friend. "It scares the shit out of me," she replied.

"How so?" Billie prompted.

Jen looked at her hands. "I love Stevie and Karissa. I really do, but I had a very difficult time through their pregnancies and deliveries. They were both very big babies. When Stevie was born, I swear I was giving birth to a baby centaur! He split me end to end. It was horrible. I was sore for weeks," she began. "The pregnancies were rough. I had morning sickness for the entire nine months with both babies. I gained a ton of weight, and with Karissa, I developed toxemia near the end and almost lost her. Those two pregnancies were the most terrifying 18 months of my life."

Cat delivered bowls of soup and grilled cheese sandwiches to the table as she listened to Jen's story. "Jen, maybe this one will be easier on you," she suggested.

Jen looked at Cat. "I don't know, Cat. Damn!" she exclaimed, nearly breaking down into tears. "I feel horrible about this, but I don't really know if I want this child. I'm afraid," she confessed.

Cat tried to comfort her friend. "Afraid of what, Jen?"

Jen sat back and breathed deeply before answering. "After Stevie and Karissa's births, I fell into postpartum depression. It was hell. I felt so out of control. I was afraid I would hurt myself, or worse, hurt my babies. I was on antidepressant medication for months after each birth. One of the primary reasons I had the tubal ligation was to prevent this from happening again. I am scared to death," she admitted.

Cat and Billie exchanged concerned glances.

Jen propped her elbows on the table and lowered her face into her hands as she cried and poured her heart out to her friends. "My youngest is in high school for crying out loud. I am supposed to start a new job in a few weeks. I'm at a point in my life where I can finally enjoy some independence, and now *this* happens."

Cat rose to her feet and wrapped her arms around Jen. Her shoulders shook with the waves of sobs that racked her body. Cat looked at Billie across the table and mouthed the words, 'Call Fred,' then talked soothingly to Jen as Billie rose and left the room.

***

Fred came home immediately after he received the call from Billie. She was intentionally vague about what the problem was...only offering that Jen wasn't feeling well, so Fred was quite a nervous wreck when he arrived home. When he entered the house, Jen was in the bathroom, trying desperately to compose herself. The minute she opened the door and laid eyes on him, she flew into his arms and once again broke down and cried.

Moments later, Cat was fanning Fred with the phone book as he slouched limply in the overstuffed living room chair mumbling, "I can't believe it...I can't believe it!"

Jen stood in the circle of Billie's arms, whimpering softly on her friend's shoulder.

Before long, Fred regained his senses and sat up with a 'deer in the headlights' look on his face. He spoke one word, "How?"

"I don't know how, Fred. I...I..." Jen tried to speak, but collapsed once more into tears as Billie helped her to the couch.

"Fred," Cat began. "It wouldn't be unusual for a tubal ligation to fail."

Fred rubbed his face hard then dropped his hands between his legs. He looked at Jen on the couch and grinned. He approached the couch, sat down, and pulled Jen into his arms. "Don't worry, love, it will be okay," he purred.

Jen looked at Fred through a veil of tears. "How can you say that?" she asked. "You're not the one who has to get sick, fat and depressed."

"Maybe this one will be different, sweetie," Fred suggested. "You know I'll be there to help as much as I can."

Jen was incapable of replying. She pulled her feet onto the couch and burrowed into Fred's side.

Billie and Cat watched the touching scene from across the room. Billie squeezed Cat's arm and motioned toward the door with her head.

Billie and Cat walked hand in hand back to their house. "Wow! That was quite a surprise about Jen, huh?" Billie asked.

"Yeah," Cat replied. "I'm really concerned about her though. I didn't realize she had such a difficult time with Stevie and Karissa. Billie, maybe this baby isn't the right thing for Jen," she suggested.

Billie furrowed her brow. "What are you suggesting, Cat?"

"I'm not suggesting anything," she replied. "It's just that Jen's right. She's at the point where she should be enjoying her freedom. She's worked hard raising her children and now that they're relatively independent, it's almost a pity that she'll be tied down again."

"What would you do if it were you?" Billie pointedly asked.

"Without actually being in her shoes, I don't know," Cat replied. "I would probably grow accustomed to the idea over time... as I'm sure Jen will. Still, it's just bad timing."

Billie nodded and held the swinging gate open for Cat to enter their front lawn. As they approached the house, the sound of loud music permeated the door. "What the heck?" Cat exclaimed.

Inside, was Tara and another girl, dancing wildly to "Old Time Rock 'N Roll" by Bob Seger. Billie and Cat exchanged wide-eyed looks before a grin broke out across Billie's face.

"You wouldn't," Cat said incredulously.

"Oh, yeah!" Billie began to gyrate to the beat and joined the girls in the living room.

Cat stood there, her arms crossed in front of her and shook her head in disbelief.

The trio danced as the strong beat vibrated through the living room…grinding and bumping hips and stomping feet. Finally, the song was over and the three collapsed side by side on the couch.

"Kelly...my mom. Mom...Kelly," Tara introduced Billie to her friend who was sandwiched between the two.

Kelly reached over to shake Billie's hand. "Nice to meet you, Mrs..." Kelly said.

"Billie. And that beautiful angel by the door is Tara's other Mom, Cat," Billie offered.

Kelly's gaze flew to the door, surprise written all over her face as she realized the family structure. She looked back to Tara with raised eyebrows and visually chastised her friend for not warning her.

Tara shrugged her shoulders in apology.

Kelly rose to her feet, approached Cat and shook her hand. "Nice to meet you too, Cat," she said cordially.

"Welcome to our home, Kelly," Cat replied as she took in the girl's appearance.

Kelly was no more than fifteen years old. She was very tomboyish, with short sandy-brown hair and an almost military-like air about her as she stood respectfully erect while shaking Cat's hand.

"Kel, wanna go play video games in the family room?" Tara suggested.

Kelly turned around sharply and grinned. "Sure," she replied. "Lead the way."

Tara led her new friend into the kitchen as Cat and Billie exchanged looks. From her position on the couch, Billie reached her hand out to Cat, who finally closed the front door and joined her. Cat sat with her feet under her.

"So, what do you think of her?" Billie asked.

"She seems nice enough," Cat answered, "a little boyish, but nice."

Billie tilted her head back and laughed. "Not all our sisters are foo-foo's like you, you know," she teased.

"Foo-foo?" she exclaimed. "I'll show you who's a foo-foo. Take this!" Cat grabbed a throw pillow from the couch and starting whacking Billie with it.

Billie could do nothing but protect her face with her arms. Suddenly the attack ceased. Billie peaked from behind her defenses and saw a confused look on Cat's face. "Cat?"

"Who said she was a sister?" Cat asked.

Billie shrugged and was embarrassed that she was caught stereotyping the girl. A red flush covered her face. "Well, I just assumed. I mean, like you said she's kind of boyish, and she acts like she's in the Army or something," Billie explained.

"Well, I'm not going to jump to conclusions until she admits it to me directly," Cat replied.

"Does it bother you that Tara is hanging with someone who might be gay?" Billie asked.

Cat propped her elbow on the back of the couch and rested her head on her hand. "I'd be a hypocrite if I said yes," she reasoned. "No, it wouldn't bother me if she had gay friends, but I guess I would be a bit concerned if she confirmed that she was gay herself," she confessed.

Billie looked at Cat questioningly. "Cat, how can you say that?"

"Honey, we went through this with Shannon and Julie the other night. You know how difficult life is for most gay people," she began. "We were lucky. Our families are supportive, we have great friends and great employers, but things are different for kids today. Hell, if I were Tara's age today and gay, I would be scared to death about starting a relationship. I mean, there's HIV and heaven forbid, AIDS. It's pretty scary stuff."

Billie nodded. "I know what you mean. In any case, Tara's a little young to be thinking about a physical relationship...at least I hope so."

"Living a gay lifestyle is tough, even for the strongest of us," Cat said. "Overall acceptance is growing—especially among the younger generation—but we have so far to go yet. I'd just hate to see any of our children have to live with that," Cat added. She paused to reflect. "I'm so torn about this. Don't get me wrong. I will unconditionally love and support our kids regardless of who they love, but as a mom, I so want to protect them from all the negative stuff in the world. We need to teach them how to be smart about their choices...and how to protect themselves. That is the least we can do for them."

"It would certainly change the nature of 'the talk' we still need to have with Tara, don't cha think?" Billie observed.

"Ugh!" Cat threw herself back onto the couch. "Don't even mention 'the talk'. I've been dreading it ever since she started her period."

CHAPTER 11

"Hello?" Cat said as she brought the receiver to her ear.

"Hi, Cat. Feel like some company?" Jen asked.

Cat furrowed her brow. She and Billie had left a very vulnerable and upset Jen in Fred's care that afternoon after learning she was unexpectedly pregnant with her third child. She looked across the room at Billie, who was flipping through the television channels with the remote and ignoring her efforts to get her attention. She turned her attention back to Jen. "Jen, are you all right?"

"I'm fine. Just a little bored," she replied.

"Bored? Billie and I just left you a few hours ago. Where's Fred?" Cat asked.

"He was called back to work. He offered to stay home, but I insisted he go."

Cat was confused. The emotional state they left Jen in just a few hour earlier was nothing like the chipper sounding woman on the phone with her right now. "Jen, are you sure you're okay? I mean, you were pretty upset when we left you this afternoon," Cat explained.

"Cat, honey, I'm fine. Fred actually left a couple of hours ago and I've spent that time thinking. Thinking about life, the baby...all sorts of things. I'd like to talk to you and Billie about it if I could," she said.

Cat mentally slapped herself for her rudeness. "I'm sorry, Jen. I'm a real clod sometimes. Yes, of course. We'd love for you to come over...or we could come to you if you'd like," Cat offered.

"No, I'll be over in a few. Bye."

"Hmm," Cat mused out loud as she hung up the phone.

Billie continued to flip through the channels. "Did you say something?"

Cat placed her hands on her hips. "Billie, you are such a guy sometimes."

"Huh?" Billie threw a quick glance at Cat before returning her attention once again to the TV.

"Ahh!" Cat marched over to Billie and sat on her lap, facing her, and successfully blocked her view of the television set.

Billie looked into Cat's impatient face. "What?" she asked innocently.

"I said you're such a guy sometimes. What is it about that remote?"

Billie looked at the remote in her hand, clearly confused about what was bothering Cat.

Cat took Billie's face in her hands and prevented her from looking around her to the TV. "Jen is on her way over. She says she'd like to talk to us about the baby."

"Jen? Is she okay?" Billie asked.

"She sounds okay. Better than okay, in fact," Cat replied.

Billie nodded. "Good," she said as Jen's voice was heard from the kitchen.

"Hey, ladies!" Jen said, announcing herself.

"In here, Jen," Cat replied from the living room as Billie clicked off the remote and placed it on the table beside her.

Tara and Kelly emerged from the basement at the same time Jen approached the doorway to the living room, causing Jen to jump.

"Oh, goodness, you scared me," Jen exclaimed.

"Hi, Jen," Tara said.

Jen hugged Tara warmly. "Hey, sweetie."

Tara pulled Kelly close and threw an arm around her friend's shoulder. "Jen, this is Kelly. Kelly, this is our neighbor, and my moms' best friend, Jen Swenson. She's Karissa's mom. Karissa is the friend I told you about," Tara explained as she made the introductions.

"Hi!" Kelly said brightly and extended her hand to Jen. "Nice to meet you."

Jen shook Kelly's hand. "Likewise, Kelly."

Tara directed Kelly to the door. "I gotta walk Kelly home. Is it okay if I call Karissa tonight? I kinda miss her."

"Sure, honey. She'd like that," Jen replied, smiling.

"Later!" Tara pulled Kelly out the door behind her.

Jen made her way into the living room and spotted her friends sitting on the couch, Cat was still perched on Billie's lap.

"Hiya!" she said brightly and dropped onto the couch next to her friends. "Cute little friend, Tara has there," she observed. "Kind of butch, but cute."

"I made the same observation," Billie said.

"Oh, stop it you two. So what if Kelly is butch. It doesn't mean she's gay," Cat said in defense of Tara's friend.

"Who said anything about her being gay?" Jen asked. She looked back and forth between her friends. "Is she?"

"I think so," Billie stated.

"Billie, you don't *know* that. Now, come on, give the poor kid a break," Cat scolded.

"All right, all right," Billie said and turned her attention to their friend. "So, Jen, you look a lot calmer than you did earlier today. Are you feeling better?"

"Much," Jen replied. "I've had a few hours to think, and to plan," Jen began. She shifted her position to face her friends and crossed her legs in front of her on the couch.

"Plan?" Billie asked.

"Yeah. I figure if I'm going to have this kid, I need to start preparing for it," Jen replied. "I mean, baby clothes, baby furniture, diapers. I gave all that stuff away when Karissa turned three."

"So you're keeping it?" Cat said. It was more of a statement than a question.

Jen cocked her head sideways. "Of course. I mean, it's not like I have a choice," she replied.

"You always have a choice, Jen," Cat pointed out. "It's all a matter of what your convictions are. No one has the right to force you to have this child."

Billie looked at Cat warily, disturbed at where her wife's comments were leading the conversation.

"Cat, you don't really think I'd get rid of it, do you?" Jen asked incredulously.

"I'm not saying you would, Jen. I'm just saying that you *do* have a choice. It's taken women a lot of years to get to this point. Don't be willing to discount your rights so easily," Cat explained.

"I'm not going to lie to you, Cat. I can't say the thought didn't cross my mind while I agonized over my situation for the past few hours, but in the end, I decided to make the best of it. I know I'm in for a tough nine months, but heck, if this kid turns out to be half as great as Stevie and Karissa, then I can't lose. In any case, I consider myself blessed just to be able to do this. I mean, the thought of a life growing inside of me again...this tiny being, created from love. Once I got over the initial shock, I realized how fortunate I am to be given another chance to bring a child into the world," Jen elaborated. "I know I have a choice, and I choose to have this baby," she finished indignantly.

Cat sat there, still perched on Billie's lap and with a grin splitting her face ear to ear.

Jen leaned forward and placed her hands on her hips. "And just what is so funny?" she asked hotly.

Cat threw her arms around her friend and embraced her tightly. She then sat back and wiped the wetness that had welled from her heart through her eyes and smiled brightly once more. "I'm sorry, Jen. I was hoping you'd say that. I was baiting you," she admitted. "I wanted to see if you were having this child out of loyalty instead of real desire."

"*That* wasn't very nice," Billie said. She stood up and intentionally dumped Cat to the floor on her rear end.

"Hey!" Cat exclaimed while Jen threw herself back onto the couch in a fit of laughter.

***

It was early evening when the phone rang. A frantic Fred was on the other end looking for his wife.

"Calm down, Fred. She's here," Billie said into the receiver. "No, she's fine...really. Okay then, we'll see you in a few. Bye."

Billie shut off her cell phone and looked at Cat and Jen with raised eyebrows. "That was Fred. He just arrived home to an empty house and immediately panicked because you weren't there. He's on his way over."

Jen looked guiltily at her friends. "I guess I should have left him a note, huh?"

"That might have helped," Cat admitted.

"So how was Fred after we left this afternoon," Billie asked.

Jen rose from the couch and stood in front of the living room window to keep watch for her worried husband. "He's nervous about it, just like I am, but at the same time, I can tell he's thrilled. When we first married, he talked about wanting five or six kids. He was kind of disappointed when we stopped after two," Jen explained. "Oh, there he is. I'll just meet him at the back door."

After Jen left the living room, Cat moved from the overstuffed chair to snuggle with Billie on the couch. "How about asking Fred and Jen out for dinner tonight?" Cat suggested. "You know, to make amends for standing them up two weeks ago."

"Sounds good to me," Billie replied.

"Hey, girls," Fred said from the kitchen doorway.

"Hi, Daddy!" Cat and Billie chimed in together. They looked at each other and laughed at their unplanned simultaneous greeting.

"Cute, girls, cute," Fred said dryly. "How's my lady been this afternoon," he asked.

Cat and Billie watched Fred lead Jen to the overstuffed chair. He pulled the ottoman over to her and lifted her legs onto it. Then he perched himself on the arm of the chair, facing Cat and Billie.

Cat smiled broadly at Fred's protective nature. "She's been great. A lot better than earlier today."

"I hated to leave her, but the call from work was important, and she insisted that I go," Fred said.

"Yeah, she told us about that," Billie replied.

"Ah, hello! Am I invisible, here?" Jen asked sarcastically. "Geesh, you guys are talking about me like I'm not even here," she complained.

Fred looked at Jen. "I'm sorry Bunny Toes," he apologized sweetly.

"Bunny Toes?" Billie replied in disbelief. "Bunny Toes?" she said again. Cat buried her face in the couch cushion to keep from laughing out loud.

Jen slapped Fred in the stomach with the back of her hand. "Damn it, Fred! Did you have to say that in front of Cat and Billie? Now I'm gonna have to kill them, or they'll tell the whole town," Jen exclaimed.

"Oops! Sorry about that, Pumpkin Lips," he teased.

"Ahh!" Jen screamed, setting off another round of laughter.

Finally, after several attempts to speak, Cat gained control of herself. "Okay, let me see if I can get this out. Fred and Pumpkin Toes... or is it Bunny Lips? Anyway, Billie and I would like to invite the two of you to dinner tonight to make up for missing our date a couple of weekends ago. Sound good?" she asked.

Fred looked at Jen. "Do you feel it up to it, hon?" he asked.

Jen readily agreed. "If it's a night off from cooking, you bet!"

Cat looked at the clock on the fireplace mantle. "Okay, then. Let's see, it's almost five. What do you say I call for a seven o'clock reservation, then Billie and I can pick you up around six thirty?" she suggested.

Jen shifted to the edge of the chair. "Perfect. That gives me time to make dinner for the kids and for us to shower and get ready."

Fred rose quickly. "Here, let me help you, sweetheart."

Jen smiled at her husband and then wiggled her eyebrows up and down toward her best friends. "A girl could get used to this." She allowed Fred to help her to her feet. "We'll see you at six-thirty."

After they heard the back door close, Billie and Cat looked at each other and grinned.

"Bunny Toes?" Billie said.

"Pumpkin Lips?" Cat replied.

Peals of laughter could be heard through the house as the ladies made their way up the stairs to get ready for their date.

***

Tara arrived home with Karissa in tow while Cat and Billie were getting dressed. "Mom! Ma! I'm home," she yelled up the stairs to announce her arrival.

"Wonderful," Cat descended the stairs while inserting her earrings. "Sweetie, I'd like you to watch your sister tonight while Mom and I take Jen and Fred out to dinner," she said. "Grandma was going to watch her, but seeing as you're home..." Cat began.

"Sure. I'd be happy to watch her," Tara replied brightly.

Cat reached the bottom step and met her daughter nose to nose. "Who are you, and what have you done with my daughter?" she demanded, only half joking.

"No, really. I don't mind watching her. 'Rissa and I were just going to watch some movies downstairs anyway, so as long as we're doing that, I can earn some money baby-sitting the rugrat," she explained hopefully.

Cat nodded her head several times, hands on her hips. "I see," she replied. "All right. I guess a couple of hours watching your sister tonight is worth a few dollars. You've got a deal," she said, extending her hand for a good faith shake, which Tara readily met.

"Cool," Tara replied. "So where *is* the rugrat?" she asked.

"She's having dinner at Missy's. I expect her home in about 10 minutes. There's plenty to eat in the refrigerator and cupboards. Help yourselves. Just make sure you clean up afterwards. Karissa, you need to call your mom to let her know you're eating here." Cat turned to address Tara. "You have our cell numbers if you need us. Oh, and if we decide to do something after dinner, we'll call you. Skylar needs to be in bed by ten okay?"

"Don't make a mess...Sky in bed by ten...call if we need help...ya, we got it, Ma," Tara confirmed.

"Awesome. Thank you, girls." Cat called back up the stairs. "Billie, honey, we've got to go in about ten minutes," she shouted.

"I'll be right there," Billie shouted from the second story.

Cat picked up the phone and cancelled the baby-sitting arrangements she had made with her mother.

"Oh, and Ma, can 'Rissa spend the night?" Tara asked.

Cat smiled at her daughter. "Sure, honey, but you'd better clear that with her mom and dad first."

Ten minutes later, with Skylar home and Tara and Karissa firmly committed to watch her, Billie and Cat set out for their date with Fred and Bunny Lips...Pumpkin Toes... ah... ah... Jen. Yeah, that's it... Jen.

***

Tara and Karissa lay side by side on Tara's bed and drew pictures on the ceiling with flashlights. "So how do you feel about it?" Tara asked.

Karissa shrugged. "I don't know. I guess it'll be all right. I mean, you have a little sister, and she isn't so bad."

"Skylar? She's a pain in the ass," Tara exclaimed. "But I gotta admit she can be pretty cute when she wants to be."

A moment of silence passed between the friends as their ceiling designs became more elaborate. "So, do you want a little brother or a little sister?" she Tara asked.

"On one hand, I'd like a little sister, but then I'd have to share my room with her, so I guess a baby brother would be good. Then Stevie can be stuck with him," she reasoned.

Tara suddenly bolted to her feet. Her hands were splayed out before her. "Ewwwwww!" she exclaimed.

Startled, Karissa pointed her flashlight into Tara's face and looked at her friend with wide eyed excitement. "What is it?" she asked quickly.

"Do you *know* what this means?" Tara asked distastefully.

Karissa shook her head side to side.

"'Rissa! It means you parents were *doing it*!" she screamed.

Now it was Karissa's turn to jump to her feet.

"Eww!" both girls exclaimed in unison.

***

Billie followed Cat into the kitchen from the back porch. "What a great evening. I really missed Jen's company over the past couple of weeks."

"I know what you mean," Cat replied. "I'm glad we invited them out."

"She seems to be really happy with the idea of another baby," Billie observed.

They made their way through the kitchen and living room and headed toward the stairs.

"Yes she does. I just hope this pregnancy goes well for her," Cat replied.

Billie ascended the stairs to the second story ahead of Cat. When they reached the top of the stairs, Cat paused for a moment to reflect on her friend's condition. Billie turned to her with concern in her voice. "Cat, is everything okay?" she asked.

Cat snapped out of her reverie and looked at Billie. "Sure," she replied, perhaps a little too quickly. "I'm fine. Just thinking about Jen."

Without another word, they ritually checked all the bedrooms, making sure their children were safe and sound for the night.

They smiled when sounds of loud snoring came from Seth's room, convincing them that he was indeed home and safe.

They moved on to Tara's room, where they found Tara and Karissa still awake, lying side by side on their backs in Tara's bed. With the lights out, they were making designs on the ceiling with flashlights. Beams of light hit the ladies squarely in the face as they opened the door, followed by squeals of giggles coming from the bed.

Billie threw the door open, ran across the room and launched an all out tickle war against the teenagers, who promptly surrendered. Cat watched the scene from the doorway with a wistful look upon her face. When it was obvious the tickle encounter was over, she joined Billie in planting kisses on the girls' cheeks and thanking them for baby-sitting duty, then bade them goodnight before moving on to Skylar's room.

Skylar was still fully dressed and lying across her bed, sound asleep. Very gently, so not to awaken her, Cat pulled off her shoes and socks and Billie turned down the covers. Billie picked her up and positioned her head on the pillow while Cat pulled the blankets up around her neck. One by one, they leaned in and kissed the young child on the cheek, wishing her pleasant dreams before tiptoeing out of the room.

Once in their own room, Cat quietly closed the door then leaned against it. Billie went directly into the bathroom to remove her clothes and slipped into a night-shirt.

Surprised that Cat was not right behind her, Billie poked her head out of the bathroom and looked around the adjoining room. "Cat?" Billie spotted her still leaning against the bedroom door. She approached Cat and stopped just in front of her. "Cat? Honey, are you all right?"

Cat blinked back to awareness and found piercing blue eyes looking at her intently. "I'm sorry, Billie. What were you saying?"

Billie frowned. "You were leaning against the door, obviously lost in thought. Are you all right? Wanna talk about it?"

Cat searched Billie's face for several moments without speaking. Finally, the words came. "Billie, how do you feel about Jen's pregnancy?" she asked.

Billie was confused. "I'm happy for her, Cat. Thrilled, in fact. Why do you ask?"

"Have you ever thought of having another baby?"

Billie's eyebrows shot into her hairline. "Me? I...I...well, yeah, when Seth was young, but I haven't thought about it for a long time," she replied. "Cat, you're scaring me. What are you getting at?"

"You're not too old to have another one, you know," Cat pointed out.

Billie was visibly disturbed by Cat's comments. She led Cat to the bed and sat her down, then knelt on the floor in front of her. Billie enveloped Cat's smaller hands between her own and looked into her eyes.

"Cat, I understand how Jen's pregnancy can spark maternal feelings in you. I half expected you to want another child after learning that Jen was pregnant, but what I don't understand is why you are so concerned about *me* wanting one. If you want another child, we'll find a way to make it happen. Believe me we will. I would be ecstatically happy about it, but if you decide never to have another one, it won't change the way I feel about you and our family.

"Cat, I love you with everything that I am. I love our kids…our home…our friends. I love our life together. I would welcome another child with open arms, but I don't *need* one to make me happy. Do you understand what I am trying to say? You complete me. Our kids complete me.

There is nothing in this world I could ask for that would make me happier than I am right now here with you. I love you, Cat."

Cat maintained eye contact with Billie throughout the entire exchange. By the end of it, the veil of tears that coated her eyes impaired her vision to near blindness. She blinked rapidly and allowed her tears to overflow and spill across her cheeks.

Billie kissed the tears from Cat's face. "Talk to me, kitten," she whispered.

"I needed to be sure, Billie," Cat began. "When we confirmed Jen's pregnancy, you were so happy for her. It made me wonder if this was something you wanted for yourself. There is nothing I would deny you, my love. You know that, don't you? I love you, Billie. I want so desperately to make you happy," she added before pausing for several moments.

"Cat?" Billie prompted once more and suspected there was more Cat needed to say.

Cat wiped the remaining moisture from her cheeks and met Billie's gaze once more. "Billie, have you felt something different about our relationship lately? Is it me, or does it feel like our lives are out of control...that something is missing?" she asked very seriously.

Once again Billie nodded. She remembered all the times she had caught Cat day dreaming and absorbed in her own thoughts. She remembered all the times Cat was either unwilling or unable to share what ever personal demon was torturing her.

Cat continued without waiting for a response. "After learning about Jen, and seeing how happy you were for her, I wondered if that missing piece was another child."

Billie took Cat's face between her hands. "Sweetheart, what can I do to convince you that I am completely happy with you and our life?" Billie continued after receiving no response. "Cat, I feel that something *has* changed, but I don't know what it is. I sense that you are unhappy, that something is bothering you. Baby, please tell me what it is. I can't help you if you don't talk to me about it," Billie pleaded.

Cat shook her head. "I don't know what it is, Billie." She looked directly at Billie with tears and desperation spilling from her eyes. "I can't tell you if I don't know myself."

The look on Cat's face broke Billie's heart. She pulled Cat into the circle of her arms and held her tight while cooing words of assurance and love.

Finally, Billie held her at arm's length and spoke to her once more. "Cat, I want to help you. I want to you look at me and our children and see hope, joy and love, not dread, heartache and anxiety. I know life hasn't been easy of late. The kids have been difficult, and I know I have made life difficult at times over the past several months, but I am not willing to give up. I won't allow us to lose what we have. Sweetheart, I am going to call your dad tomorrow and ask for the name of a good doctor. Someone you can open up to. Someone who can help you, and I will be there with you every step of the way. Okay?"

Cat nodded as new tears coursed down her face.

"Good," Billie replied. "Now, let's go to bed. We're both tired."

With great care, Billie removed Cat's clothing and slipped an oversized T-shirt over her head, then tucked her into bed. She extinguished the light and climbed in beside her then gathered her into her arms. Billie hummed softly, the tune of a newly released song that Cat loved to listen to, until she felt her relax in her arms and drift off to sleep.

CHAPTER 12

Billie encouraged Cat to stay in bed and rest over the next two days. Cat enjoyed writing, but with precious little time with their busy lives, she rarely had the opportunity to do so. With time on her hands that weekend, Billie encouraged her to write about their lives and about the things that were bothering her. It was her hope that by putting her thoughts on paper, they might gleam some clues to help them through this troubling time.

On Saturday morning, Jen let herself into the kitchen. Billie stood by the counter, making a cup of coffee.

"I'll take one of those, big guy. Decaf, if you would," Jen said.

Billie smiled when she saw her friend. "Good morning, Jen. Wanna grab the creamer from the fridge?" Billie inserted a new pod into the coffee machine and pressed 'go.'

"Where's Cat this morning?" Jen asked.

Billie carried the coffee mugs to the table and placed the decaf one in front of Jen. "Still in bed, I'm afraid."

Jen glanced at the clock on the wall. "At ten o'clock? Seriously? Is she okay?"

Billie wrapped her hands around her coffee cup. She stared at the dark liquid swirling around inside it.

"Billie? Is Cat okay?" Jen asked again.

"Yes…and no. Physically, I think she's okay. I mean, she doesn't appear to be sick, but something else is wrong that I can quite put my finger on. She's depressed or something."

"Have you talked to her about it?"

"I've tried, but she doesn't seem to know what's wrong either, so she's having a bit of a problem explaining it to me."

"Maybe she'll talk to me. I'm not as close to the situation as you are."

"Maybe." Billie was a bit taken aback by Jen's persistence. "As much as I hate to admit it, you might be more impartial than I would be."

Jen covered Billie's hand with her own. "Don't worry, love. We'll get her through this."

Billie struggled to hold tears back. "Thank you, Jen. You're a good friend. I don't know what we'd do without you."

***

At one point during the weekend, Billie called Doc and filled him in on Cat's behavior. She agreed with his advice to schedule a full physical as well as a visit to a counselor. She was able to secure the physical for Cat on the following Wednesday afternoon and a session with the counselor on that Friday. Billie immediately rearranged her own schedule so that she would be able to accompany Cat to the appointments.

When Billie called Cat at work to inform her of the scheduled visits, Cat was reluctant to go and claimed that her melancholy was bound to be 'just a phase' that would pass with time. Unwavering, Billie insisted.

Wednesday morning rolled around, and as usual, Cat was reluctant to get out of bed at the sound of the alarm. It took several nudges by Billie, both verbal and physical, to get her moving that morning.

"Cat, sweetheart, it's getting late. They'll start your first surgery without you if you don't get your butt into gear," Billie warned as Cat sat on the edge of bed, eyes closed, and her head resting on her right shoulder.

Cat dragged herself out of bed and headed for the shower. "I'm moving...I'm moving," she complained.

Billie watched Cat move sluggishly across the room. Worry etched her brow. Cat was never an early bird and frequently required a nudge or two to get her moving in the morning, but this was different. This was more than Cat wanting a little extra sleep after the alarm went off. This was a serious reluctance to enter the human race. This was fueled by a strong desire to seclude herself from the world, and for someone as social and outgoing as Cat, Billie had reason to be concerned.

Billie leaned her backside against the bathroom sink and kept Cat company while she showered.

"Cat, don't forget that you have a physical scheduled for two o'clock this afternoon."

Billie could see Cat's silhouette through the shower curtain. Her heart sank as she watched Cat's head fall backward in exasperation.

"Billie, I really don't want to keep that appointment," she whined.

"You have to, Cat. Honey, we need to understand why you've been feeling out of sorts lately. Being a doctor, you should understand that."

Cat groaned.

"I'll pick you up in front of the hospital at one-thirty. That should give us enough time to reach Dr. O'Brien's office before two," Billie offered.

"Billie, I think I can make this appointment by myself. I am a grown woman after all."

"Yes, you are," Billie agreed, "but you are a grown woman who tends to put her needs last, and in this case, that won't do. I'll be there at one-thirty. I don't want to hear an argument about it, okay?"

Billie waited several moments for Cat to answer, to no avail.

"Cat?"

"All right! All right! One-thirty. I heard you," Cat said sharply.

Billie lowered her face into her hands and sighed just as Cat shut off the water and slid the shower curtain aside. Billie looked up.

"Cat, I don't want to fight with you. I just want to help. I'm concerned about you, and I'm scared to death of losing you. I will do everything in my power to prevent that. Going to this appointment with you is more for me than for you. Can you understand that?"

Cat stood there naked, covered with tiny drops of moisture and with streams of water running down her face from her soaking wet hair. She furrowed her brow and looked at Billie. After several moments of silence, she held out her hand. "May I have a towel?"

Billie grabbed Cat's towel and enveloped her in its white fluffiness and then pulled her into an embrace. Billie breathed in her freshly showered scent. Tears filled her eyes as her heart and mind acknowledged how right it felt to be holding the woman she loved. A shudder of fear and uncertainty shook her body as she released Cat and began to towel dry her skin. Sorrow pulled heavily at her heart while Cat stood there, relatively unresponsive.

A short time later, Billie stood on the back porch and watched Cat pull her car out of the driveway. Billie continued to wave until the car was out of sight...never once having received a wave in return.

***

Billie sat distractedly at her desk for most of the morning and tried hard to concentrate on the folder before her. She had a court appearance that morning to present Shannon and Julie's case before the judge, and had to make a supreme effort to keep her mind on business rather than on Cat as she prepared for the hearing.

Billie felt particularly confident about winning this case based on legal merit alone however, if the attorney for the prosecution—or the judge for that matter—decided to turn this into a case about the morality of homosexual adoptions, then she would have her work cut out for her. Luckily for her, she had fought and won her own case years earlier for the right to same-sex marriage, and subsequently, her adoption of Tara and Skylar, and Cat's adoption of Seth. She had the law on her side and she planned to use these events as precedents if necessary. What bothered Billie is why this case had progressed as far as it had. With the legal precedence already established, it should have never made it to court.

She looked at the clock on her desk and uneasiness settled in the pit of her stomach. She closed the folder in front of her and prepared to leave for court.

***

"All rise and come to order. The court of the Honorable Judge Jonathan P. Williams is now in session."

Billie watched a distinguished looking gentleman in a black robe enter the courtroom from a door adjacent to the bench.

Shannon and Julie shifted nervously in their seats beside Billie. Billie gave her clients reassuring glances. She looked at the opposing attorney and was met by a smug grin. *He knows something I don't.*

"Now hearing the case of Shannon and Julie Crawford Nash vs. Mr. and Mrs. Howard Crawford," the bailiff announced.

"All right, Ms. Charland, Mr. Mercier, I have read the case, and I believe I understand the issues. I will however, interrupt you with questions if necessary. Is that clear?" the judge asked both attorneys.

"Yes, Your Honor," Billie and the prosecutor responded nearly simultaneously.

"Ms. Charland, you may begin with your opening statements," the judge instructed.

"Thank you, Your Honor." Billie collected a few papers from the table and walked in front of the bench.

"Your Honor, I am at a loss as to why this case had made it to this level. Based on State Statutes, Title 15A, Chapters one through seven, Shannon Nash has the legal right to adopt her partner's seven-year-old daughter, Kaleigh Crawford. Let me explain," Billie continued. "Chapter two, Adoption of Minors, subchapter one, Placement of minors for Adoption, indicates the following. First, the statute requires that a minor be placed for adoption only by a parent having legal and physical custody of the minor. In this case, that parent is Julie Crawford Nash. Second, that parent has the legal right to place a minor for adoption if the other parent's whereabouts are unknown and/or if the other parent has not exercised his or her legal visitation rights for two or more consecutive years. In this case, the other parent is Kaleigh's father, Gary Crawford, who has not been seen for the past seven years. Furthermore, the statute allows the parent with legal custody to place a minor for adoption if the other parent provides written consent, which Julie has done.

"Our state statutes further indicate that the court may order a termination of rights if the other parent has failed or neglected to provide regular and substantial support for the child for a period of two or more years, or if the other parent has not visited, contacted, nor communicated with the child for a period of two or more years. I would like to point out to the court that because of his disappearance seven years ago, the court has already awarded Julie Crawford Nash a divorce based on desertion, and has awarded her full legal custody of her daughter, Kaleigh. Had it not been for Mr. Crawford's parents, the plaintiffs in this case, objecting to Shannon Nash adopting their granddaughter, it is highly probable that legal termination of Gary Crawford's parental rights, and a legal adoption would have been granted at that time as well."

Billie paused and walked back to her table where she lifted a glass of water to her lips and drank sparingly. She returned the glass to the table, winked at Shannon and Julie and turned to face the judge once more.

"If I may continue, Your Honor, Shannon Nash fully realizes the consequences of adopting Kaleigh Crawford. She has made a long-term commitment to Kaleigh's mother through legal marriage just three months ago, and is willing to make that same long-term commitment to Kaleigh. She understands that she will become legally, morally and financially responsible for this child until she reaches the age of eighteen. She fully accepts this responsibility, as she has done since Kaleigh was four months old, the age of the child when her biological father deserted her and her mother. Ms. Nash truly loves this child and already considers herself to be the child's mother. This adoption is merely a legal formality designed to protect the child's future.

"As you know, Your Honor, this fine state of ours honors the laws of marriage equality. With a marriage certificate, Shannon and Julie Nash are legally entitled to all the rights of heterosexual married couples, including the right to fair and just consideration in adoption proceedings. I should point out that in adoption cases involving prospective heterosexual parents, sexual preferences are never an issue, so it should not be an issue in any cases involving prospective homosexual parents.

"Mr. and Mrs. Crawford seem to be concerned that Shannon and Julie Nash cannot give their granddaughter a normal family life. Your Honor, gay parents express the very same feelings about what is necessary for a successful family that heterosexual parents do, specifically, love, care and respect. In other words, it is the quality of parenting which matters above all else, even above the gender of the parents.

"For the past five years, Shannon and Julie Nash, and Kaleigh Crawford have been living happily as a family. It is not in the child's best interest for the court to turn her over to her fraternal grandparents when she has enjoyed a stable, healthy, and happy family life for many years. We encourage the court to consider the facts of this case, to immediately terminate Gary Crawford's parental rights, and to consider Shannon Nash's petition for the adoption of Kaleigh Crawford with legal, swift, and unbiased due process. Thank you, Your Honor," Billie concluded before returning to her table.

Shannon and Julie greeted Billie with broad smiles as she approached them. Their expressions confirmed a sense of confidence in their lawyer and their case. As Billie sat, the judge called for the prosecution to make their opening statements.

"Thank you, Your Honor. I will make this brief," John Mercier said as he approached the bench. "Quite simply, Mr. and Mrs. Howard Crawford feel that their granddaughter's future would be better served if she were raised in a home with not only a loving mother figure, but a loving father figure as well. Mr. and Mrs. Crawford mean no ill will to Shannon Nash, nor do they mean to damage the reputations of either of these women, but the fact still remains that they are both women and cannot provide the type of balance seen in a normal, healthy family."

"Mr. Mercier, you *do* understand that there is legal precedence in this state for gay and lesbian couples to adopt children?" Judge Williams asked.

"Yes, Your Honor, we do understand that. However, we have ample evidence and testimony to prove that Mr. and Mrs. Crawford will be able to provide the type of well-balanced, healthy home environment children need to be raised in. I beg the court's patience, but I assure you, we will prove our case shortly," the prosecuting attorney replied.

Billie eyed John Mercier suspiciously as Judge Williams allowed him to continue.

"In conclusion, Your Honor, we believe that Shannon and Julie Nash have provided young Kaleigh Crawford with an adequate home to date, however, as she progresses through elementary school, and then into high school, it will become increasingly important that her father's presence is felt in her life. Mr. and Mrs. Howard Crawford believe they can provide that for her, and we will strive to prove that point in the next hour. Thank you, Your Honor." Mercier once more shot a smug look at Billie and returned to his seat.

"Billie, they can't do that, can they? I mean, it's sexual discrimination, isn't it?" Shannon whispered hoarsely in Billie's ear. Her tone clearly conveyed her agitated state.

"Shannon, you need to calm down. We have the law on our side. This is a sure win for us, unless Julie's in-laws have something up their sleeve. If there's anything you haven't told me, now's the time to do it," Billie replied.

The judge allowed the prosecutor to sit before he picked up his gavel and brought it down on the strike plate. "This promises to be an interesting case. Ms. Charland, you have the floor. Call your first witness," he announced.

Billie's attention was drawn from Shannon to the case at hand when the judge mentioned her name.

She rose to her feet, straightened her skirt and placed her fingertips on the table. "Your Honor, I call Shannon Nash to the stand." She continued to look straight at the judge while Shannon took the stand and pledged to tell the truth.

Billie walked around the table, and approached Shannon. She stopped directly in front of her and made eye contact. "Ms. Nash, how long have you known your wife, Julie?"

"I've known Julie since we were in grade school. She was my best friend," Shannon replied.

"How long have you been in love with her?"

Shannon looked across the room to where Julie was sitting at the defendant's table and smiled. "I have always loved her, but I didn't realize I was *in* love with her until high school."

"And did she return that love?"

Shannon looked at Billie and frowned. She looked at Julie once more before she responded. "No, she didn't. At least not right away."

"And why is that, Ms. Nash?"

"For several reasons," Shannon began. "She had been dating Gary for a few months when I told her how I felt. I could see how he treated her, and I was hoping she would see my love for her as a way out of her relationship with him."

"And just how did he treat her?" Billie prompted.

Billie watched Shannon's knuckles turn white from gripping the top of the rail. "He beat her," Shannon replied.

"Beat her?" Billie repeated. "Can you elaborate?"

"Gary was a jock. He was full of self-importance and more concerned with his self-image than anything else. Julie was his trophy. She was—and still is—a beautiful woman, who was extremely popular with both the boys and girls at school, so of course, he had to have her. He did his best to win her over. He sent her flowers, arranged for her to have a special seat at the school football games, escorted her to the senior prom. By the middle of their senior year, she was committed to him. By the end of the school year, she was pregnant with Kaleigh, and he was trapped. He blamed her for the pregnancy and felt forced into marrying her," Shannon explained.

"So when did you enter into the picture, Ms. Nash?" Billie asked.

"Like I said, Julie and I were best friends. She told me everything. She told me how she hated being alone with him because his treatment of her in private was very different from when they were in public," Shannon began.

"I object! Hearsay on the witness' part," Prosecutor Mercier exclaimed.

"I'll allow it. Continue, Ms. Nash," Judge Williams instructed.

Shannon looked from the judge to Billie and continued. "Gary was sadistic He'd pull her hair, pinch her, burn her with his cigarettes. The final straw came when she told him she was pregnant. He beat her...called her a whore and claimed the child wasn't his." Shannon paused, visibly shaken.

"I was the one she called that night when he left her lying behind the bleachers in the football field, barely able to stand. He was smart, though. He was careful not to hit her where the bruises would show. It was then that I told her how I felt about her. I begged her to stay away from Gary. I promised to take care of her and the baby for the rest of our lives. She allowed me to take her home with me that night. I called her mother and asked if she could stay over. Like I said, she and I were best friends, so her parents thought nothing of her spending the night. I held her all night as she cried and trembled. It broke my heart to see her in such pain," Shannon finished.

"Did she profess her love for you that night?" Billie asked.

Shannon nodded her head. She wiped away the tears that escaped her lids during the painful recall and looked across the room once more and met Julie's gaze. "Yes, she did."

After a short pause, Billie continued with her questions. "Julie married Gary against your wishes anyway, and despite the fact that she was in love with you. Why was that?"

"I wondered that myself at first. I offered to take care of her and the baby. I offered to raise and love the child as my own. I went away to college feeling betrayed. It wasn't until later...until after Gary repeatedly mistreated her through their marriage, and after he deserted Julie and Kaleigh that I learned Julie made that decision for my benefit. She didn't want to ruin my future, so she had decided to accept the hand that fate had dealt her by marrying Gary."

"So, after Gary deserted her…" Billie prompted.

"After Gary deserted her, I transferred to the state college close to home, found a part time job, and helped to support them while I finished school. Julie and Kaleigh lived with Julie's parents until I graduated, but I helped out financially as much as possible. When I graduated, Julie and Kaleigh were there, sitting in the front row, beaming with pride. Just moments after I accepted my diploma, I asked Julie to marry me. Because she was legally married to Gary, we had to wait out the seven years required to have him declared legally dead, releasing her from their marriage," Shannon explained.

Billie walked a few steps away from the bench and then turned around to face Shannon once more. "Ms. Nash, if you would, describe for the court your living arrangements with Julie and Kaleigh for the past five years," Billie instructed.

"Well, like I said, Gary had to be missing for seven years before he could be declared legally dead. By the time I graduated, two of the seven years had already passed. For the next five years, Julie, Kaleigh and I lived together as a family.

I love Kaleigh as though she had come from my own womb. In every respect except the biological, she is my child. Three months ago Julie's divorce was finalized, and we were legally married. Now, we want to make our family complete with my adoption of Kaleigh." Shannon sat back in her seat, exhausted from her explanation.

During Shannon's explanation, Billie made her way to the defendant's table and leaned her backside against it, crossing her ankles and arms in front of her. "So, Ms. Nash, are there other factors involved that have led you to enter this petition for adoption?" she asked.

Shannon nodded. "Yes. In fact, the primary reason for the petition is to protect Kaleigh. You see, unless I legally adopt her, my health insurance does not cover her, nor is she protected from being placed in foster care if something were to happen to Julie." Shannon turned to the judge. "Your Honor, I love this child and her mother with all my heart. I have been there for her since she was four months old. Together, Julie and I have given her a stable, loving home. She has known nothing else. Please don't take our little girl away from us." Shannon's voice broke with unshed emotion.

Julie gave up all efforts to control her own emotions as loud sniffles could be heard coming from the defendant's table. Judge's Williams attention was drawn in that direction.

"Is that all Ms. Nash?" Judge Williams asked. When Shannon nodded affirmatively, he turned to the prosecution. "Do you wish to question this witness, Mr. Mercier?" he asked.

The prosecuting attorney rose quickly to his feet. "No questions, Your Honor," he replied.

"You may step down, Ms. Nash." Judge Williams turned to Billie. "Call your next witness, Ms. Charland."

"The defendants wish to base this case on legal precedence, Your Honor, not on the moral platform the plaintiffs wish to pursue. We believe the law clearly states that Ms. Nash has the right to petition the courts for the adoption of her legal partner's daughter...that is, given the girl's biological father has had his parental rights terminated. We believe Gary Crawford's desertion seven years ago constitutes cause for the termination of those rights, and we respectfully ask the court to grant that termination, and accept Ms. Nash's petition for adoption. There are no other legal facts to be presented in this case, Your Honor. The defense rests," Billie stated as she seated herself beside Shannon and Julie.

"Very well, Ms. Charland. Mr. Mercier, you may call your first witness," Judge Williams instructed.

John Mercier rose to his feet and with much fanfare, waved his arm in the direction of the door at the back of the courtroom. "I call, Gary Crawford to the stand," he said loudly.

Julie froze as Shannon's head snapped around to the back of the room. "Oh, my God," she said just loud enough for Billie to hear as a well dressed, clean-shaven, still handsome Gary Crawford walked into the courtroom.

Billie was immediately on her feet. "Objection! Your Honor, the defense was not informed of this witness, and we are unprepared to cross-examine him at this time. I respectfully request a recess."

Judge Williams looked at the prosecuting attorney with raised eyebrows. He lifted the gavel and brought it down loudly on the strike pad. "Request approved. Mr. Mercier, Ms. Charland, I expect to see you both in my chambers in five minutes. We will discuss a delay in the proceedings at that time."

Billie busied herself gathering her papers while Julie sat in shock and Shannon went into panic mode.

"Billie! Holy shit! Can they do that? Oh, my God! Can he take Kaleigh away from us? Please don't let that happen," Shannon ranted.

Billie placed both hands on Shannon's shoulders and urged her back into the chair beside Julie. "Shannon, panic will get us nowhere. I will get to the bottom of this, I promise.

Right now, I want you to take Julie home. She needs you now, more than ever. Okay?"

Shannon looked at Julie who sat rigidly by her side, gripping the edge of the table. Her gaze stared straight ahead, and she was trembling. "Jules," Shannon said softly. "Come on, honey. Let's go home."

Julie looked at Shannon as a trail of tears ran down her face. She rose to her feet and allowed Shannon to lead her out of the courtroom.

Billie paced back and forth in front of Judge Williams' desk. Her arms gyrated wildly as she read John Mercier the riot act. Judge Williams sat back and watched the tirade play out before him.

"John, how could you do this? You know in your heart that this child is better off with her mother. Where in God's name did you find him? My clients have tried for seven years to locate this man, and suddenly, he appears on the day his daughter is placed for adoption. This smells pretty dirty to me."

"Billie, it's my job to represent my client to the best of my ability," Mercier replied. "Mr. and Mrs. Crawford produced him at the last minute…miraculously it seems. He *is* the child's father after all."

"It's a dirty trick and you know it! He's not her father. He's nothing but her sperm donor." Billie resumed pacing and then stopped to run a hand through her hair. "I need time to prepare for this witness. You owe us that much, John," she demanded.

"How much time do you need, Ms. Charland?" Judge Williams asked.

Billie thought for a moment. "I need at least a week."

"That sounds reasonable," Judge Williams replied. "This case will resume then; oh, and Mr. Mercier, I will not tolerate further theatrics in my courtroom. Is that clear?"

Billie grabbed her briefcase and thanked the judge for his consideration. John Mercier was on his feet quickly and reached for the door handle before she could. He opened the door and stepped back to let her pass through ahead of him. Before doing so, Billie stopped directly in front of the man and glared at him. "I play by the book, John. If you do anything underhanded, so help me God, I will see you disbarred."

John Mercier smiled weakly at her before following her out of the judge's chambers and closing the door behind him.

CHAPTER 13

Billie rushed out of the courthouse with barely a moment to spare and raced toward the hospital to pick Cat up for her doctor's appointment. Cat was waiting for her when she pulled up to the curb.

Billie apologized as Cat climbed into the car. "Sorry I'm late, love. I've had a really bad morning,"

Cat sat in the passenger seat, nervously worrying her fingers into knots. Billie noticed her distress and covered Cat's hands with one of her own. "Sweetheart, are you all right?"

"Billie, I don't want to go to this appointment. I have a bad feeling about it."

"All the more reason to go, Cat. We need to get to the bottom of what's bothering you, and ruling out physical causes is the first step. I'll be there with you, love," she replied soothingly.

Cat nodded and continued to clench her hands as Billie drove through traffic to the doctor's office. Once inside, Cat sat in the waiting room in the same worried state while Billie checked her in and filled out insurance paperwork.

After what seemed like an eternity, Cat was called into an examination room, was weighed, produced a urine sample, and stripped down to total nakedness. She then donned a hospital gown that did little to cover her up, after which, she sat stoically on the end of the examining table and allowed the nurse to take her temperature, pulse and blood pressure. Finally, they were left alone to wait for the doctor's arrival. Billie's stomach was in knots with anticipation of what the doctor would find. She could only imagine how Cat felt.

Dr. O'Brien entered just a few minutes later. "Hey there!" she said a cheery voice.

Dr. Patricia O'Brien was a gregarious physician, full of life and laughter. Her easy bedside manner immediately put Billie at ease, but did little to calm Cat's tender emotions.

"Well, Ladies, it's nice to see you again. Are you here for a physical, or is there a specific reason you're gracing me with your beautiful presence today?" she asked.

Cat looked at Dr. O'Brien with a worried expression on her face and said nothing. Billie offered an explanation for their visit.

"Patty, we're here because Cat has been out of sorts of late...more emotionally than physically, but Doc suggested we start with a complete physical to see if there is some underlying condition that might be causing her problems," Billie explained.

"Ah, Doc. How is the old codger these days?" Patty asked playfully. Without waiting for an answer, she turned to Cat and addressed her directly. "So, Cat, talk to me. What has been bothering you lately?"

Cat shrugged and looked down rather than meeting Patty's eyes head on. Patty reached under her chin and lifted Cat's face so she could see her eyes. "Cat?" she prompted.

Cat started to cry, causing Billie to fight back tears of her own. "I don't know," Cat said. "I just don't know. My life is so overwhelming lately. I feel like I am out of control...like my life is in a tailspin," she explained. "I'm so afraid of pushing Billie and the kids away, and I don't know how to stop it," she admitted.

Billie took Cat's hand. "Kitten, I'm not going anywhere. You get that thought right out of your mind. Okay?" she said reassuringly, which only caused Cat to cry harder.

Patty wiped a tear from her own eye and cleared her throat. "Okay. Let's have a look at you."

Cat lay back on the table and Patty started with the normal examination...heart, lungs, reflexes, and digestive tract. "So far, everything looks good," she said as she instructed Cat to place her heels in the stirrups. Several uncomfortable moments later, the pap smear was complete. "Okay, one more thing," she said as she pulled the gown from Cat's shoulders. "Left hand behind your head, please," Patty instructed and she proceeded to do a thorough exam of Cat's left breast. She moved to Cat's right breast, she began her examination, and stopped short, seconds into it. A concerned look crossed her brow and she locked gazes with Billie sitting across the room. An expression of panic immediately crossed Billie's features. Patty continued the exam and maneuvered Cat's breast tissue around until she returned to the spot she had started before starting a second trip around the breast. One again, she stopped in the same spot she had before.

Alarmed at the noticeable change in Patty's demeanor, Cat demanded an explanation. "What is it?" she asked shakily. She looked at Billie and noticing the white pallor on her wife's face which further confirmed that something was not quite right. Cat grabbed Patty's hand and demanded eye contact with the doctor. "Patty?"

Patty stood erect and looked at Cat, and then Billie. Returning her gaze to Cat, she explained. "I can feel a lump in your right breast. It is about the size of a pea and it's located right here." Patty took Cat's hand and directed it to the upper left quadrant of Cat's right breast, just to the left of center. "I doubt very much that this is causing the emotional trauma you seem to be experiencing of late, but it is serious enough that we must do further tests. Do you understand?"

Cat felt around in the spot indicated by Patty. Billie was on her feet instantly when she saw the terror cross Cat's face. She placed her hand above Cat's and was also able to locate the lump quite easily. Cat scanned Billie's face carefully for verification, and once she had it, reality sunk in.

"I'm going to be sick," Cat said as her emotions and stomach played tag-team mutiny. She retched into the basket that Patty produced just in time to avoid a mess. Billie wrapped her arms around Cat and held her as her nerves purged her system. After a few moments, the retching ceased and Cat lay down weakly on the table. She held tightly to one of Billie's hands.

Cat apologized for her sudden sickness. "I'm sorry."

Patty was by her side in an instant. She pushed back the bangs from Cat's now clammy forehead. "It's all right, Cat. That's a pretty normal reaction to news like this."

For a few moments, no one spoke as Cat struggled to regain control of her emotions.

Finally, she was able to speak again. "Is it cancer?" she asked weakly.

Patty replied as honestly as she could. "We don't know yet. There is a whole series of tests we'll have to do first," she explained.

Cat nodded and both she and Billie fought to hold the tears back.

"Cat, how often do you do self breast exams?" Patty asked.

"She's pretty good about doing them monthly," Billie answered for her. "In fact, she usually reminds me when it's time to do one. The last time was about two weeks ago."

Patty nodded. "If it wasn't there two weeks ago, then it's either a cyst, or a fast developing tumor of some sort," she explained. "If it is a cancerous tumor that can be contained to the breast, the survival rate is 85% to 90%. If the disease spreads beyond the breast, the survival rate drops to about half that," she continued, "so if it is cancer, hopefully we've caught it early, and early diagnosis almost always improves the chances of a cure. I'm going to send you across the hall for a mammogram before you leave today. Hopefully we'll have the results in a couple of days then we can plan our next step from there. I'll be right back." Patty left the room to schedule the X-ray.

Cat's emotions bordered on a state of shock as she began to tremble. Billie helped her into a seated position and held her close. Neither spoke as scenarios of what this could mean flew across their conscious minds.

Finally, Cat broke the silence. "Billie, I don't want to die." She broke down into violent sobs. "My babies. What will happen to my babies?" she cried.

Billie gulped deeply and willed herself not to cry. She knew she had to be strong for Cat. "Cat, sweetheart, you are not going to die. Baby, I won't let you. We are destined to be together. I won't let you leave me." Billie tried desperately to calm her nearly hysterical wife. "Shhhh. It's going to be okay, love. This could be nothing. Please don't give up. I need you."

Finally, after several moments, Cat became calmer and the crying subsided. Billie continued to hold her close...so close she could feel Cat's heart beating.

Patty returned to lead them to the mammography lab. "Okay ladies, follow me."

Upon their arrival, Patty introduced them to the radiology technician and explained the procedure to Cat. "Cat, I know you're a doctor but you might not be familiar with mammography, considering you're a little young to have your first mammogram, so I'll just explain the procedure to you. This here is the X-ray machine. You'll need to stand against it and place your breasts, one at a time on this surface. The technician will then compress your breast tissue from above with as much force as you can physically tolerate, and an X-ray will be taken. The compression will be released and then another film will be taken compressing the breast from the sides rather than from above. The procedure will then be repeated on the other breast. Any questions so far?" she asked. Receiving none, she continued. "Okay then. Oh, one more thing, the higher the compression you can tolerate, the better the film will be. We don't want to make you too uncomfortable, but the plain truth is, if you can tolerate the discomfort level for five or ten seconds, the results will be more conclusive."

Cat's emerald green eyes were wide and full of fear as she clutched the gown tightly in front of her. She nodded, unable to speak for fear of breaking down into tears again.

"Billie," Dr. O'Brien said. "You can wait across the hall. You're not allowed to be in here while X-rays are being taken. After the films are done, you and Cat can go home. I'll call when we know something."

Billie nodded, unable to speak. She approached Cat and took her into her arms. "It will be okay, Cat. I promise." She placed a kiss on Cat's head and left the room.

Billie paced back and forth across the waiting room, unable to sit for more than a few seconds at a time. Fear tore at her heart...fear that she actually might lose Cat. She brought her hands up in front of her and clasped them together as she walked. *Please don't take her away from us. The kids need her. I need her. I can't live without her. God, please spare her.* Billie prayed and wore a path across the rug, tears blurring her vision.

Moments later, a very emotionally fragile and vulnerable Cat was led to the waiting room by the X-ray technician.

"She did great," the woman told Billie. "She was able to take full compression." To Cat, she added, "Caitlain, I'll need you to sit for a moment while I develop the film to determine if we need to take any more slides. Okay?"

Cat clutched the robe in front of her and nodded. As soon as the technician was gone, Cat fell into Billie's arms.

Billie held Cat close, laying her head on top of Cat's. Neither was able to speak as they stood there together, sharing their love as well as their fear.

A few moments later, the technician poked her head back into the room. "We're all set. The doc should be here in the next day or two to read the films. We'll call you with the results as soon as we get them…good or bad. Unless you have questions, you can go ahead and get dressed," she said.

***

Cat leaned against the passenger door in silence all the way home. After several attempts to get her to speak, Billie finally gave up and assumed she needed to sort out the chaos that their lives had become.

By the time they had reached home, it was nearly four o'clock. Cat walked directly through the living room to the second-story staircase. She climbed it quickly and ran to their bedroom where she threw herself across the bed and began to sob violently. Billie followed close behind.

Cat's sobs were heard throughout the upper floor of their home, drawing Tara and Skylar out of Sky's bedroom where the girls were listening to music and reading.

"Mom?" Tara stood at their closed bedroom door. "Mom, is everything all right?" Tara clearly expected the answer to be no, based on the sounds coming from behind the door. After a few moments with no response, she tried another approach. "Mom, you're scaring Skylar," she added.

"Tara, Mama isn't feeling well," Billie replied shakily. "I'll be out soon to fix dinner for you and Sky. Okay, honey?"

Tara narrowed her eyes at the response. She didn't believe Billie for a moment.

"Tara, what's wrong with Mama?" Skylar asked in her little-girl voice.

Tara turned to look at her sister. "I don't know, Sky, but I think I know how to find out."

***

Tara paced back and forth across the kitchen until she heard footsteps on the porch. She went to the back door and opened it wide to admit Jen.

"Where are they?" Jen asked.

"In their room."

Tara's response sent Jen on a mad dash for the stairs.

Jen reached the end of the hall and knocked loudly on the bedroom door. "Billie? Billie, its Jen. I'm coming in." She grabbed the handle and pushed the door open. Cat was sitting on the bed, her face puffy and ravaged with tears. Billie sat beside her. Her body was slumped over in a defeated posture and her hands were clasped tightly in front of her. Fear radiated from both women.

Jen turned to close the door and saw Tara and Skylar, who stood worriedly in the hall. She smiled at them to dispel their fears and then pushed the door closed. She turned to face her friends. "Out with it," Jen demanded.

Billie looked at Jen and started to cry. She had been trying so hard to stay strong for Cat, but Jen managed to break through her defenses with just a glance.

Jen sat between them and threw her arms around them both. Both women leaned in toward her and allowed themselves to be held. "Talk to me," Jen said hoarsely.

Billie sat up and wiped her face. She took Jen's hand and said very shakily, "Cat had a physical today. They found a lump in her breast."

Jen's eyes flew open wide and her stomach nearly rebelled at the news. She wrapped both arms around Cat and held her close. "Sweetie, it will be all right. I'm here for you, okay? If you need anything...anything at all, I'm here. I will always be here for you both." Jen reached one hand out to Billie, who grasped it thankfully.

The trio sat there for long moments, and tried hard to regain control over their emotions. Finally, Cat sat erect and wiped her face dry. "I have to feed the kids," she said. "They're probably starved."

"Actually, they're scared. Tara is the one who called me. Have you told them?" Jen asked.

Both women shook their heads. "We came straight to this room from the doctor's," Billie said. "We need to figure out how to tell them. I don't want to scare them unnecessarily. After all, we don't really know how bad it is yet," she added.

Jen nodded. "You're right. It might turn out to be nothing. Pretty scary stuff nonetheless," she replied. "Look, I'll take the girls home with me. They can have dinner with us, and maybe even spend the night. Okay?" she suggested.

Billie smiled. "You're a good friend, Jen. We love you. You know that, don't you?"

"Yeah, I know," Jen replied. "Right back at 'cha." She stood and leaned in to kiss them both. "Don't lose hope, my friend. We're gonna make it through this. You got that?" she said sternly. "I won't accept anything less."

Cat's eyes filled with tears once more at her friend's tone. "Okay," she said softly.

"I'll give you a call later tonight. Get some sleep. It looks like you can use some," she suggested, noting the dark circles under Cat's eyes.

"Thanks, Jen," Billie said.

Jen just nodded and quietly slipped out, closing the door behind her.

Billie slipped to her knees on the floor in front of Cat and pulled off Cat's shoes and socks. Next, she loosened the waist of Cat's jeans and pulled them off as well, followed by her shirt and bra. After slipping a soft nightshirt over Cat's head, she pulled down the bedcovers and tucked her in. Moments later, dressed in her own nightshirt, Billie crawled in beside her and gathered Cat into her arms. She held Cat close until she relaxed and fell into a much needed deep sleep. Sleep for her own weary soul was a long time in coming as she lay there for several more hours, dreading a future without the woman she loved.

***

"Sweetheart, it will be all right. Relax and sleep. Things will look better in the morning."

"It breaks my heart. I can't bear to lose her. What if she dies? Life wouldn't be the same without her. My God, the poor children. What will they do without their mother?"

"Jen, you need to calm down. This is not good for the baby," Fred warned.

"I know," Jen replied, "but I can't get Cat out of my mind. She's so young. Fred, if I lost you, I would want to die too. I can only imagine how Billie feels."

"She's not gone yet, Jen. We have to keep hope alive for her. She can beat this. I know she can."

Jen nodded. "I hope you're right, Fred. I hope to God you're right."

CHAPTER 14

Billie shut off the alarm and then rolled over to give Cat a ritual hug, only to find her side of the bed empty. She sat up quickly and looked around the room. "Cat?" she called out.

Cat poked her head out of the bathroom. "Yeah?" she asked, comb poised above her head.

Billie frowned. "What are you doing up so early?" she asked. "That's not like you."

"I couldn't sleep."

Billie climbed out of bed and approached Cat. She rubbed Cat's arm and looked at her closely. Cat appeared to be indifferent, detached. "Sweetheart, are you all right?"

Cat stared straight ahead and nodded her head slightly in response to Billie's question.

"Cat, I think you should stay home today. You're not in any condition to assist in surgery."

Cat snapped out of her trance and looked at Billie. "I'm fine." She brushed past Billie on her way out of the bathroom.

Billie moved to intercept her. "No, you're not. If you go to work like this, they'll just send you home. You need to take the day off. I'll reschedule today's appointments and stay home with you," Billie urged.

Cat walked a few feet away and then turned around to face Billie. "I can't stay home, Billie. I spent the entire night tossing and turning with thoughts of dying running through my mind...thoughts of leaving you alone to raise the kids. I had too much time to think. I need to stay busy. I need to keep my mind occupied. I need to think of anything but this disease growing inside of me," she exploded, hands raised into the air.

"You're not dying, Cat. I won't let you," Billie said softly.

Cat rushed forward and stopped within inches of Billie's nose. "Well here's a news flash for you, Billie, you may not be able to stop it. I have seen people die of cancer. I have seen people's hopes dashed after years of remission. I have seen the agony each and every family member goes through as they watch their loved one waste away to nothing. You may not be able to stop it. Don't you understand that?" she shouted.

Billie grabbed Cat by both arms and pushed her up against the wall. "I will *not* give up on you, Cat. Don't you dare dig your grave before we've had a chance to fight this. We need you. We love you. We won't let you go without a fight. Do *you* understand *that*?" she shouted back.

Cat's eyes filled with tears at each word that left Billie's mouth.

Billie suddenly realized she had been rougher with Cat than she intended. She released her hold on Cat and sunk to her knees on the floor. She lowered he face into her hands and began to cry.

Cat looked down upon a normally strong Billie, so raw and vulnerable at her feet. Her anger and fear eased and she slid down the wall and landed on her own knees in front of Billie. She wrapped her arms around her and laid her head on top of Billie's. "Yes, my love, I understand."

***

Not too long after Seth left for work, Billie talked Cat into returning to bed while she called the hospital to inform them that Cat would not be in for the rest of the week. She retreated to the kitchen so as to be out of earshot of Cat and then called Doc the break the news to him.

At first, there was silence at the other end of the line.

"Doc?" Billie said softly into the phone.

"I'm here." His voice cracked with emotion. "Ummm... you said she's had a mammogram?" he asked.

"Yes. It was done yesterday. We expect the results in a day or two," Billie replied.

"I see. Did Patty give you any indication of what it might be?" he asked.

"Not really. The lump wasn't there two weeks ago, so she said it might be a cyst, or..." Billie began.

"Or a fast growing tumor," Doc finished for her.

"Yes. We won't know for sure until the mammograms are read."

Billie could hear Doc take a deep breath at the other end of the line. "Well," he said. "I have seen numerous tumors turn out to be benign. As far as I know, there is no breast cancer in the family, which is a statistic that holds favorable for Cat. I'm not going to tell Ida until we know more. I don't want to upset her unnecessarily," he informed his daughter-in-law.

"We feel the same way about the kids, Doc. We've decided not to say anything to them until the results are in," Billie agreed.

"You said she has an appointment with a counselor tomorrow?" Doc asked.

"Wow! I almost forgot about that. Yes, she does. Maybe it will help if she talks it out with someone who isn't personally involved," Billie said hopefully.

"You may be right. Encourage her to go. She may refuse, but encourage her anyway," Doc urged.

"I will," Billie replied.

"All right then. I want to know the results as soon as you get them. In fact, I may put out a few feelers of my own. I'll let you know if I learn something before you do. Take care of my kitten, Billie," Doc said. "Bye."

"Goodbye Dad. We love you," Billie replied, her voice heavy with emotion.

"I love you too, daughter."

Billie hung up the phone and sat for long moments staring at the floor and fighting back her fears. She hoped she was overreacting. All they had was a lump. They had no real results yet from the mammogram. They had no clinical test results. It was just a lump. It suddenly amazed her how something the size of a pea had thrown their lives into such chaos. Cat was right. It did feel like their lives were in a tailspin. Billie took a deep breath, rubbed her face hard with both hands, and determined to keep her mind productive until they had the test results.

Billie resolved to place her focus elsewhere while they waited for the mammogram results, so she forced herself to deal with the problematic court case she was currently working on. Her whole case had been thrown into chaos the day before when Gary Crawford walked into the courtroom after a seven-year absence. She picked up the phone and dialed Jimmy in criminal law.

Jimmy was a genius. An older gentleman who had been with the law firm for years, his specialty was finding things... people, facts, leads. He had helped her locate Tara's adoptive parent…Cat's partner at the time, when she was looking for her consent to adopt the girl. How Jimmy found the woman was a mystery to her. As much as Jimmy complained about 'new fangled technology', he was a master of the Internet and managed to harness its powers to further enhance his investigative skills. Jimmy always came through for Billie, and she had no doubt he could help her out now.

"Criminal Justice, James P. Buchanan, speaking," Jimmy said, using his formal name.

"Hey, Jimmy," Billie said.

"No, no, don't tell me," Jimmy replied. "Six foot, long legs, silky black hair, piercing blue eyes. Am I right?" he teased.

"Damn, you're good!" Billie said, humoring the older gentleman.

"What can I do for you, Billie?" Jimmy asked.

"Well, I've got a tough one for you this time," Billie began.

"Good, I love a challenge," Jimmy interjected.

"Okay then. Gary Crawford, age 25, disappeared seven years ago. He was the captain of the football team at the local high school. Graduated in 1993. His picture should be in the yearbook. Married right out of high school. His wife was named Julie. One daughter, Kaleigh, who was four months old when he disappeared. Parents, Irene and Howard Crawford," Billie said.

"Got it. So, why are you looking for this guy?" Jimmy asked.

"Actually, I'm not looking for him. He showed up suddenly as a witness for the prosecution in court yesterday. He deserted his wife and daughter and now that the child is up for adoption by the mother's partner, he suddenly surfaces. What I need to know is where he's been for the past seven years, what he's been doing, how he's been living, and why he's suddenly made an appearance. Is that possible?" she asked.

"Well, let me have a crack at it and I'll let you know. When do you need the information?" he asked.

"Court convenes next Wednesday, but it would be nice to have the information by Monday so I have time to build a case around it," Billie replied.

"Okey Dokey, Billie. I'll give it a go and get back to you as soon as I know something," he quipped.

"Thanks Jimmy. I owe you…again!" Billie exclaimed.

Billie heard an audible click as Jimmy hung up the phone.

Billie put her cell phone on the table and picked up the teapot from the stove to fill it.

Billie's attention was drawn to the kitchen door. "Hey there!" Jen said, who as usual, let herself into the house.

"'Morning, Jen. Care for some tea?" Billie asked as she finished filling the teapot and held it up in front of her.

"Sure, as long as it's decaf," Jen replied, patting her stomach.

Billie placed the teapot on the stove and turned the burner on beneath it. "I think we have decaffeinated tea," she mumbled as she searched the pantry. "Ah, here it is."

Jen retrieved two mugs from the cupboard and joined Billie in front of the stove where she was watching the teapot.

"A watched pot never boils," Jen quipped, grinning.

Billie stuck her tongue out at her friend.

"Where's Cat?" Jen asked.

"In bed," Billie replied. "She was bound and determined to go to work this morning, but she was acting like such a zombie, that I convinced her to stay home," she explained. "She didn't get a lot of sleep last night."

Billie placed a tea bag in each mug and filled them with hot water. She handed one mug to Jen and the two ladies sat down at the table.

"I can understand why she might be having trouble sleeping," Jen remarked. "She's dealing with some pretty heavy stuff."

Billie sipped her tea then placed it on the table, cupping the mug between her hands, and stared into the amber colored liquid. Without saying a word, she acknowledged Jen's comment with a nod.

"So, when do you expect the results?" Jen asked.

"Hopefully by tomorrow," Billie replied.

Jen rubbed Billie's back. "It'll be all right, Billie. I just know it," she said softly.

Billie looked at her friend. "I hope so." Then, suddenly she remembered that Jen had kept her daughters over night. "How were the girls last night?"

"They were great. They always are when they spend the night," Jen replied. "They were chowing down on pancakes and sausage when I left to come over here."

Billie smiled and once again fell silent and stared into her teacup.

"Speaking of the kids, I'd better get back over there." Jen rose to her feet and wrapped her arms around her friend. She kissed Billie on the head and hugged her once more. "Don't lose hope, my friend. Just remember I'll be here for you if you need me, 'kay?"

Billie closed her eyes and nodded her thanks.

Jen stood erect and immediately grabbed her side as well as the back of Billie's chair to prevent her from doubling over.

Billie swung around sharply. "Are you all right, Jen?" she asked.

Jen smiled. "Yeah. Just growing pains, I think. I'm fine. I'll send the girls home whenever. Okay? See ya later this afternoon." With that, she was gone.

Billie watched her friend go then headed upstairs to check on Cat.

***

Billie spent a good part of the morning pacing back and forth across the living room as she painstakingly waited for the phone to ring with news of Cat's mammogram results. She checked on Cat several times as the hours passed, each time finding her sound asleep. Billie saw this as a good thing, as each hour spent asleep was one less hour Cat would spend torturing herself with worry.

Tara and Skylar returned home from Jen's late morning, trailed closely by Karissa.

"Mom, we're home!" Tara called as they entered the kitchen.

"I'm in the living room, sweetie," Billie called out.

The girls found Billie standing by the mantel, looking intently at the numerous family pictures proudly displayed there. She turned as she felt Tara touch her shoulder.

"Mom? Are you all right?" the astute girl asked.

Billie looked at her daughter. For the hundredth time, it stuck her how much this beautiful young girl resembled her mother. She cupped the side of Tara's face with her palm.

"You look so much like Mama, it brings tears to my eyes," she said softly.

Tara narrowed her eyes. "Mom, what is it that you're not telling me? Is Mama all right?" she asked directly.

Billie realized she was scaring her daughter, so she forced a smile to her face. "Mama will be fine," she replied. "She's just a little tired," she said in half-truths. She then turned to Skylar. She dropped to one knee and held her arms open for the little girl. "Hey baby-cakes. Were you a good girl for Jen last night?"

"Mom, Karissa and I are going to the mall. Do you want us to take the runt along?" Tara asked.

Billie looked at the sincerity on Tara and Karissa's faces, and then at the eager face of Skylar. "Do you mind?" she replied hopefully. "That would be really great if you would. I think your sister would enjoy it," she confirmed, seeing Skylar nod vigorously.

"Sure. No big deal. Come on, rugrat," Tara said affectionately to her excited younger sister.

"Tare..." Billie said, halting the girls' departure, and causing her older daughter to turn around. "Here, have a sundae and a coke on me." She handed Tara a twenty-dollar bill to treat the three of them.

"Cool!" Tara shoved the money into her pocket. "We'll be back later this afternoon. Love you, Mom!" she called over her shoulder as the trio quickly departed for an afternoon at the mall.

"I love you too, baby," Billie said softly as she turned back to the pictures on the mantel.

***

Billie stealthily made her way across the bedroom carpet and knelt on the floor beside the bed. She gently propped her elbows on the comforter, and placed a light kiss on Cat's lips. Cat squirmed slightly beneath her touch, but remained asleep.

Billie smiled at the peaceful look on her face. Once more, she placed a kiss upon her lips.

Cat's eyes fluttered open. "Hi!" she said as she made eye contact with Billie.

"Hi, yourself!" Billie watched the relaxed look fade from her wife's face, only to be replaced by worry etched across her brow.

"Any word yet?" Cat asked.

Billie shook her head. "Not yet. If they don't call in the next hour or two, I'll call them," she replied.

"What time is it?" Cat asked. She looked at the alarm clock to answer her own question.

"Just after one," Billie answered. "You were really tired. I was glad to see you sleep."

Cat maneuvered herself into a sitting position. "Where are the girls? Have they come home from Jen's yet?"

Billie sat on the edge of the bed to face Cat. "Come and gone. They're gone to the mall with Karissa."

"Skylar too?" Cat asked.

"Skylar too. She was thrilled to be included," Billie responded.

Cat stared at the hands she had folded in her lap. Long moments passed in silence this way.

Billie tucked a long strand of red-gold hair behind Cat's ear. Before she could retract her hand, Cat grabbed it and brought it to her lips. She kissed it gently and then clutched it fiercely to her chest. A few teardrops fell into her lap.

Billie sat there in silence and struggled to hold back her own tears. Moments later, Cat regained her composure and released Billie's hand.

"Cat?" Billie said softly. "Sweetheart, talk to me. I can understand why you would be upset and preoccupied with this breast lump, but things weren't right even before that. Have I done something to upset you? Have the kids?" she asked, desperation tingeing her voice.

Cat looked into her wife's eyes. Tears threatened to spill out as she fought to keep her composure. "I... I don't know," she began. She drew her knees up and clutched the bed sheets to her chest. "Life has just been so hectic and so overwhelming. The kids...Jen...the horrible disease that may be growing in my body. I feel so out of control, Billie. I feel like I'm disappearing under this dark cloud that is hanging over me. I'm scared, Billie," she cried.

The vision of Cat sitting there—knees clenched into a fetal position, tears pouring from her eyes—broke Billie's heart. She wrapped her arms around Cat and drew her close while she cried.

Finally Billie spoke. "Cat, you need to talk to someone about this. Someone who can help you. You have an appointment tomorrow with a counselor, remember? I'll go with you."

Cat nodded and Billie visibly relaxed under her approval.

"Good. Now, I've got a pan of stew simmering on the stove, and a nice ham sandwich waiting for you in the kitchen. What do you say?" Billie asked, hoping Cat's appetite had returned.

Not really hungry, but needing to diffuse the tense situation she had created, Cat looked at Billie and asked incredulously, "*You* made stew?"

Billie threw her head back and laughed. "Not exactly. I had a little help from Chunk E. Soup."

"Whew! For a moment there, I thought I'd have to eat your cooking," Cat dead-panned.

***

Brrrring . Brrrring!

"Come on, answer the damned phone!" Billie growled into the receiver.

Brrrring . Brrrring!

"Hello? Hi, this is Billie Charland. I'm calling to see if you have my wife's mammogram results," she said into the phone. "No, this is not a joke. Look, I know I'm a woman," Billie stammered frustrated.

"Billie, let me have the phone," Cat instructed. "Hello... This is Cat, I mean, Caitlain Charland. I'm calling about my test results. Yes. They were done yesterday," Cat supplied. "Yes, I'll hold."

Billie paced impatiently back and forth across the kitchen as they waited for the technician to return to the line.

"Yes. Ah, huh, okay. So, when? Tomorrow? Are you sure? Okay. Good bye," Cat replied haltingly through the conversation.

Billie stood with hands on her hips. She knew from listening to Cat's end of the conversation that she made little progress with the test results. "Well?"

Cat sighed deeply, and then turned around to face Billie. "Tomorrow," she said. "The radiologist covers the entire region and won't be there until then."

Billie threw her hands up. "Great! That's just great," she complained. "Don't those doctors have one shred of compassion? They've got to know we're worried out of our minds over this. Jesus Christ!"

Cat had nothing to say. One part of her wanted to defend her chosen profession. The other part was just as upset and worried as Billie. All she could do was shake her head.

Billie realized her behavior was only adding to Cat's stress, so she willed herself to calm down. She took Cat into her arms and rubbed her back. "Hang in there, my love. We'll get through this. One more day. Just one more," she said soothingly.

"Hey, Ladies," Jen said as she once more let herself in. "How goes it?" she asked, and embraced the two ladies in a giant bear hug.

No response was necessary as raw emotions permeated the trio. "Any word from the hospital yet?" Jen asked.

"Tomorrow," Cat replied wearily.

"That sucks!" Jen exclaimed.

"My sentiments exactly," added Billie.

"Is there anything I can do?"

Cat touched the side of her friend's face. "You're doing it, Jen... you're doing it," she replied.

CHAPTER 15

The phone rang bright and early the next morning. Billie jumped up from the kitchen table and grabbed for it. Her heart was in her throat as she anticipated the results of Cat's mammogram.

"Hello?" she said breathlessly into the receiver.

"Billie? Billie, this is Art. Look, I know you planned to work from home for the rest of the week, but I really need you to come in for a few hours this morning. We've received an intent-to-audit notice concerning the government anti-trust suit you worked on a few months ago and we're meeting with our records department this morning. Can you make it in?" Art asked.

Billie hesitated. She really didn't want to leave Cat alone. "Ah, is it really necessary to have the meeting today, Art?" she asked.

"I'm afraid so. The first meeting with the auditors is on Monday. That leaves just today to go over the facts and set the records department up to work on it over the weekend," he replied.

Cat listened to Billie's end of the conversation, and realized that Billie was hesitating because of her. She approached Billie and covered the receiver with her hand. "Sweetheart, I'll be all right. Go ahead. If I hear from the hospital before you get home, I'll call you," she urged.

"Are you sure, Cat?" Billie felt uneasy about leaving Cat alone.

Cat nodded her assurance.

"Okay, Art. I'll be there in about an hour. Is that all right? Oh, and I've got to leave around one," she added, remembering Cat's appointment with the counselor. "Good.

Okay, I'll be in soon. All right, goodbye." Billie hung up the phone and turned to Cat. "Are you sure you'll be okay?"

"Billie, go to work. I'm fine."

***

Cat was consumed in thought as she sat by herself on the edge of her bed. She was alone in the house, the kids having gone to their respective friends' homes. Part of her mind logically analyzed the problem and invented ways to prepare her family for her impending demise. Another part screamed in heartbroken agony at the thought that she might possibly leave everyone she loved. She knew she was thinking irrationally, but part of her was terrified that Billie wouldn't be strong enough to endure her death. Part of her was concerned that Billie would fall apart, and their children would be left with no parent to provide emotional support for their pain. She knew her own parents would be there for them, but it wouldn't be the same. Waves of fear ravaged her heart as she sat there fretting over what might be.

She glanced at the clock and realized it was already after noon. Acknowledging she had a one o'clock appointment with the counselor, she rose to her feet and headed toward the bathroom to shower, only to be interrupted by the phone. Cat stopped short and stared at the offending appliance. Fear once again welled in the pit of her stomach. She forced herself forward and reached for the receiver.

"Hello?" she said softly. "Yes, this is Caitlain Charland."

Cat silently listened to the voice on the other end of the line, the creases in her brow deepening with each second that passed. Finally, it was her turn to speak.

"Ah, yes...I understand. Monday? Okay. All right," she said, haltingly and somewhat in shock. "Good bye."

She placed the receiver back on the cradle, lowered herself to the bed and stared at the floor as her shoulders shook.

***

Billie closed the last manila folder of audit material at noon. She interlocked her hands behind her head and stretched before looking at the clock. *Damn! I've got to get home. Cat's appointment is in an hour.*

Billie grabbed the folder and tossed it on her secretary's desk on the way out. "That should be the end of it, Deb," she said. "I'll be home later this afternoon if Art has any questions, okay?"

"Sure thing, Billie," Deb replied. "Will you be in next week?"

"I'm planning on it," Billie responded.

"All right then, have a great weekend," the secretary offered.

"You too."

Before heading home, she stopped at Jimmy's office to see if he had made any progress reconstructing the last seven years of Gary Crawford's life.

She stood in the older gentleman's doorway. "Hey Jimmy, have you got anything for me?"

Jimmy looked up. "Have I got anything? You know better than that. Take a look at this." He handed Billie a piece of paper with neatly written notes.

Billie's eyebrows shot into her hairline. "Holy shit!" she exclaimed. "Damn, you're good!"

Jimmy retrieved a folder from his desk and removed a few photographs from it, which he handed to Billie.

Billie picked up the photograph and stared at it. "So how does this explain his sudden appearance?" Billie commented out loud, more to herself than Jimmy.

"My guess is that he's motivated by money. Why else would a guy like this show a sudden interest in a child he hasn't seen in seven years?"

"You may be right, Jimmy," Billie said, smiling. "Once again, you've come through for me, my friend. What can I do to repay you?" she asked.

"Seeing that smile is payment enough, Billie. Glad to help," he replied.

Billie glanced quickly at her watch. "I've got to run. Thanks again, Jimmy." She planted a kiss on the older man's cheek before heading out the door.

***

Billie rushed into the kitchen and glanced at the clock. They had only twenty minutes to make it to Cat's appointment.

"Cat, are you ready? We're going to be late." Billie made her way toward their bedroom. She found it odd that Cat was not responding. "Cat?" she repeated.

Billie hesitated as she entered their bedroom. "Cat?"

Billie heard a faint noise coming from behind the closed bathroom door. She reached for the handle and found it locked. She shook the handle. "Cat, open the door," she demanded.

The only response was Cat's angry voice sputtering something indiscernible from behind the door.

Panic began to rise in Billie's chest. "Damn it, Cat! Open the God-damned door!"

Billie began to pound on the door. "Cat, please. Open the door. Don't make me break it down," she warned.

The door remained locked.

Billie looked around frantically for something to break through the door and then suddenly remembered that the small key that came with the lock was sitting just inside the nightstand drawer. She rushed to the nightstand and yanked the drawer out, spilling its contents all over the carpet. She grabbed the key and quickly returned to the locked door. She fumbled and dropped the key twice as she tried to insert it into the hole.

"Son of a bitch!" she exclaimed, angry at her own clumsiness. "Cat! Talk to me," she shouted as she retrieved the key from the floor. Once again, all she heard was angry mumbling.

Finally, she managed to insert it into the lock and felt the tumbler surrender. She grabbed the handle and flung the door open. There before her was Cat, standing in front of the bathroom sink, shears in hand, surrounded by the long red-gold tresses that had once adorned her head.

"Oh, my God, Cat! What are you doing?" Billie snatched the shears from Cat's hands before she could do any more damage. Cat's eyes were wild with rage, fear and confusion.

Billie threw the shears to the floor and grabbed Cat by the shoulders.

"Let go of me!" Cat shouted.

Billie captured Cat's face between her palms. "Cat. Honey, talk to me," Billie pleaded. Tears filled her voice as she took in the shredded mass of hair that remained on her wife's head. "Why?" she asked.

A look of pure sarcasm crossed Cat's face. "I'm going to lose it any way," she shouted. "So, I'd rather lose it by my own hand!"

Billie's brow knit together in a confused frown. "What are you talking about?" she demanded.

Cat broke free of Billie's grasp and stomped out of the bathroom, strands of her once-long hair falling off her shoulders to the floor along the way. Half way across the bedroom, she stopped and swung around to face Billie.

"What am I talking about?" she asked angrily. "I'm talking about cancer, Billie. I'm talking about my hair falling out from chemo."

Billie's face went ashen. "The results came in, didn't they?" she stated more than asked.

Waves of anger crossed Cat's face. Clearly, she was struggling with the news she was given by the hospital.

Billie once again approached her wife and took her by the shoulders. In a much calmer voice, she asked once more. "Sweetheart, tell me. What did the hospital say?"

Intense fear and anxiety replaced the anger in Cat's face as she locked eyes with her wife. "It's what they didn't say that's alarming me," she replied.

Thoroughly confused by the riddles coming from Cat's mouth, Billie tried once more. She led Cat to the bed and urged her to sit down. She pulled a chair toward her and sat facing Cat. "Cat, I need you to tell me exactly what the doctor said," she instructed.

Misty green eyes met blue. "They said the results were 'suspicious'. They said they need to do a needle biopsy to determine if the lump is cancerous," she explained softly.

Billie felt like she had been punched in the stomach. Trying to control the emotion in her voice, she looked at Cat. "When?" she asked.

"Monday, at ten o'clock."

"Today is Friday. Can't they get you in sooner? Don't they realize Monday is two days away?" she pointed out.

Cat sat there in silence, already resigning herself to a weekend of emotional hell.

Seeing how vulnerable Cat was, Billie decided not to pursue the line of questioning. Instead, she looked intently at her wife. She took in the choppy appearance of her once flowing hair. Feelings of intense regret filled her heart as she chided herself for taking the extra time to speak with Jimmy instead of heading straight home. She quite possibly could have arriving in time to prevent what Cat had done to herself.

Cat pulled away when Billie reached to touch her hair, her own regret flowing freely from her eyes.

"Baby, I'm going to call the counselor to cancel and reschedule your appointment, then ask Marge to come over to fix this," she said, referring their friend, and Art's wife, who was a hairdresser.

Cat nodded slightly, but continued to stare down at the carpet.

Billie retrieved the shears from the bathroom floor and took them with her down into the living room where she made her calls without Cat overhearing. When she returned to the bedroom, Cat was lying on her side, still awake and staring at the wall.

Billie sat on the edge of the bed and rubbed Cat's arm. "Marge is on her way, love. She'll be here soon, and your appointment has been rescheduled to Monday afternoon."

Once again, Cat nodded, and then in a tiny voice, she added, "I don't want to die, Billie."

Billie took a deep breath and held back her emotions. "I won't let you die, Cat. I need you too much to let that happen," she said. She fell to her knees, and placed her cheek against Cat's. "Sweetheart, you were so strong when Skylar was sick. You never gave up hope. We need you to be strong now. Please don't give up," she pleaded.

"I was able to help Skylar," Cat whispered hoarsely, "I can't do a damn thing to help myself."

Billie lifted her head and placed a kiss on Cat's cheek. "That's not true, love. I've heard you say that fifty percent of any cure is attitude and willpower. You're a doctor, Cat. You know there is always hope. Your babies need you. I need you. Don't give up. Please fight."

Cat nodded and closed her eyes, squeezing tears out from between her lids.

Billie stood and looked down on her wife. "Rest a while. Marge will be here soon," she said as she returned to the bathroom to collect the golden strands that had fallen victim to fear.

***

Billie walked in a circle around Cat. "I like it! It will take some getting used to, but I like it. You outdid yourself, Marge."

Cat subconsciously touched her now short pixie-cut hair, feeling sick at heart for what she had done to herself. Her gaze met Billie's as she looked to verify the words that were coming from her wife's mouth. Cat was always able to tell when Billie was being sincere just by looking into her eyes.

What she saw there brought relief to her fears. "Really?" she asked.

"Really," Billie replied. "In fact, it looks kind of sexy," she added, growling.

"Stop it!" Cat blushed in front of their friend.

Billie pulled Cat to her feet. "Come on. Let's take a look at it." She led Cat to the bathroom, followed closely by Marge.

Cat stepped in front of the mirror and gasped. "I look like a little girl!" she exclaimed. She was unable to keep a small grin from forming in the corner of her mouth.

Billie stood behind Cat and noticed that despite herself, Cat liked the cut. "I think she likes it," she said to their friend. "You're a miracle worker, Marge. We can't thank you enough."

"My pleasure," the dark-skinned woman replied. She hugged Cat. "You look beautiful, my friend."

Cat leaned her newly shorn head against Marge's. "Thanks, Marge. I owe you," she exclaimed.

"The only thing you owe me is a promise that you'll fight this thing, and to keep your chin up. Okay?" Marge declared.

She looked at herself once more and then addressed Marge's reflection in the mirror. "One more thing," she said.

"What's that?" Marge asked.

"Promise me it will look this good when it grows back in, just in case chemo ends up sending me to Kojak's barber at some point along the way." Cat tried her best to distill the tension her question raised by grinning ear to ear.

"I promise," Marge replied. "After all, I work miracles, remember?"

***

"Cool! A cookout," Tara exclaimed as she entered the back yard, followed by Karissa and Kelly.

Billie looked over from where she was smoothing out the tablecloth on the picnic table. "Hey sweetie, I'm glad you're home. Could you run across the street to collect your sister from Missy's? Dinner should be ready in about a half-hour," she called out.

"Sure, Mom," Tara reversed her direction and led her entourage back down the driveway.

Moments later, Jen made an appearance. "Hi, neighbor. Was that my daughter I just saw crossing the street?" she asked as she deposited her salad and three bags of chips on the picnic table.

"Sure was. I sent them to fetch Skylar. How are you feeling?" Billie asked as she hugged her friend.

"A little tired, but other than that, okay, I guess," Jen replied. "Fred will be along in a few minutes. He's gone after ice for the cooler. So, how's Cat?" she asked.

"Cat is fine," came the reply from behind the two women.

Jen turned around sharply at the sound of Cat's voice. "Holy shit!" she replied loudly. "Wow! Cat, I love it!" she exclaimed loudly as she noticed her friend's new hairstyle. She held her at arms' length to admire the cut. "Whatever possessed you to do it?"

Cat's hand automatically went to her newly shortened locks. "Possessed is a good way to put it," Cat replied lightly.

The sound of a car door drew their attention to the driveway.

"That will be Fred," Jen remarked, still not able to take her eyes from her friend.

"Hidey-ho Neighbors," Fred called out in his best 'Mr. Rogers' voice as he crossed the back yard lugging a cooler full of ice and soft drinks.

Jen furrowed her brow as she responded to Fred's greeting. "Fred, you are such a nerd some times."

"Yeah, but you love me anyway," Fred replied. He put the cooler down at the end of the table.

Jen stood on tiptoe to kiss her husband. "Honey, I'd like you to meet our new neighbor, Cat Charland," she said. She pulled Cat from behind Billie, where she was hiding, hoping to surprise Fred with her new look.

Fred's eyes nearly popped out of his head. Whistling loudly, he replied, "Oh, baby! Wow, what a knockout!"

"I'll knock *you* out if you don't put those eyes back into their sockets," Jen said jokingly. She punched him on the arm as Cat blushed under the praise and Billie puffed with pride.

Amidst the commotion, the adults didn't hear the kids arrive home.

"Mama?" Tara asked incredulously. "Is that you?"

Cat turned sharply to see a look of suspicion on Tara's face

"Hi, sweetie," Cat replied.

"Mom! What did you do to your hair?" Tara exclaimed.

Cat frowned and said the obvious. "I cut it," she said. "Don't you like it?" she added.

"Ah, sure...but why?" the girl asked.

"I guess I needed a fresh start," Cat replied. "It feels good. I kind of like it."

"Mama, can Missy eat with...us?" Skylar shouted as she ran across the yard, followed closely by her friend Missy. The little girl stopped in her tracks as she spotted her newly coiffured mother.

"Hey, rugrat." Cat dropped to one knee to greet her youngest daughter.

Realizing this woman was indeed her mother; Skylar continued across the yard and hugged Cat tightly. "Mama, you cut your hair!" she exclaimed.

"Yes I did. Do you like it?" Cat asked.

Skylar nodded vigorously before remembering her mission. "Can Missy eat dinner with us?' the little one asked.

"Sure," Cat replied.

"Cool!" shouted Skylar as she hugged her friend, and totally forgot about her mother's new look.

Cat noticed that Tara, Karissa and Kelly were still looking at her oddly. "Tara, why don't you ask Kelly to stay for dinner too?"

"Sure Mom, sure," Tara replied. She walked away, shaking her head. "Come on, Kel, let's go call your mom."

Suddenly, the sound of a very loud wolf whistle came from across the yard.

"Yo, Mama! What a fox," Seth shouted as he spotted his mother. He crossed the yard quickly and scooped her up into his arms. "Cool cut. If you weren't my Mom, I'd ask you for a date," he joked.

"Well, if I wasn't your Mom, I might accept," replied Cat jovially. "I'm glad you made it home on time for dinner, Scout," she added.

"Is Stevie with you?" Jen asked.

"He's gone home to take a quick shower. In fact, I need to do the same. We've been playing basketball with the guys for the past two hours."

"Well, that went over pretty easily," Billie remarked as she watched Seth walk toward the house. "None of them seemed too upset by your sudden change."

"All except Tara." Cat glanced absent-mindedly at the house.

"So, wanna tell me the truth about why you cut it?" Jen said pointedly as Billie and Fred went off to warm up the grill.

Cat looked at Jen and threw her arms into the air. "How do you do it? How do you know when I'm not being totally honest with you?" she asked.

"Well, my friend," Jen said, throwing her arm around Cat's shoulder and drawing her in for a quick hug. "You see, I think we are sisters from different mothers. We have a connection...a bond. Know what I mean?" she asked.

"All I know, is I feel guilty as hell keeping things from you," Cat replied.

Jen threw her head back and laughed. "Works for me," she exclaimed. "Now spill it."

Cat locked arms with her friend and led her toward the house. "Why don't you help me carry the salads out and I'll tell you all about how I was possessed by Edward Scissor-hands."

***

"So, what you're saying is the mammogram is inconclusive...that it still might be something to be concerned about," Jen parroted back to her friend.

Cat placed the salad on the picnic table. "Exactly." She wrapped her arms around herself. "I'm really scared, Jen. I mean, what if it's cancer?" she asked.

Jen took Cat by the shoulders. "If its cancer, then we'll deal with it. You're a doctor Cat. You must know there are all kinds of advancements in medicine today that make cancer more curable," she said.

"I also know there are some types of cancer that can't be cured. I've seen so many people suffer and die from the disease. What it does to their families is heartbreaking," Cat explained. "Jen, my emotions are in such turmoil over this. I'm angry at becoming a victim. I'm terrified that I may die before I see my children grown. I'm scared to death about what it will do to Billie if I die."

"C'mere, you," Jen said as she embraced Cat. "It will be okay, Cat. I can feel it."

Suddenly, a bolt of pain pierced Jen's side as she released Cat and grabbed the edge of the table in one swift movement.

Cat immediately knew her friend was in trouble. "Jen? Jen! Honey, are you all right?" she asked.

The tone of Cat's voice drew Fred's stood by the picnic table. "Jen, sweetheart, sit down," he urged as she slowly lowered herself to the bench. While Fred assisted his wife, Cat sprinted into the house to retrieve her medical bag.

After several deep breaths, Jen's face, and her death grip on the edge of the table finally relaxed as the pain subsided. Billie's face was ashen with fear for her friend.

"Jen, are you all right?" Billie asked as Cat rejoined them.

Cat pulled her blood pressure cuff and stethoscope from her bag. "Left arm," she demanded. She wrapped the cuff around Jen's arm, pumped it up and slowly released the pressure as she read the valve. "180 over 110," Cat announced as she removed the cuff from her friend's arm. "You'd better get your ass to the doctors, ASAP!" she ordered.

"Cat, I'm fine." Jen tried to make light of the situation. "Look, the pain is gone. I feel fine," she repeated.

Cat looked at Fred. "She needs to see her doctor, Fred."

Fred looked at Jen and opened his mouth to lend support to Cat's orders.

"Don't even say it, Fred," Jen interrupted before he could speak. "Cat, I have an appointment on Monday. I'm feeling fine now. If it happens again before then, I promise I'll go to the emergency room. Okay?"

Cat narrowed her eyes at Jen. She came nose to nose with her friend. "Obviously I can't force you to go Jen, but for your own sake, and the sake of this unborn child, I'm going to hold you to that promise. Don't you dare do anything to put your life at risk. I need you here. Do you understand that?" she asked, quite seriously.

Jen nodded and whispered, "I promise."

CHAPTER 16

Saturday morning found Cat sitting at the kitchen table with her hands wrapped around her coffee cup. She stared blindly ahead. It was unusual for her to rise before Billie, but this morning she had awakened with the dawn, unable to sleep. Her mind raced with thoughts of the detours life had placed in her path.

Cat tried to look at her situation without emotion clouding her mind. She had to be pragmatic and practical. She had to plan for her family's future, even if she wasn't in it.

Financial issues were not a concern. Billie made an exceptional amount of money as a partner in her law firm. The children would be well provided for. There would be adequate money for college. They would never want for anything.

Of utmost importance to Cat was not that her children would be well taken care of, but that they'd be happy. They were at such tender points in their lives. Seth was on the verge of becoming a man. He needed guidance, understanding and patience. Tara struggled with her identity and coming into her own maturity at an alarming rate. And Skylar...well, Skylar would forever be her baby. She craved the attention she received from both her mothers. Billie would have a difficult role to fill for both of them.

Cat agonized over what it would mean to the children if she were no longer with them. She thought about how she would feel if she had lost her own mother at such a tender age. Such thoughts led her to how Billie surely had felt when she discovered the people who raised her were not her biological parents. Deep feelings of lost and despair filled her heart as she realized for the first time how Billie must have felt.

Cat inhaled deeply. She closed her eyes and allowed waves of fear and anger to rush over her. *Should they tell the children?* Billie had urged her not to until they had conclusive information. Cat guessed Billie was right. There was no need to unnecessarily alarm them until they knew what they were dealing with. Doc knew, but thought it best not to tell Cat's mother. Cat wished her mother knew. She needed the comfort of maternal arms at a time like this. Cat felt so isolated and so alone in her confusion. *Thank God I have Billie and Jen to confide in.*

As these thoughts fleeted through her mind, she felt warm hands slide down the length of her arms and envelope her own hands that were still wrapped around her coffee cup. Eyes still closed, she savored the feel of the body pressed against her back as moist breath tickled her neck. She felt safe and surrounded in love.

"Good morning, my love. You're up early." The sultry purr came from behind her as warm lips delicately touched her cheek.

"Hmmm. Good morning." She tilted her head back to complete the closeness. "I couldn't sleep."

"Are you all right?" Billie asked.

Cat opened her eyes and looked at the coffee cup now surrounded by four hands. She nodded silently and released the cup from their grasps. She picked the cup up and handed it to Billie. "How about a refill?"

Billie took the cup without reply and carried it to the counter to retrieve a cup for herself while she refilled Cat's. She returned to the table and sat on the side of the table opposite Cat. Billie slid the now full cup toward her. "Here you go love."

"Thanks, sweetie," Cat said.

Billie looked intently at Cat. Even with sleep-stained features, the woman was beautiful. Billie smiled as her eyes took in every detail of Cat's appearance.

Cat met Billie's eyes. "What are you smiling about?" she asked softly.

Billie's smile broke into a full grin. "This smile is my inability to hold the love inside," she responded. "Cat, you are so beautiful, right down to the sleepy eyes and disheveled hair. You are so damned cute, I just want to squeeze you!" she explained. "Every day I wonder how I was so lucky to have found you," she added.

Cat held Billie's gaze as her wife's words filled her heart and tears filled her eyes.

Concerned that she had said something to upset her, Billie reached across the table and covered one of Cat's smaller hands with her own. "Cat?" she whispered softly.

Cat allowed several large tears to fall to the tabletop. Billie waited patiently for her reply.

"Billie, I'm afraid," she admitted, not able to elaborate further.

Billie placed two fingers under Cat's chin and raised her face. "Are you really afraid, or are you angry?" she asked.

Cat realized at that moment how wise and perceptive Billie really was. Cat tended to think that Billie lived in the moment, reactive rather than proactive…spontaneously emotional, and not prone to deep intuition. She now realized she was wrong. Here before her was a very tender and sensitive creature whose own intuitive abilities had seen right through her.

Cat smiled at her own realization. She looked down into her coffee cup and composed herself before she looked back at Billie. "I must be pretty transparent, huh?"

Billie released Cat's chin. "Not really. I just put myself in your shoes. I would be royally pissed," she explained.

"That's putting it mildly," Cat admitted. She sat back in her seat and wiped the tears from her face. "Billie," she continued, "I feel so powerless. I feel like my future has been taken out of my hands. Pissed? You're damned right I'm pissed!" she complained. "I didn't ask for this."

Billie leaned forward. "I know you didn't ask for this. Who would? Cat, you are not powerless. We can beat this. We can beat this together."

Billie looked at Cat for several long moments in silence before she spoke again. "Look, Cat. I know this is scary stuff, and I can understand how terrified you are, but you are allowing this to consume you. This doesn't have to be a death sentence. Hell, we don't even really know yet if it's serious. Tara is already suspicious. Let it go for now...at least for the weekend."

Cat sat back once more, defeat clouding her features. "All right, Billie," she replied. "I'll try."

***

Later that afternoon, Cat elected to stay indoors and write while Billie mowed the lawn. Normally, that was a chore Seth took care of; however' as much as Billie had just lectured Cat about dwelling on the issue, she was crawling out of her skin with anxiety and worried about what they were bound to live through over the next several weeks...or even years. She needed to get out of the house, move around, and take her mind off the troubles that plagued her family.

Billie finished mowing the front yard and was starting on the back when Karissa came running across the lawn.

"Billie! Billie! Mom needs help! Where's Cat?" she asked, nearly hysterical with fear.

Billie immediately shut off the mower and took Karissa by the shoulders. "'Rissa, honey, what happened?" she asked.

"Mom is bleeding," she rasped out between sobs. "She fell on the floor with pains in her stomach, and she's bleeding."

"Oh, my God!" Billie exclaimed. "Is she alone?" she asked.

Karissa nodded. "Stevie is working and Dad went after groceries. Billie, she needs help," the girl cried.

"Run back home as fast as you can so your mom isn't alone, okay, sweetie? I'll get Cat and we'll be there right away."

Billie sprinted into the house as Karissa turned and ran back across the lawn.

"Cat! Come quickly, Jen is in trouble," she shouted before she even made it through the kitchen.

Cat was on her feet in seconds, her own problems totally forgotten. "Billie, what is it?" she demanded, meeting Billie at the doorway between the kitchen and living room.

"Jen is bleeding. She's alone with Karissa. God, Cat..." Billie said, fearful for her friend's life.

Dr. Charland took over as she began to bark orders. "Billie, call an ambulance then do what you can to find Fred. I'm going to Jen's." Cat grabbed her doctor's bag from the kitchen closet and ran out the door.

***

Cat burst into Jen's house to find her laying on the living room floor, clutching her stomach, a pool of blood collecting under her. Karissa was kneeling by her mother's side, trying hard not to cry.

Cat dropped to her knees next to her friend and brushed the hair from Jen's face. She fought her own tears as she began to examine the fallen woman. "Jen. Jen, honey, Billie is calling an ambulance. You're going to be all right, do you hear me?" she asked. Cat wrapped the blood pressure cuff around Jen's arm.

"Cat...the baby," Jen said painfully. "Oh, God..." Jen drew her knees into her chest as a round of cramps wracked her abdomen.

"Help is coming, my friend. Hang in there." Cat tried not to let her personal attachment to this woman affect her professional competence as she took Jen's pulse. "Karissa, fetch a cold face cloth, will you honey?" Cat asked, giving the teenager a reason to remove herself from the crisis for a moment.

"Cat, it hurts. My stomach...shoulder." Jen gasped as another cramp doubled her over. "Cat, please tell me I'm not losing the baby. Please," she pleaded.

Cat looked at her friend and cursed the fates that were condemning the unborn child whose life was ebbing away at that very moment. "I'm sorry, Jen," was all Cat could say. Jen closed her eyes and released the tears that were trapped under the lids.

Billie crashed through the door. "Cat, the ambulance is on the way...oh, my God!" Billie felt sick to her stomach at the scene before her.

Cat once more took charge. "Billie, grab that throw off the back of the chair. She needs to be kept warm."

Billie snapped into action and spread the blanket over Jen. She too knelt by Jen's side. "Jen, we're here with you. You're going to be fine," Billie assured her.

"The baby..." Jen repeated weakly.

"Here's the face cloth." Karissa offered it to Cat as she knelt once more beside her mother.

Cat looked assuredly at the girl. "Wipe the sweat off her face with it, would you sweetie?"

Karissa looked down at her mother and began to wash her face. Pain distorted Jen's normally jovial features. Karissa had never seen her in this state before. Her mother was always the strong one. She was the one who took care of *them* when they were ill. She leaned in and placed a kiss on Jen's flushed cheek. Jen forced a smile onto her face for her daughter and mouthed a silent 'thank you' to the girl, bringing a teary smile to the young girl's face.

The ambulance arrived at the house at the same time Fred did. Billie did what she could to calm Fred while Cat identified herself as a doctor then filled the EMT's in on Jen's condition.

"She needs you to stay calm right now, my friend," Billie told Fred. She physically held him back so the EMT's could strap Jen onto the stretcher.

Fred was frantic. "Billie," he said shakily. "Billie, I can't lose her." His voice was choked with emotion.

Billie had her hands on Fred's shoulders. "She'll be okay, Fred. She's in good hands."

One EMT approached Fred while the other discussed Jen's condition with Cat and made arrangements for to ride to the hospital in the ambulance.

"I'm going with her." Fred moved immediately to Jen's side and took her hand.

"I wanna go too," exclaimed Karissa.

Cat shot a look at Billie who immediately caught her meaning.

"'Rissa, honey, why don't you come home with me and spend some time with Tara. Your dad will call with news when they get to the hospital," Billie suggested.

"Baby girl, do as Billie says," Jen rasped from the stretcher. "Honey, I'll be okay. I promise." She reached her hand out to her distraught daughter.

Karissa immediately went to her mother's side and buried her face in Jen's neck. "Please come home," Karissa whispered tearily.

"I will, baby. I will," Jen assured her daughter. "Now, go with Billie, okay?" she asked.

Karissa nodded and went to stand next to Billie who immediately tucked the teenager into her side with a reassuring arm around the girl's shoulder. She mouthed a silent "I love you," to Cat, and then led Karissa out the door.

***

It was late into the evening when Cat called from the hospital.

"Cat?" Billie answered the phone with the single syllable.

"She's resting under sedation," Cat said stoically.

An uncomfortable silence followed. Neither of them wanted to discuss the obvious. Finally, Billie spoke. "The baby?" she asked.

"Gone," was all Cat said, sadly.

Billie wrapped her arms around her middle and stifled a sob, the silence of which Cat heard loud and clear over the phone.

"Are you all right, Billie?" Cat asked.

Billie sniffed away a tear. "I'm fine. How are Fred and Jen taking it?" she inquired.

"Fred's main concern is Jen's health. He's sad over their loss, but he's relieved that Jen will be okay. Jen? Well, Jen is devastated. She blames herself, of course," Cat explained.

"It's not her fault, Cat," Billie replied.

"No, it isn't, but she is too emotionally raw right now to accept that," Cat said.

"And you?" Billie asked. "How are you doing?"

"I'm tired, and I'm ashamed. I'm ashamed that I have been too self-centered and too wrapped up in my own problems to see that Jen needed me."

Billie immediately regretted the distance between them. "Cat, don't talk like that. This is *not* your fault. Look, come home. There's nothing else you can do for Jen and Fred tonight. Okay?"

"I'll be home soon."

"Okay. I love you, Cat."

"I love you too."

***

Billie was sitting in the dark living room when Cat arrived home. She instinctively knew Billie was there and went directly to the chair she was sitting in and lowered herself into her Billie's lap. Billie placed a light kiss on Cat's head and wrapped her arms around her.

"What happened, Cat? Why? Why Jen?" Billie asked softly.

Cat sat up. The light from a street lamp partially illuminated Billie's features and enhanced the strong lines of Billie's jaw. Cat ran her index finger along the side of Billie's face and inhaled deeply.

"Jen had what is called an ectopic or tubal pregnancy. This happens with the fertilized egg becomes stuck in the fallopian tube and begins to grow there. Most of the time, ectopic pregnancies resolve themselves without the woman even knowing she's pregnant, but sometimes they grow and can be pretty dangerous if they rupture. That's what happened to Jen. Thank God, Karissa was home with her, or she could have bled to death," Cat explained.

"But why, Jen?" Billie asked once more.

"Jen had her tubes tied after Karissa was born. Because her tubes were damaged, there wasn't a clear path for the fertilized egg to travel to the uterus," Cat replied.

"Those pains she had at the cookout must have been the beginnings of the rupture," Billie observed.

"You're probably right," Cat answered. "If she had only gone to the doctor like I told her to, it wouldn't have gotten to the point it did. She could have died," Cat explained, choking up on the last sentence.

"Are you saying they could have saved the baby?" Billie asked.

"No. Ectopic pregnancies never end with a live birth, but the massive bleeding and cramping could have been avoided. Poor Karissa. She was scared out of her mind seeing her mother like that," Cat recalled. "By the way, how is she?" she asked.

"She was pretty quiet for most of the evening. Tara and Skylar did their best to entertain her, but she was pretty down in the dumps. Finally, they all went to bed. I checked on them just before you came home. She seems to be sleeping pretty soundly," Billie explained.

Cat suddenly bolted upright. "Oh, my God! Stevie! Has anyone told him? Where is he?" she exclaimed.

"Don't worry, Cat. Stevie and Seth are camping out in the family room tonight. I left a note for him to come over here as soon as he got home from work. With Seth's help, I broke it to him as gently as I could. He seemed pretty shook up, but after I assured him Jen would be okay, he seemed to handle it all right," Billie replied.

Cat relaxed once more and settled back into the protection of Billie's arms. "You're a good mom and a good friend, my love," she whispered.

"It's no more than Jen would do for us. Heck, it's no more than Jen *has* done for us," she explained.

Cat yawned loudly.

"All right love, time for bed." Billie rose to her feet, still cradling Cat in her arms.

Cat laid her tired head on Billie's shoulder as they ascended the stairs to their room.

CHAPTER 17

Early the next morning, Billie and Cat were awakened by a knock at their bedroom door.

"Whaa...?" Billie sat up in bed and looked at the clock flashing 6:18 a.m.

The knock came again.

"Cat, wake up, someone is knocking at the door," Billie said, nudging Cat awake. "Who is it?" Billie called out.

"Karissa. Can I come in?" the young girl's voice said through the door.

Cat sat up. "Karissa, sure, honey, come in," she replied.

Karissa turned the handle and slowly pushed the door open. "I couldn't sleep," she said. "I'm worried about Mom."

Cat threw back the covers and patted the bed, inviting Karissa in. Within seconds, the teenager crawled into bed and allowed herself to be wrapped in Cat's arms. Billie joined the fray by throwing her arm over both of them.

"Cat, is my mom gonna be okay?" Karissa asked softly.

"She's going to be fine," Cat replied. "She was sleeping comfortably when I left last night."

"Did the baby die?"

Billie tightened her hold on the two girls as Cat prepared her reply.

"I'm afraid so, sweetie," Cat confirmed.

"Why?" she asked.

Cat brushed the hair away from Karissa's forehead while she thought of how to answer. "The baby started to grow in your mother's fallopian tube instead of the uterus, so your mom's body rejected it. Nature has a way of taking care of things that aren't right, honey. It's really sad that the baby is gone but sometimes things are just not meant to be. It's nobody's fault. It just happened," she explained.

Karissa nodded while Billie marveled at how delicately Cat had handled the questioning. She lay there for long moments with her arm still wrapped around them, waiting for the next question that never came. Finally, Billie lifted her head from the pillow to see that both Karissa and Cat had drifted off to sleep. She smiled and rested her head once more on her pillow, where she soon joined them in dreamland.

***

Karissa was gone when Billie and Cat awoke the next morning.

Billie wrapped her arms around Cat as she stood before the bathroom mirror brushing her teeth. "You were very gentle with her this morning,"

Cat rinsed her mouth and tapped the toothbrush on the side of the sink to rid it of excess water before she returned it to the caddy mounted on the wall. She raised herself on tiptoe and kissed Billie full on the lips. "Thank you," she said.

Having just stepped out of the shower, Billie continued to towel dry her hair while Cat dressed herself. "Are you going to call the hospital this morning?" she asked Cat.

"I didn't have to. Fred called us while you were in the shower. They're releasing Jen around noon. Fred asked that we come to pick them up since they both rode in the ambulance and don't have their car," Cat replied.

"Did you speak with Jen? How is she this morning?" Billie asked.

Cat slipped a shirt over her head. "No, I didn't. Fred called from the lobby. He left the room while the doctor examined Jen and took advantage of the break to call us."

"Did he say how Jen was?" Billie asked again.

"He didn't say much, except that she was pretty quiet. She's going to need a lot of moral support over the next few weeks. I can imagine she's feeling pretty guilty about losing the baby," Cat replied.

Cat slipped her shoes on and tied the laces while Billie combed out her long dark hair. "I'm going to make a pot of coffee if you're interested," she offered.

Billie mentally noted the upbeat mood Cat was in. "Coffee sounds great. I'll be down in a few minutes." Billie dressed quickly and carried her shoes down the stairs and into the living room, where she found Karissa, Tara and Skylar splayed all over the furniture as they watched cartoons and ate bowls of cereal. She stopped and looked at the girls. "You know you aren't supposed to be eating in here," she observed.

"Mama saw us and didn't say anything." Tara replied, without taking her eyes from the television.

Billie frowned and went into the kitchen in search of Cat. She found her humming lightly while filling the coffee machine with water. She stood there in the doorway with her shoes still in her hand.

Cat turned around and looked at her. "Billie, I'm going to run over to Jen's after breakfast and clean up the mess we left behind. She doesn't need to come home to that reminder." She turned back to filling the reservoir.

"If you don't mind, I'll join you." Billie sat in a kitchen chair to put her shoes on while Cat continued to hum happily.

"Oh, and while we're there, remind me to grab a change of clothes for Jen. All she has with her is the soiled ones from yesterday," Cat said with her back still to Billie.

Cat turned off the faucet and slipped a pod into the coffee machine to brew. She stepped into the sunlight coming in through the open kitchen door and looked out over the back yard. "Looks like a beautiful day today," she remarked.

Billie stood there with eyebrows raised into her hairline.

Cat turned from the door and tipped her head inquiringly to one side. "Is something wrong, Billie?"

The question snapped Billie into awareness. "Wrong? No, not really. It's just that I haven't seen you in this kind of mood in a week," she replied.

Cat looked apologetically at her and sighed. "I have been kind of a bitch for the past few days, haven't I?"

Billie approached Cat and stopped in front of her. She took Cat's hands in her own and kissed each one before holding them close to her heart. "No, Cat. I wouldn't say that exactly. I can understand how you would be preoccupied with everything that has been going on lately."

"Well, I realized this morning when Karissa came to our room, that we have a lot to be thankful for. Here was this helpless child, worried sick about her mother...a mother she could have easily lost yesterday, and there *I* was, feeling sorry for myself." Cat paused for a moment and then looked once more into Billie's eyes. "I'm sorry, Billie."

Billie placed a finger on Cat's lips. "Shhh. There's no reason to be sorry, love. Just remember, we're in this together, okay? I'll be right by your side tomorrow during the biopsy, and no matter what the results are, we'll deal with it. We'll get through it. I promise," she said softly.

Cat smiled and tilted her head to accept a delicate kiss. "I love you" Cat whispered.

"And I love you."

"Oh man! Are you guys at it again?" Tara complained as she walked in on the tender moment. "Geesh, get a room!" she added, laughingly.

Billie and Cat looked at each other with raised brows. "Time for 'the talk'!" they said in unison.

***

Cat entered Jen's hospital room and found her sitting on the edge of the bed, clad in a hospital gown. Billie followed close behind. Cat sat beside her and hugged her affectionately. "Hey sweetie, how are you feeling?"

Jen shrugged and looked at the hands she had folded in her lap.

Billie sat down on the other side of Jen and looked over her head at Cat. Instinctively, they both wrapped their friend in loving arms, sandwiching her between them. Jen sat very still, as though absorbing the love radiating from her friends.

"We're so very sorry for your loss, sweetheart," Cat said.

"We're here for you, Jen...always," Billie added.

Jen squeezed her lids tightly and allowed liquid sorrow to seep down her cheeks. Unable to manage a verbal reply, she reached her hands up to squeeze the pair of arms crossed before her and nodded slightly.

Billie reached for the tissues and handed one to her friend, then with a quick pat to Jen's thigh, she rose from the bed to join Fred who stood at the window overlooking the parking lot. She rubbed his back then wrapped her arm around his waist. "And how are *you* doing?" she asked, not forgetting that he too had lost a child.

"I'm okay," he replied. "I guess it just wasn't meant to be. I'm more concerned about Jen. She's been so quiet," He looked at Cat and Jen on the bed. "She's supposed to start as a teacher's aide at the school in a few weeks. Maybe that will take her mind off things."

Billie just nodded.

Cat reached to the floor where she dropped the bag containing Jen's clothes. "Here's the change of clothes you requested, although I really have to say, you look ravishing in that hospital gown."

Jen smiled. "Do you think the neighbors would mind me arriving home with my bare butt sticking out the back?"

"Works for me!" Fred chirped from his position by the window, drawing an elbow to the ribs from Billie.

"Owwww!" he responded.

Jen chuckled and then went into the bathroom to change. Moments later, she emerged from the bathroom, fully dressed and ready to go. Fred moved immediately to her side, and wrapped an arm around her waist.

An uncomfortable silence ascended over the four friends as they waited by the elevator. Cat made the first attempt to dispel the tension.

"Did your doctor leave you with any special instructions?" she asked.

Fred volunteered the answer before Jen could speak. "Just lots of bed rest for the next few days."

"Well, don't you worry about the kids. They can stay with us for as long as they need to," Billie offered.

Jen was drawn out of her silence by the mention of Stevie and Karissa. "The kids! Are they okay? Karissa...she must be out of her mind with worry,"

"The kids are fine," Cat replied. When we left this morning, Karissa, Tara and Sky were happily munching on cereal in front of the TV, and Seth and Stevie were still camped out in the family room. Karissa was a little concerned this morning, but we assured her that you'd be fine."

Jen offered a weak smile at Cat's reply as the elevator door opened to admit them. Within moments, they were in the car and on the road to home. Silence once again prevailed. Billie glanced into the rear view mirror to see Jen sound asleep on Fred's shoulder.

"I'm afraid she didn't sleep well in the hospital last night," Fred explained.

Cat nodded. "I don't blame her. The hospital is the last place I'd suggest for getting any rest," she replied. "Kind of ironic, isn't it?"

Billie pulled into neighbor's driveway, and then jumped out of the car to open the door for Fred and Jen.

Fred gently nudged Jen awake. "Jen, honey, wake up."

Jen lifted her head from her husband's shoulder and looked around, sleepy and disoriented. "We're home already?"

Once outside the car, Jen allowed her friends to hug her and wish her well and promised them she'd call when she felt well enough for visitors.

"Fred, don't hesitate to call us if you need anything, okay?" Cat handed him the bag of soiled clothes she had grabbed as they left Jen's hospital room.

"The kids have been worried about their mom and will probably want to see her, but like we said, they are welcome to stay for a long as they want. Keeping them at our house for the next day or so might allow Jen to get more rest," Billie added.

Jen stopped on the landing and turned to face her friends. "You really don't need two extra kids around. You'll have your hands full tomorrow with your own medical issues."

"They really are no bother," Cat said.

"It'll be fine, Cat. I'm taking tomorrow off to spend with Jen, so I'll be able to keep things relatively quiet, even with the kids around," Fred replied, "But if you can keep them for the night we'd really appreciate it. It will give Jen a chance to catch up on her sleep."

"It's absolutely no problem," Billie responded as they headed back to their car.

Jen stopped them with the sound of her voice. "Oh, Cat, I want to hear from you as soon as you get home tomorrow, okay?"

"Okay, Jen. Get some rest. We'll see you tomorrow," Cat replied as she climbed into the car.

Upon pulling into their own driveway, Billie switched off the ignition and turned to Cat. "That was just a little too uncomfortable for my tastes."

"It *was* a little tense, wasn't it?" Cat replied. "It's so hard knowing what to say when something tragic happens. All we can do is give her all the love and support we can. She'll never really forget about it, but with time, the pain of losing the baby will diminish," she added.

Billie was intently watching Cat as she spoke, emotions running rampant across her brow.

Cat noticed the change in Billie's demeanor. "Billie, are you okay?" she asked.

Billie smiled. "You know me so well, my love." She reached across the seat to touch the side of Cat's face.

"What are you thinking about?" Cat asked softly.

"Cat, I know I've been lecturing you about your fears, and about making a big deal of this breast lump when it may turn out to be nothing." She looked down at the seat between them and tried to gather her thoughts. "Truth is, I've been secretly worrying enough for both of us. I can't help it, Cat. I would die if I ever lost you," she confessed. "I can't imagine the pain ever diminishing, no matter how much time passed by."

Cat became misty-eyed as Billie spoke. She took Billie's hand in her own. "I know exactly what you mean. Now you know how I felt when you were lying in the hospital with a gunshot wound to the head several years ago, and then later, when you woke up after an epileptic episode and didn't know who I was. God, Billie, it was like losing you even though you were still with me. I went through agonizing moments, knowing I would never get over losing you," Cat recalled.

Billie took Cat's face between her hands. "Cat," she said seriously. "Cat if this *does* turn out to be something serious, promise me you'll fight it with every ounce of strength you have. I can't lose you. Promise me," she demanded, her voice broke with emotion.

Cat smiled through tears. "I promise, my love. I promise. Even if I died and went to Heaven, it couldn't possibly be better than being here with you," she replied.

Billie lowered her forehead to touch Cat's. "Thank you," she whispered. Billie planted a gentle kiss on Cat's lips. "Now maybe we should get inside and let Jen's kids know that she's home."

As expected, both Karissa and Stevie were eager to hear news of their mother, and quite relieved to know she was home and would be all right. After strict instructions to return later that afternoon so their mother could get some rest, Stevie and Karissa went home.

Sunday evening at the Charlands' was a quiet one. Karissa and Stevie returned in time for dinner, and afterward retreated to their respective friends' rooms for 'teen time'. Stevie and Seth played video games. Karissa and Tara talked incessantly on the phone with Kelly, and Skylar and her friend Missy colored quietly on the living room rug in front of an oft-watched video of Mary Poppins.

Billie sat comfortably in the living room recliner with her notebook computer on her lap and compiled notes for the final hearing on Shannon and Julie Nash's custody battle, scheduled for the following Wednesday.

As for Cat…she sat curled in the corner of the sofa and divided her attention between Billie, the children, her family and friends and the pad of paper in her lap on which she was attempting to put her thoughts, all the while acutely aware at that moment of how blessed she was to be surrounded by such love, warmth and good fortune.

Her mind wavered, yet continued to return to the one shadow that loomed over her happiness…the shadow of what awaited her tomorrow...the shadow of what may or may not be. *Never is one so appreciative of what they have as when they are threatened by the loss of it.* Such were the thoughts she penned to paper as the sun set on the Charland household that evening.

CHAPTER 18

Traffic was particularly heavy on Monday morning as Billie maneuvered the car through the streets. Cat sat beside her with her hands clasped firmly in her lap and a frown worrying her brow.

Billie and Cat had awakened in the wee hours, but chose to stay in bed, wrapped in each other's arms. Neither spoke, but shared their silent agony...fearing the worst, yet hoping for the best. An occasional shudder passed through Cat, and she fought back her emotions. She wondered how many more mornings she would have the luxury of lying in Billie's arms. It was hours before they finally rose, showered and set out for the hospital.

Cat looked at Billie from the passenger seat of their car. "Billie, I'm really nervous about this biopsy."

Billie nodded, but did not take her eyes off the busy road. "I know, Cat. I am too." She rubbed Cat's thigh with her right hand. "I'd be lying if I said otherwise."

Silence descended over the car for the rest of the trip to the hospital. When they arrived, Billie pulled into a parking space and turned off the engine. "Are you ready?" she asked softly.

Their eyes met. Fear was clearly written all over Cat's face. Billie reached across the front seat and caressed Cat's cheek with her palm.

Cat pressed her cheek into Billie's touch and closed her eyes. "I'm being a baby, aren't I?" Cat asked.

"You're being human," Billie replied. "No one is immune to sickness, Cat, not even doctors. I know you're trained to distance yourself personally from a patient's illness, but when it's yourself, or a family member, I can understand how fear reigns over reason."

"Thank you for coming with me, sweetheart," Cat said.

"There is no way I would allow you to go through this alone. I will always be here for you. You know that, don't you?" Billie asked.

"I know," Cat replied.

She took a deep breath and looked at her watch. "It's nearly time. I guess we'd better get in there."

Billie and Cat sat in the waiting room of the Breast Care Center, having pre-registered and checked in. Soon, a nurse came by to direct them to an examination room where she was instructed to unclothe from the waist up and don a hospital gown.

It seemed like an eternity before the ultrasound technician arrived. Cat sat stiff-backed. Her right knee bounced up and down in nervous agitation. She clutched tightly at the gown, and held it together between her breasts. Her knuckles were white with tension. She looked around wildly, as though dreading the moment when the door would open and her name would be called. It broke Billie's heart to see Cat consumed by fear and on the verge of near panic.

Finally, it was her turn.

They were led to a room with an examination table, an ultrasound machine and a tray laden with various needles and anesthesia. The nurse instructed her to lie on the table, and assured her the doctor would be with her soon. Cat was grateful that Billie would be allowed to stay by her side during the procedure. She clung tightly to Billie's hand and waited for the procedure to begin.

Cat was cold and trembled with fear, unable to stop her traitorous body from shaking so violently. Billie was near tears herself, unable to help calm Cat's fears. She was tense; her jaw hurt and her head ached. She sat beside Cat and laid her head on Cat's stomach. It was a move that seemed to calm them both.

Suddenly, the door swung open and Billie's head snapped up. A pleasant looking middle-aged woman clad in blue scrubs entered. "Caitlain Charland?" she asked. Without waiting for confirmation, she circled the table and sat on the stool opposite Billie.

Cat nodded weakly and accepted the hand the woman extended to her in greeting.

"Hi, I'm Jenny Moore and I'll be your radiologist today. She shook hands with a silent Cat and then turned her attention to Billie. "And you are?"

"Billie. Billie Charland. I'm Cat's partner," she said, and accepted the firm handshake from the doctor.

Jenny placed an assuring hand on Cat's shoulder. "Okay, Cat, let me explain what's about to happen. We're going to perform what is called a Needle Aspiration Biopsy. This procedure is usually used to differentiate between cysts and solid tumors. If it is a cyst, it will usually contain fluid and will all but disappear after aspiration. Cytological or pathological examination of the material we remove will be done at the lab for possible identification of cancer cells. We will use this ultrasound machine over here to help locate the lump, and then once located, we'll numb the area above the lump and insert the needle into it to extract the material. If all goes well, in a few days, we'll have the results. Do you understand?"

Billie wanted to scream that Cat was a doctor, and of course she understood; however, a quick glance at Cat's face made her realize that the radiologist's explanation was actually having a calming effect on her.

"Good! Now all we're waiting for is the ultrasound technician," she said.

As if on cue, the door opened and a twenty-something woman entered.

"Ah! Here she is. Marissa, this is Caitlain Charland and her partner Billie. Ladies, this is Marissa, and she'll do us the honor of running the ultrasound machine," Jenny explained.

While Marissa calibrated the machine, Jenny opened Cat's gown and asked her to point to the location of the lump. Then, with practiced movements, Jenny did a breast exam and easily located the offending tissue. "There it is," she said.

Cat watched her every movement with clinical detachment. Billie, on the other hand, was scared to death, and clutched Cat's hand more for her own peace of mind than for Cat's.

Marissa held the tube of jelly above Cat's breast. "This might be a little cold."

True to her word, Cat gasped as the cold gel touched her skin. Within seconds, Marissa passed the ultrasound wand over the area. Cat's eyes were glued to the screen as she saw the lump before they did. "There it is!" she exclaimed as the lump passed in and out of view.

"You have good eyes, Caitlain," Jenny remarked.

"Cat."

"Cat?" Jenny repeated.

"Cat," she said again. "That's what I'm called. Only my mother and Grandma Alex call me Caitlain," she explained lightly.

"Okay, Cat it is. I'm just going to use this marker to place a dot on the skin over the lump so we'll know where to insert the needle," Jenny explained.

Once the dot was positioned, Jenny wiped the jelly from Cat's breast and thoroughly cleansed the area with Betadine solution to sanitize it from any bacteria that might cause an infection later on. Billie grasped Cat's hand tightly as Jenny picked up the needle containing the anesthesia and gently inserted it into Cat's breast. Cat tensed slightly as the burning liquid entered her skin, but soon relaxed as the numbing agent worked quickly.

Jenny extracted the needle. "You tolerated that well. We'll give that a few moments to really settle in before we aspirate the lump. Do you have any questions while we wait?"

"I have just one," Cat replied. "Most breast cancers occur in the upper outer quadrant of the breast, which my lump is not. They are also usually irregular in shape, are poorly delineated, non-mobile and painless. I want to know if you can tell through the ultrasound if this lump meets any of those descriptions, or if it is an invasive ductal carcinoma. Is it radiating into the surrounding breast tissue?" she asked with clinical coldness.

Jenny looked at Cat and frowned. She tilted her head to one side. "Are you holding out on me? You're a doctor, aren't you?" she asked.

Cat had the decency to blush. "An anesthesiologist, actually," she replied.

Billie beamed with pride.

The radiologist smiled broadly. "Well, that certainly makes my job easier." she chucked. "Okay, I guess it's time. Can you feel this?" She picked the surface of Cat's breast with the needle.

"Feel what?" Cat said facetiously.

"Good. I'm going to insert the aspiration needle into the skin, then employ the ultrasound once more to help guide us into the lump. Here goes." Jenny punctured the skin above the lump.

Billie's stomach threatened to mutiny as she watched the procedure. Cat was very calm. Her gaze was glued to the ultrasound screen as they literally watched the needle pass through Cat's breast tissue and into the lump.

"How are you doing, Cat?" Jenny asked.

"Fine. I don't feel a thing," Cat replied.

Within moments, the material inside the lump had been aspirated into the needle and the needle slowly extracted.

"There. All finished." Jenny placed the specimen on the tray and grabbed a cloth to wipe off the excess lubricating jelly and the small amount of blood resulting from the invasion. She cleaned the area thoroughly and then placed a bandage on the point of insertion. "Nice job, Cat. You can sit up now. "If you feel any discomfort in your breast as it thaws, simple Ibuprofen should help. If you notice any inflammation or swelling, call your doctor," Jenny instructed.

Cat sat and tied the gown together in front of her. "So, you didn't answer my question. "Is this an invasive ductal carcinoma?"

Jenny looked at Cat. "Normally, I don't answer questions from patients on what I did or didn't see. Thankfully, that job belongs to their doctors. However, since you are a doctor yourself...no, it didn't appear to be an invasive ductal carcinoma." Seeing the relief on Cat's face, she quickly added. "Don't be fooled though, Cat. That doesn't mean it can't still be something serious," she warned.

Billie wanted to drop Jenny right there for dashing Cat's hopes, but Cat seemed to take it in stride. "I know, but it does mean I have something to hope for," she explained.

"That you do," Jenny agreed. "Well, I'd better get this over to the lab. You should hear from your doctor in a day or two. Good luck, Cat."

***

"Hi, Daddy. This is Cat."

"Cat, honey, you had the biopsy today, didn't you? How did it go? Did they tell you anything?" Cat could hear the hope in his voice.

"It went fine Daddy, and no, they didn't tell me anything definitive. It'll be a few days before the results come back. Daddy, I'm calling because I think we should tell Mom. It doesn't feel right keeping it from her."

"I'm not sure that's a good idea, Cat. I mean, why worry her until we know what we're dealing with?" Doc suggested.

"Look, I put myself in her shoes. If Tara or Skylar, or even Billie had something seriously wrong with them, I would be devastated if they kept it from me. I would be crushed. Hell, I'd be highly insulted. Don't you realize that we'd be sending the message to her that we don't think she can't handle it?" Cat explained.

Doc was silent for long moments.

"Daddy?"

"I'm here," he replied, followed by another short period of silence. "Maybe you're right, Cat, but she'll be worried sick until we know for sure."

"She's stronger than you think, Daddy. After all, she survived four daughters," Cat pointed out.

Doc chuckled slightly. "Okay, you win. I'll tell her," he said. "But you need to be prepared for lots of phone calls and 'mother henning'," he warned.

"Right now, that's just what the doctor ordered, Daddy, but I think I should be the one to tell her. It's not fair to dump that on you," she offered.

"No, Kitten, let me do it. She's bound to be less emotional that way," Doc replied.

"Daddy..." Cat began.

"I insist, Caitlain."

When Doc used her given name, she knew he was serious. "Okay, Daddy. Tell her she can call me any time, okay?"

"Don't worry, she will. I'll talk to you later, daughter. I love you."

"I love you too, Daddy."

***

The alarm sounded as usual at five a.m. on Tuesday morning. Cat reached for the alarm and shut it off and then sat up in bed. She rubbed the sleep from her eyes and threw the covers back. As she attempted to climb out of bed, Billie captured her with an arm around her middle and pulled her back into the warm comfort of her embrace.

"You're not going to work today, are you?" Billie asked.

Cat snuggled into Billie's neck. "Yes, I am."

"Honey, why don't you stay home until we hear from the doctor?"

"Now you sound like my mother. Billie, I *want* to go to work. It will help to take my mind off things," Cat explained. "There's no reason why I can't work. I feel fine. And besides, if I stay home, I'll be on the phone all day with my mother or Jen assuring *them* that things will be fine. I swear they're more worried about this than we are," Cat said.

"Well, I don't know about that," Billie said. "I've been sick with worry myself over the past few days."

"Look, sweetie, I'm fine. And besides, you have a lot of work to do yourself to prepare for Shannon and Julie's hearing tomorrow. Go to work, and I will too. Trust me, it will be fine. *I* will be fine," Cat pleaded.

Billie chuckled. "Trust you. I guess I haven't been doing a very good job of that lately, have I? I'm sorry for hovering, Cat."

Cat sat up. "Billie, I love you. I'm not sure I've said that often enough over the past few days. I've been pretty self-absorbed. Thank you for caring so much. I don't know what I'd do without you, my love."

"Well, I don't plan to give you a chance to find out," Billie said. "Now, I suggest you get that cute little butt of yours out of bed before I do something that will make us both late for work."

Cat raised her eyebrows. "Late? My first surgery isn't until 9 a.m."

Billie grinned ear to ear and pulled Cat down for a kiss. Cat splayed herself directly on top of Billie so that they were nose to nose, breast to breast. Cat traced her tongue around Billie's mouth, delving deep inside when the opportunity arose. Billie wrapped her arms around Cat, mindful of not crushing her sore breast. She placed her hands on the small of Cat's back and pulled her closer as she lifted her own pelvis in response.

The closeness and intimacy of the movement drove Cat wild. She pressed herself into Billie and took Billie's ear lobe between her teeth.

"Make me late for work," she breathed huskily.

And she did.

***

Cat stood before the sink and scrubbed for her third procedure of the day. Her mind once more returned to the test results. Physically, she felt fine. The biopsy had gone exceptionally well, with so little pain from the procedure that the only reminder was a slight tenderness when she leaned into the operating table while adjusting anesthesia or when she reached across a patient to check vital signs.

Mentally, she was a nervous wreck. Now more than ever, she understood why patients were so vocal about how slow their doctors were in responding to health issues. She also understood that even doctors fell into the bureaucracy when they became patients. The amount of work lab technicians had to do was overwhelming. Cat marveled that the average response time wasn't even longer than it was. What weighed more on her mind was not the response time, but the level of accuracy. She sighed deeply, shook the excess water from her hands and headed into the operating room.

***

Billie sat at her desk and leaned on her elbows. Her fingers formed a teepee in front of her as she stared out the window at nothing in particular. She'd tried hard all day to concentrate on Shannon and Julie's case, but her thoughts repeatedly returned to Cat. She was very proud of how Cat handled the biopsy the previous day, although she supposed being a doctor and understanding the clinical aspects of the procedure helped her to look at things more objectively. What really surprised her though, was Cat's attitude since the biopsy. She seemed less worried and more hopeful. At least it seemed that way.

A beep on the intercom returned her to reality. She blinked rapidly and quickly composed herself before she pressed the call button on the telephone. "Yes Deb?" she asked.

"Billie, John Mercier on line three. He says he has something very important to discuss about tomorrow's hearing," Billie's secretary replied.

"Thanks, Deb. Tell him I'll be with him in a moment."

Billie sat back in her chair and stared at the phone for a moment. She reached for the receiver and pressed the number three. "Hello, John. What can I do for you?" she said so sweetly, she even made herself sick.

"Billie!" he replied like she was his best friend. "Billie, I'd like to come over to discuss the details of the Nash case with you. Do you have some time this afternoon?" he asked.

"Hold on and let me check my calendar," she said. She put the defense attorney on hold. She knew full well her afternoon was free of meetings. She sat back in her chair and picked up the Nash folder to skim through the contents once more and to re-familiarize herself with all the aspects of the case before she spoke to the Crawford's attorney again. Several moments passed before she picked up the phone again. "John, thank you for waiting. It looks like I have three o'clock open. Can you make it then?" she asked.

"Three sounds fine. I'll see you then."

Billie sat back and propped her elbows on the arms of her chair, once again making a teepee with her fingertips. She tapped the tips of her fingers on her chin and narrowed her eyes in contemplation. *What have you got up your sleeve, John? Better yet, what has Gary Crawford got up his sleeve?*

***

Cat gave herself a pep talk as she entered the operating room. "Okay, Cat, last one of the day. You can make it." She sat down at the head of the table and looked into the face of a young woman who could not have been but a year or two older than herself. She glanced at the chart hanging in front of her and looked for the woman's name.

"Hi, Gwen, I'm Cat, your anesthesiologist. I'm going to be your best friend for the next hour or two. You see, it's my job to send you off to dreamland while the docs here fix you up. I'm going to put this mask over your face and ask you to take several deep breaths and to count backward from one hundred. If you feel sleepy, don't fight it. The less you fight, the more comfortable you'll feel. Okay, sweetie?" She saw the woman nod slightly.

This was the one part of her job that Cat enjoyed the most. Nearly every patient, no matter how young or old, strong or weak, lay there on the operating table with such raw, intense fear in their eyes, it hurt to look at them. But when Cat started to administer the anesthesia, she would talk to them soothingly, sometimes joke with them if their condition wasn't too serious, but most importantly, she would watch their eyes as the anesthesia took effect. Without exception, even the most intense fear would fade away into peaceful slumber. She understood how important it was to keep the surgeons up-to-date on the patient's vital signs. She understood the importance of keeping the patient as safe and comfortable as possible during surgery, but the part she liked the most was easing the fear.

Cat watched Gwen closely until she was completely anesthetized. She checked her vitals and relayed the information to the surgeons as they prepared for the operation. She looked up from the woman lying before her and watched as the OR nurses opened the front of Gwen's gown and started prepping her skin. Suddenly, the importance of this operation struck Cat. She caught the surgeon's gaze and whispered *breast cancer*, to which she received a silent nod. Cat closed her eyes, sat back in her chair and took a moment to compose herself and then once more donned her professional manner and focused on her job.

***

At three o'clock on the dot, John Mercier stepped into Billie's office and smugly sat himself in front of her desk.

Billie looked up from the file she was reading. She removed her glasses and placed them on the desk in front of her. "John."

"Billie, I'm here to save us both a lot of trouble tomorrow," he started.

"Trouble?" Billie pretended she didn't know what he was talking about.

"Yes. You see, my client is the biological father of Kaleigh Crawford, and without him agreeing to terminate his parental rights, your client doesn't stand a chance in hell of winning."

Billie propped her elbows on the arms of her chair and clasped her hands in front of her. "John, your client deserted his daughter more than seven years ago. Why, all of the sudden, does he care about her welfare?"

"Well, my client was incapable of taking care of himself, never mind a child, but we'll get into that in more detail tomorrow," he said, "that is, unless you want to cut a deal."

"A deal?" Billie raised her eyebrows into her hairline. *Jimmy, you old son of a gun, you were right!*

"Yes, my client is interested in negotiating a deal with the two Mrs. Nashes."

Billie feigned interest in his proposal. "Go on."

"He is willing to forego his parental rights, for say, a monetary payment of $500,000," he said.

Billie smiled. "$500,000? A half-million dollars?"

"Yes, that is what I said," Mercier replied condescendingly.

Billie sat back and pretended to consider the proposal. "A half-million dollars, huh? I'll have to approach my clients before I can give you an answer. But, if you would, I'll need this request in writing so the price doesn't mysteriously rise for some reason," she replied. "If you see Deb on her way out, she'll draft the documentation for you."

Mercier's eyes flew open as if in disbelief that Billie was actually taking the bait. He quickly jumped to his feet. "No problem. You'll have the proposal on your desk before I leave this building. You won't regret this, Billie." He extended his hand to Billie, who remained seated behind her desk.

Seconds later, the phone rang. "Billie, Mr. Mercier said..." Deb began.

"Don't ask any questions, Deb, just type up his dictation. Trust me on this one," she said.

***

Cat arrived home that evening to find all three children home and lounging around the living room watching TV. It was rare that all three were home at the same time. She entered the living room, kissed each one gently on the head, and asked about their day. As usual, their answers consisted of one word responses like, 'okay', 'fine' and 'good'. None of them wanted to draw their attention away from the television long enough to have a real conversation with her. Such was the life of a mother. The only thing that managed to get their undivided attention was her question about what they wanted for supper. After several suggestions, they all happily agreed to goulash and tossed salad, which Cat headed to the kitchen to make.

Seth poked his head into the kitchen while Cat was retrieving an onion from the refrigerator. "Ma, Mom called a little earlier and said she'd be late tonight and not to wait dinner for her."

Cat looked up, disappointment all over her face. "Oh. Did she say what time she'd be home?"

"No, just that she'd be late."

Cat nodded. "Okay, sweetie, thanks." Heaviness settled over her heart as she began to fix dinner for the children. She had been looking forward to seeing Billie this evening. She needed to see her. Needed to be held and comforted as she recalled her last surgery of the day. Gwen had died on the operating table. Terminal breast cancer had taken her life.

CHAPTER 19

Billie struggled to get herself out of bed the next morning. She'd arrived home late from work the night before and it was midnight before she finally lay down to sleep. She called Cat late in the evening to apologize for the long hours and promised to make it up to her when Shannon and Julie's case was closed. She spent the evening cursing John Mercier repeatedly as she did research and prepared a reaction to his client's last minute offer to negotiate an out of court settlement with the Nash's. She would have much rather curled up on the living room sofa watching an old movie with Cat.

Billie rubbed her face vigorously to help her wake up and then looked at Cat who was still asleep. Billie marveled at how she could sometimes sleep through the alarm. She noted the peaceful look on Cat's face and the smoothness of her brow that seemed chronically crinkled with worry of late. She longed to soothe Cat's fear and relieve the burden of sadness she had been carrying around with her for the last several weeks. *I need to reschedule the appointment with the counselor,* she thought. Billie placed a delicate kiss on Cat's cheek and then got out of bed to take a shower.

Several moments later, and feeling much refreshed, Billie reentered the bedroom to find that Cat was no longer in bed…and in fact, she was nowhere in sight. She spent the next several minutes rummaging through her closet to find an appropriate suit for court and finally settled on the pinstriped skirt and jacket, white silk blouse, and a light gray scarf , the knot of which, when tied, settled just below the last open button of her blouse. She slipped nylon-clad feet into pumps, brushed her now-dry hair until it shone, applied minimal makeup and then went downstairs to find Cat in the kitchen making her breakfast.

Cat stood at the kitchen counter dressed in her knee-length nightshirt. Her hair was all askew and her feet were bare. She reached into the cupboard for a second cup when she heard Billie approach from behind her. She finished brewing both cups of coffee, and then turned around to wish a good morning to her wife.

Cat fought to catch her breath at her first sight of Billie. "My, God, you're beautiful!" she exclaimed. The impact of Billie in her business suit and with her shiny hair and long sculpted legs sent waves of heat to her abdomen. She felt woefully inadequate at that moment and reached up to smooth her disheveled hair and to straighten her nightshirt.

Billie wrapped her arms around Cat and whispered, "And you, my dear are quite ravishing at this very moment yourself. You make it difficult for me to go to work when you look like you so desperately want to be made love to."

All feelings of self-pity flew out the window as Billie's words turned her legs to jelly. "Keep that up and I won't *let* you leave," Cat purred seductively. She pressed herself into Billie, allowing her hands to roam quite freely over Billie's backside to reinforce her point.

Billie groaned. "You are quite the seductress, Cat Charland."

Cat laughed and slapped Billie's butt. "You'd better have your breakfast before *I* get too hot, and *it* gets too cold!" She handed Billie a mug of coffee and then grabbed her own cup and headed toward the table where a breakfast of cereal, bagels, fruit and juice awaited them.

During breakfast, they talked of the upcoming day's events. Billie explained her court strategy for Shannon and Julie's case, and Cat described the full plate of surgeries she was scheduled to assist in that day.

Cat walked Billie to the door when it was time for her to leave or work. She reached as high as she could on tiptoe and kissed Billie, and received a passionately probing kiss in return.

As she pulled away from the kiss, Billie looked deep into Cat's eyes. "Promise you'll call if you hear from the Breast Center today, okay?"

A wave of sadness washed over Cat when Billie mentioned the Breast Center. I reminded her of losing Gwen the day before on the operating table. Billie arrived home so late the previous evening that Cat never did have the chance to talk to her about it.

A parade of emotions crossed Cat's features…sadness, fear, anxiety, and finally anger.

"Cat?" Billie asked. "Honey, are you all right?"

Cat forced a smile onto her face. "I'm fine. I promise to call you if I hear anything today, okay?"

Billie smiled. "Okay. I'll see you tonight then. Wish me luck in court!" She gave Cat one last kiss before turning to go.

"Good luck...and I love you," Cat called to Billie's retreating back.

"Love ya back," Billie shouted and then disappeared into the interior of her car.

Moments later, Billie drove away and left Cat to pull herself together to face the day.

***

Tara was sleeping soundly with the covers pulled up tightly around her neck and an expression of peaceful slumber on her face...that is, until the phone on her night stand suddenly rang. She looked at the time and noted it was nine o'clock. She grabbed the receiver and brought it to her ear. "Karissa, this had better be good," she growled.

"Ah, excuse me? Is Caitlain Charland there?" the voice asked on the other end of the line.

Flustered, Tara stumbled over her words. "Oh! Sorry, I thought you were someone else. No, my mom isn't home right now. She's working. Can I take a message?" Tara replied.

"Yes, please tell her to call Jenny at the Breast Center Oncology Unit for her test results," the woman replied.

Tara fell silent.

"Hello?" said the woman on the line.

Tara suddenly had an intensely sick feeling in the pit of her stomach. "Uhm...yeah...yeah, I'll tell her. Breast Center...Oncology Unit. Thanks."

Tara hung up the phone before the woman could say anything else, and lay on the bed, stunned. Numbness began to spread through her legs. She pulled the covers up over her head. "Oh, my God," she said. She scanned her memory for what the word 'oncology' meant. It was a word whose meaning was burned into her brain forever. She heard the word so many times when Skylar was ill with leukemia, she could spell it in her sleep.

Cancer? Does that mean Mama has cancer? Now what did the lady say...oh, yeah, call the Breast Center Oncology Unit for her test results, she repeated to herself again. Tara closed her eyes tightly and tears escaped between her lids. *Oh, God, no! Don't let her have cancer!*

***

"Shannon, Julie, I need to talk to you before we go into the courtroom," Billie said. She ushered the two women into an interview room and closed the door behind them. "Please sit." She motioned them into the chairs on one side of the table and proceeded to pace back and forth in front of them.

"Look, is there anything you know about Gary, or his family that you haven't told me?"

Both women replied by shaking their heads no.

"Good. Okay. You need to know that whatever happens in there, and no matter what I say or do during the course of this trial, I am doing it for your benefit, and I expect you to be supportive. No unsolicited comments, no sensational reaction...at least not until it's over. You hired me, you're paying me a lot of money, and you've got to trust me. Any questions?"

Shannon stood and extended her hand to Billie. "You've got our total support, Billie. We are counting on you to come through for us."

"And that's exactly what I aim to do. All right, it's nearly nine. We'd better get in there." Billie once more ushered the women to their next destination.

Billie noted that Gary, his parents, several supporters, and his lawyer were already in the courtroom when they entered. John Mercier sent a sly, knowing look in Billie's direction. She made herself comfortable at her table and ignored his obvious attempt to make eye contact. Instead, she neatly placed her papers and notes on the table in front of her before she sat stiff-backed in her chair and looked straight ahead. She was the picture of professional confidence. Shannon and Julie on the other hand sat beside her, holding hands and looking nervously at each other.

Finally, the bailiff entered from a door to one side of the judge's bench. "All rise and come to order. The court of the Honorable Judge Jonathan P. Williams is now in session," he announced. Everyone in the courtroom rose to their feet while the judge entered and sat himself comfortably behind the large wooden bench. Judge Williams looked first at John Mercier and then at Billie. "Mr. Mercier, Ms. Charland, I am familiar with your case. Ms. Charland, you may begin with your opening statements."

Billie rose to her feet. "No opening statements, Your Honor."

Shannon gasped audibly beside her.

Judge Williams raised his eyebrows. "Very well," he said. "Mr. Mercier?"

John Mercier rose to his feet. "I too would like to waive opening statements, Your Honor," he said. Again, he looked slyly in Billie's direction.

Judge Williams sat back in his chair and narrowed his eyes. "Ms. Charland, Mr. Mercier, approach the bench please," he ordered.

Billie and Mercier both rose and approached the bench, and looked at the judge expectantly.

"This is highly unorthodox," he remarked. "I trust we are not going to raise a circus tent over the proceedings again today?"

Billie smiled. "No, Your Honor. My clients and I are well prepared to make this as short and uncomplicated as possible."

"And you, sir?" Judge Williams said to Mercier.

"I agree with Ms. Charland, Your Honor. Short and sweet."

"Good. Then we may proceed." He sat back in his chair as Billie and Mercier returned to their tables. Once both lawyers were seated, the judge spoke. "Ms. Charland, you may call your first witness."

Billie stood and sorted through her papers. Finally, she found what she was looking for. Holding the paper in front of her, she announced. "I call Shawn Bennett to the stand."

Gary Crawford instinctively stood and started walking toward the stand, and then stopped half way across the room when he realized what he had done. The entire courtroom fell silent. He looked at Billie with a 'deer in the headlights' expression on his face.

Billie waved him on toward the stand. "Please continue, Mr. Bennett," she said.

John Mercier shot to his feet. "I object!"

Billie looked at the judge.

"This had better be good, Ms. Charland," Judge Williams warned. "Overruled,"

Mercier sat tentatively on the edge of his seat, a very worried expression on his face.

Billie smiled and waited for the bailiff to swear the witness in. She approached a very nervous looking Gary

Crawford and rested her hands on the railing in front of him. "Please state your name for the court, if you would," she said.

"Gary David Crawford," he replied.

Billie took a step away from him, and then turned back. "Mr. Crawford," she said, "Could you tell the court who Shawn Bennett is?"

Crawford shifted uncomfortably in his seat. "Shawn Bennett is my alias," he explained.

"Alias? Why do you need an alias, Mr. Crawford?"

"I object," Mercier exclaimed once more. "I fail to see what this testimony has to do with this trial."

Billie looked at the judge. "I promise this will all make sense in a few minutes, Judge."

"Overruled!" came the judge's reply. "You may continue, Ms. Charland."

"So, Mr. Crawford, why do you need an alias?" Billie asked again.

Crawford cleared his throat. "I'm a writer. Shawn Bennett is my pen name," he explained.

"A writer?" Billie repeated. "Have you been published?"

"Well, no, but..." he stammered.

"Mr. Crawford, how many children do you have?" came Billie's next question, completely changing the subject.

Gary Crawford looked dumb struck. "Ah, one. I have one. Kandy. Julie is her mother," he replied.

Billie smiled. "So, Mr. Crawford, how do you intend to support your daughter if you should win custody?" she asked. "Are you counting on your writing skills, or do you have other employment?"

Billie could see from the expression his face, that Crawford was totally unprepared for these questions. She was sure his lawyer assured him that the trial would be over before it could begin.

"We'll...we'll live with my parents for a while...until I'm published, that is, and then we'll buy a house," Crawford answered.

"I see." Billie walked back to her table, turned around, and leaned her backside against it. She crossed both her arms and legs in front of her. "One more question, Mr. Crawford. Where have you been for the past seven years?"

"I have been Shawn Bennett," he replied. "I have been suffering from amnesia from a car accident, and I truly believed I was a writer named Shawn Bennett. I regained my memory about a month ago," he explained.

Billie stood and once more turned her back to the man. "That is all, Mr. Crawford...oh, except for one thing. Your daughter's name is Kaleigh."

Mercier lowered his head into his hands on the table and Crawford turned ten shades of red. Loud murmurs came from the audience. Shannon and Julie looked at each other and grinned. Billie simply returned to her seat and sat stoically.

Judge Williams did his best to keep the grin from his face. "Your witness, Mr. Mercier," he said to Crawford's lawyer.

Mercier reluctantly rose to his feet. "I have no questions at this time, but reserve the right to recall this witness," he said.

"Mr. Crawford, you may step down," the judge said and made notes on the pad before him.

Crawford was quite angry as he sat down next to his lawyer. The proximity of the defense and prosecutor's tables was such that Billie was easily able to hear his rasp to his lawyer, "I thought you said she would settle."

"Call your next witness, Ms. Charland," the judge instructed.

Billie once again rose to her feet. "I call Marie Wentworth-Bennett," she announced.

"Oh, my fucking God," Gary groaned and sank down into his chair as a beautiful redhead entered the room. Dressed to the nines, she walked sexily toward the witness stand. She stopped by the prosecutor's table along the way. "Hello, Shawn," she said.

From her peripheral vision, Billie could see the excitement build in Shannon's and Julie's body language. She squeezed Shannon's hand to remind them to remain composed.

Billie approached the stand after Ms. Wentworth-Bennett had been sworn in. "Please state your full name," she said.

"Marie Wentworth-Bennet," she replied.

"May I ask how you know Gary Crawford?"

"You mean Shawn? He's my soon to be ex-husband," she replied. A loud rumble spread throughout the room.

Mr. Mercier jumped to his feet. "I object, Your Honor!"

"Mr. Mercier, I fail to see where you have grounds to object. Overruled!" the judge said.

"Ms. Wentworth-Bennett, how long have you been married to Gary...I mean Shawn Bennett?" Billie asked.

"Six years. Six years too long to tell you the truth."

"Six years. Do you have any children with Shawn Bennett?"

"Two boys, ages 3 and 4," the witness replied.

Billie smiled and pointed to Julie. "Were you aware when you married him that he was already married to Julie over there?"

Marie sent a hateful look in Crawford's direction. "No, I didn't. In fact, I didn't find out until you came to see me yesterday."

Mercier looked at Billie with a shocked expression on his face.

"Ms. Wentworth-Bennett, you said Gary Crawford was your soon to be ex-husband. I assume then that you have begun divorce proceedings?" Billie asked.

"The divorce will be final in about a month...none too soon," she replied sternly.

"Will Mr. Crawford receive alimony, a separation allowance or assets?" Billie probed.

"That deadbeat asshole will not receive a red cent from me, or my family," she replied. "I was smart enough to insist on a prenuptial agreement before we were married."

"I understand your family is wealthy," Billie commented.

"Daddy is the CEO of one of the Fortune 500 companies. We are very comfortable to say the least," she admitted.

"So is it fair to say that Mr. Crawford's life style is about to change dramatically?" Billie asked.

"That is an understatement," Wentworth-Bennett said smugly.

"Thank you, Ms. Wentworth-Bennett. That is all," Billie returned to her table.

"Mr. Mercier," the judge said to Crawford's attorney.

Billie noticed that Mercier been whispering to Crawford during her questioning of Crawford's soon to be ex-wife. Mercier now stood to address the court. "Your Honor, Mr. Crawford withdraws his bid for custody, but retains his parental rights," he stated.

Billie felt like she had been punched in the stomach. If Crawford refused to give up his parental rights, it meant that Shannon could not adopt Kaleigh. She decided to play her last card.

"Ms. Wentworth-Bennett, you may be excused. Ms. Charland, do you have any more witnesses to call?" the judge asked.

Billie rose to her feet. "Your Honor, I do not have further witnesses, but I do have one more piece of evidence that I will ask the court to consider in Shannon and Julie Nash's bid to request the termination of Gary Crawford's parental rights."

Billie approached the bench with a neatly typed one-page letter. She handed the letter to the judge and then walked back to the table and stood behind it while Judge Williams absorbed its content.

When he finished, he placed the letter on the desk in front of him and looked at Billie. "Continue, Ms. Charland," he said.

Billie picked up a copy of the letter from the table in front of her. "For the benefit of the court, the letter in question is a proposal from Mr. Crawford, delivered to me by his lawyer yesterday afternoon, with an offer to relinquish his parental rights for a sum of $500,000. Your Honor, Mr. Crawford is in effect offering to sell his child to Shannon Nash. I urge the court to consider this cold-hearted proposal during deliberations and to rule in favor of terminating Gary Crawford's parental rights. We further urge the courts to grant an adoption of Kaleigh Crawford by Shannon Nash. Thank you, Your Honor. My clients rest."

Billie returned to her seat and let out a long sigh. Julie cried softly beside her, protected in the circle of Shannon's arms. Shannon caught Billie's eye and smiled reassuringly.

Judge Williams sat back in his seat and for long moments said nothing. An uncomfortable silence settled over the courtroom. Finally, he leaned forward and rested his weight on his forearms. "Mr. Crawford, to your feet, sir," he commanded. "Sir, it is clear to me that you willingly deserted your wife and child seven years ago, and contrary to your claim of amnesia, I tend to believe you found a wealthy woman to take care of you, and settled in for the ride. Now, you return, in the throes of a divorce, just days before your biological daughter is about to be adopted by another, and propose a trade—your child for a half-million dollars—money you will certainly need once your divorce leaves you penniless. In addition, it is also clear that you have committed the crime of bigamy, having married Ms. Wentworth while still married to Julie Nash."

Gary Crawford stood before the court with his chin lowered to his chest while the judge continued.

"Mr. Crawford, I am appalled that you believe you still have the right to be a parent to Kaleigh Crawford. You gave up that right when you deserted her seven years ago. Never once, did you visit or contribute to her upbringing, yet you stand there and smugly deny a happy, healthy home life for your daughter in the adoptive custody of Shannon Nash and the child's biological mother, Julie. Sir, I am truly appalled. Therefore it is the ruling of this court that your parental rights are to be terminated immediately and permanent adoptive custody is awarded to Shannon Nash."

The judge looked at the bailiff. "Mr. Keene, please take Mr. Crawford into custody, to be charged for the crime of bigamy and then to be released on his own recognizance until a formal hearing can be scheduled. This case is closed." The judge picked up the gavel and brought it down hard.

Billie, Shannon and Julie all rose as the judge left. Shannon and Julie were about to explode with happiness. Billie looked at Shannon and grinned. "Congratulations, Mom." She extended her hand to Shannon, who brushed it aside in favor of an uncharacteristic hug.

"Billie, we can't thank you enough," Shannon said.

"My pleasure." Billie collected the folders and papers from her desk and re-packed her briefcase.

"How about we take you and Cat to dinner tonight? I'm dying to know how you dug up all that dirt on Crawford," Shannon offered.

Julie vigorously nodded her approval.

"I appreciate the offer, ladies but now is really not a good time for Cat and me to commit to a date. Maybe next week?" Billie countered.

"It's a date," Shannon said and extended her hand once more. "Once again, Billie, you have our undying gratitude."

Billie returned the handshake. "Go home and spend time with your daughter. Be happy in your life. If you're happy, she'll be happy, and once more, congratulations."

Billie continued to pack her brief case when Mr. Mercier approached her.

"That was dirty pool," he said.

"I warned you I play by the book, John. Producing Gary Crawford at the last minute was underhanded. You knew that child was better off with those two women. Why in God's name did you even agree to represent him?" Billie asked.

"I'm not the bad guy here, Billie. Believe it or not, I had no knowledge of the other wife. All I know is that his parents contacted me and said they were representing their son in an effort to save his daughter from being adopted against his will. I was unaware of the dirty laundry behind all of this.

You did your homework well," he said, extending his hand. "Congratulations."

"Thank you." Billie picked up her briefcase and glanced at her watch. "Time to go," she announced. "I'll see you later, John."

***

Cat and Billie arrived home nearly simultaneously that afternoon. After the custody trial that morning, Billie went back to the office and completed filing the paperwork associated with the case, and then worked to clear her calendar for the next two days. By midafternoon, she was ready to go home and informed her secretary that she was taking a four-day weekend and not to disturb her unless Art designated it an emergency.

When Cat arrived at work that morning, she had a full schedule of surgeries that would take her well into the afternoon. As luck would have it, her last surgery was canceled, which was fine by her, since she struggled to keep her mind on her job. All she could think about was her test results. Her nerves were on edge all day as she waited for the phone to ring. By the end of the day, her nerves were frazzled. She would have even welcomed bad news at that point. Any news was better than no news at all.

Cat pulled into the driveway just as Billie stepped out of her own car. She waited for Cat to meet her in the driveway and then embraced her affectionately

"Hi, my love," Billie said. "You're home early. How was your day?"

"It was fine. My last surgery was canceled, so here I am."

Arm in arm, they let themselves into the back yard and headed toward the house.

"Any news from the breast clinic?" Billie asked.

"None," Cat replied. "It's starting to worry me."

They walked past the gate into the back yard and noticed Skylar sitting in the sandbox, with an array of dolls around her. "Hey, rugrat," Billie called. She directed Cat across the yard to greet their daughter.

"Mommies!" Skylar shrieked. She jumped to her feet and ran to meet them.

Several hugs and kisses later, Billie set Skylar back onto her feet and asked her how her day went.

"Okay, except for Miss Grumpy," Skylar replied. She crossed her arms across her chest and pouted.

"Miss Grumpy?" Cat asked.

"Yeah, Tara. She's been mean to me all day," the little girl replied.

Billie ruffled Skylar's hair. "Well, maybe she's just having a bad day."

Skylar immediately plunked herself back down into the sand and started playing with her dolls again.

Cat took Billie's hand and pulled her toward the house. She called back over her shoulder to Skylar. "Dinner will be ready soon, Angel. I'll give a yell when its time."

"Okay, Mama."

"What's the hurry?" Billie asked as Cat pulled her along.

"I'm anxious to see what's ailing Miss Grumpy."

"Tara?" Cat called out when she entered the kitchen, followed closely by Billie.

Before Billie could close even the door behind them, Tara was in the kitchen, looking like a Banshee on a rampage.

"Why didn't you tell me?" Tara demanded sternly.

Both mothers were taken aback. They looked at each other in confusion.

"Tell you what?" Billie asked.

"Do you think I'm stupid? Do you think I'm so weak that I couldn't handle it?" she asked.

Cat saw the wild look of fear and anger in Tara's eyes.

"Tara, sweetheart. Come into the living room and sit. Tell us what's wrong," she suggested.

Tara paced back and forth and ignored Cat's suggestion. "You two are really good at keeping secrets from me, aren't you? First, I find out about how Sky was born…and now this!" she shouted.

"*This*? What is *this*?" Cat asked. She took Tara firmly by the shoulders. "Tara, you are talking in riddles. I don't understand what you're trying to tell us."

Billie stepped forward and wrapped her arms around both Cat and Tara and held them tight until the tension abated. Finally she released them. "Okay. Sit," she commanded and led them both to chairs at the table. "Now talk. Tara, you first."

Tara looked at her mother. "The crying…the haircut. It didn't make sense to me until this morning."

"Okay, stop right there. You need to get to the point, Tara. Mama and I have no idea what is upsetting you," Billie said.

"You got a phone call this morning," Tara said.

Cat immediately reached across the table and grasped Billie's hand.

"It was from someone called Jenny," Tara continued.

"From the Breast Center?" Cat asked softly.

"Yeah, from the Breast Center," Tara slammed her hand on the table. "Mama, look at me."

Billie rose to her feet and leaned over the table toward her daughter. "Tara, you will not speak to your mother that way, do you hear me?" she asked sternly.

Tara looked at Billie and narrowed her eyes. "Mom, I have a right to know."

"She's right, Billie. Please sit down," Cat said. She reached once more for Billie's hand.

Cat met Billie's gaze and looked for support before turning to speak to Tara. "Tara, honey, we didn't want to say anything until we knew for sure. There was no need to worry anyone. After all, it could turn out to be nothing."

"But, Mama. I'm not just *anyone*. I'm your daughter!" Tara said, almost in a whisper. She struggled to mask tears she was trying desperately to hold back.

For the same reason Cat insisted on telling her mother, she now realized she should not have kept this secret from her daughter. Tara was right. She didn't trust her enough to handle it, and by doing so, she was cheating Tara out of chance to show her strength and support. She was wrong.

Cat nodded and raised her eyes to meet Tara's. "I'm sorry, Tara." She leaned forward in her chair and reached for Tara's hand. "I went to the doctor's for a regular checkup almost two weeks ago, and Dr. O'Brien found a lump in my right breast. They could also see it on a mammogram. On Monday, I had a needle biopsy. Mom went with me. That phone call you took this morning was supposed to be the results," she explained.

Cat sat back in her chair and forced the lump down that was rising in her throat. She suddenly realized that their daughter was no longer a child. She covered her mouth with her hand to hide the sob that threatened to erupt from her throat.

"Is it cancer, Mama?" Tara asked directly.

"We don't know yet, sweetie. But if it is, we'll fight it together, okay?" Cat replied.

"You can count of me. Both of you can," Tara said. She reached her free hand out to Billie, who immediately lost it and began to cry.

CHAPTER 20

"What do you mean by abnormal cells?" Billie asked.

Cat called the Breast Center after the emotional confrontation with Tara, and was informed that her results had been sent to her doctor. She cursed her own profession for its sometimes cold-heartedness, and contacted Dr. O'Brien who made an immediate opening for her that very afternoon. After a quick call to beg a babysitting favor, Cat, Billie and Tara dropped Skylar off at Jen's and then headed to the medical center.

"Does that mean cancer?" Tara interjected before Dr. O'Brien could answer Billie's question.

"Well sweetie, there is a whole range of cell types between normal and cancerous. Just because cells are abnormal, it doesn't necessarily mean its cancer," the doc explained.

"So what *does* it mean then?" Billie asked.

Cat sat back and smiled. As long as she had these two with her, she didn't *have* to ask any questions.

"Let me put it this way. If you started to grow healthy cells in the center of a Petri dish, they would stop growing as soon as they hit the sides of the dish. In other words, they would grow to fill the confines of the container they are in. Abnormal cells on the other hand, would start to pile on top of one another once they reached the sides of the dish. They aren't programmed to recognize their container, so they keep growing, and soon, they form a mass of tissue that may or may not turn into a tumor," Dr. O'Brien explained.

"So a tumor means cancer?" Tara asked.

"Only if the tumor has the ability to metastasize or spread from where it originally appeared to other locations in the body. Metastases occur when cells break away from the tumor, travel around the body through the blood and become trapped in the capillaries of other organs. From there, they infiltrate the organ and start to grow into a new tumor. That type of tumor is called malignant. If it doesn't do any of those things...and what I mean by that is…if it doesn't have the ability to spread, it is called a benign tumor. Do you understand?"

"Yeah, I guess it makes sense. So what kind of tumor does Mama have?"

"Well, we won't know that until we take it out and do a biopsy," the doc explained.

"Are they gonna cut Mama's breast off?" Tara asked

"No, Tara. That's a little dramatic for this stage of the game. That would only be recommended if she had malignant tumors that couldn't be cured through minor surgery, radiation or chemotherapy. No, what they *will* do to your mom is called an excisional biopsy which is done under general or local anesthesia when the lumps are small. In this case, the entire tumor and a margin of good tissue around the tumor are removed. The tissue is then frozen, sliced and examined for cancer cells. They won't be taking off her whole breast, just a small section inside it. This procedure is sometimes called a lumpectomy," Dr. O'Brien explained.

"So when can we schedule that, Patty? And before you answer...the sooner the better. We've already been living in hell for almost two weeks," Cat interjected.

Patty laughed. "I knew you were going to say that, Cat, so when you called this afternoon, I contacted the breast clinic and set up an appointment for tomorrow morning. I hope you don't mind," she said, smiling sheepishly.

"Mind? I could kiss you right now!" Cat exclaimed.

"Whoa, there, don't you dare! I don't think I could go one-on-one with the big guy over there," Patty said. She nodded in Billie's direction.

"Actually, I could kiss you too," Billie added.

"Oh. Please!" Tara said. "You guys are sick."

***

Early the next morning, Cat, Billie and Jen found themselves in the family room of the breast clinic, nervously waiting for Cat's turn in the operating room. Karissa talked Tara into staying home with Skylar and promised to stay with her until her mom was out of surgery.

Cat broke the silence. "I think Tara will be okay, regardless of the outcome."

Billie nodded. "I guess we underestimated her strength. I guess we've been underestimating her a lot lately."

"So has she said anything to you about being gay?" Jen asked.

Cat shook her head. "She hasn't said anything to me. I'm not even sure she'd know at this stage if she was gay or not. Some of us don't realize it until we're adults."

"You're right, Cat. *I* didn't know until I was an adult. But if Tara *is* gay—and I'm not saying she is—but *if* she is, all we can do is give her unconditional love and support," Billie added.

Cat nodded and another awkward, nervous silence fell over the three women.

"I am so glad I arranged for the rest of the week off," Billie commented.

Cat suddenly perked up. "Oh, Billie, honey, I'm sorry. I've been so wrapped up in myself that I forgot to ask how Shannon and Julie's case went yesterday," she exclaimed apologetically.

Billie raised her eyebrows. "Well, Jimmy worked miracles for me again, as usual. He found that Gary Crawford had an alias, and a whole other life, including a wealthy wife and two children. Apparently he wasn't happy with one wife—ah, make that two wives—so he started roaming again. Wife number two found out and threw his sorry ass out with nothing more than the clothes on his back. So, there he was, penniless and in the position to bargain for the custody of his daughter. What he didn't count on was that we would discover the second family." Billie chuckled. "You should have seen his face with I called his wife as a witness. It was priceless."

"Wow! So why did he suddenly show up? Has he been keeping tabs on Kaleigh all these years?" Cat asked.

"Are you kidding? He couldn't even get Kaleigh's name right during the trial. No, I think his parents knew where he was all along and alerted him when they heard Shannon was trying to adopt her."

"It sounds like she's better off with your clients," Jen observed. "Imagine having a child and deserting it like that. Doesn't he realize what a gift children are?" Jen's voice cracking slightly as her own recent loss hung over the group.

Cat took her friend's hand, squeezing it lightly.

"Ms. Charland?" a voice said from the doorway. All three women looked up to see a scrubs-clad technician standing before them.

"Yes?" Cat and Billie answered together. A deep crease formed across the brow of the technician.

The technician scanned the papers attached to the clipboard in his hand. "Caitlain Charland?" he asked.

"That would be me." Cat rose to her feet and reached for Billie's hand.

Billie placed a protective arm around Cat.

The technician looked at the women. "I'm afraid you'll have to stay here," he said to Billie. "She'll be in good hands. The whole procedure should only take an hour or so."

Billie frowned and looked at Cat.

Cat placed her head on Billie's chest, just above her heart. "It'll be okay, Billie."

Billie wrapped her arms around Cat and placed her cheek on top of Cat's head. "I love you, kitten," she whispered.

"Love you too."

Cat stepped out of Billie's embrace and followed the technician out of the room.

Billie turned to Jen just in time to see her wipe the moisture from the corners of her own eyes.

"Jen patted the chair beside her. "Come, sit."

Billie sat and reached for Jen's hand.

"I can't lose her, Jen," Billie said softly. "I've tried to be strong, but if truth be told, I'm scared to death."

"Me too," Jen confessed. "I've tossed and turned many a night thinking about how unfair it would be if she were taken from us prematurely. But I've decided that isn't going to happen," she declared.

"How can you be so sure?" Billie asked. She desperately wanted some sort of guarantee.

Jen looked Billie straight in the eye. "Because my child made the ultimate sacrifice so she could live—that's why," Jen reasoned. "There's a balance to life, Billie. Something dies so something else can live. My child is living through Cat. I *have* to believe that. Do you understand?"

Billie felt a chill run through her body as Jen's meaning sunk in. "Yes, I do," she replied.

***

"Hi, Caitlin, I'm Dr. David Bradbury. How are you feeling?" the surgeon asked.

"I'm feeling wonderful, Doc. Cut away!" she replied. Euphoria settled in from the Valium that Cat had taken several minutes earlier. Cat distractedly thought about how her own patients felt while under the general anesthesia she usually administered during surgery. She suddenly appreciated, more than ever, what her work meant to her patients.

"Okay. The first thing we need to do is to locate the tumor again using ultrasound so we can familiarize ourselves with its appearance and the structure of the tissue surrounding it. Then we're going to administer a local anesthetic by injecting a medicine that will cause a lack of sensation into a wide area around where we'll make the incision. This will allow us to perform the surgery without you feeling any pain. If at any time during the surgery, you feel any discomfort at all, let us know and we'll inject more local anesthetic into the area, okay?" he instructed.

"So, you're not going to administer a sedative intravenous medication," Cat observed, "...which is good, because I'd like to stay awake for the procedure, if you'd please," she concluded.

Dr. Bradbury raised his eyebrows. "You are correct. You will be awake during the procedure. So, are we ready?" he asked.

"Go for it!" Cat giggled.

Dr. Bradbury applied the ultrasound jelly to Cat's breast and passed the wand over it several times to locate the lump. "There it is," he said. He studied the images on the screen for the next several minutes. "Okay, I think we can begin." He wiped the jelly from her breast and sanitizing it thoroughly.

"Caitlin, we're going to..." he began.

"Cat," she stated.

"What was that?" the surgeon asked.

"Cat. My name is Cat," she replied, giggling again.

He nodded his head and smiled broadly. "Okay, Cat. We are going to start by making an incision in the skin above the lump and then we'll actually cut away the tissue with a cauterizer to reduce the risk of bleeding. Don't be alarmed to see a little smoke rise from the incision," he warned.

Cat laughed out loud. "Ha! Billie always said my breasts were smoking hot! Hee-hee! Wait 'till she hears this!"

"Billie?" Dr. Bradbury remarked as he made his incision.

"That's my wife," Cat replied. "Been together for nine... or maybe it's ten years now. She's a lawyer, you know. A real smart one too."

Dr. Bradbury grinned. "Okay, Cat, the incision is made, now I'm going to switch from the scalpel to the cauterizer," he informed her.

"So Doc, how much margin of normal tissue are you going to take around the tumor? You want to make sure to use a non-transected tumor margin as clear margin. I'd hate for you to have to re-excise the site at a later time. Oh, and if you don't mind, please use a periareolar incision," she commented. "For cosmetic reasons, of course," she added.

"Okay, identify yourself," Dr. Bradbury teased. "You are obviously in the medical field."

"Yep! Dr. Caitlain Charland, anesthesiologist extraordinaire!" she bragged.

David Bradbury smiled. "Glad to meet you, Dr. Charland," he said as the first puff of smoke rose from Cat's breast.

"I'm driving in my car...I turn on the radio," Cat began to sing. "You move a little closer. I just say no. You say you don't like it. I know you're a liar. When we kiss...Ooooo, FIRE!" Cat giggled as another puff of smoke rose.

Now it was Dr. Bradbury's turn to laugh. "Do you serenade all your patients like that, Cat?" he asked.

"Are you kidding? I can't carry a tune in a bucket with a lid on it. Now Billie...*she* can sing!" Cat exclaimed.

"All right, like you so eloquently reminded me, I am using a non-transected tumor margin. There it is," he said as he lifted a mass from Cat's breast that was about the size of a small brussel sprout.

Cat looked at the slightly yellow, lumpy mass. "Hey, it looks like chicken fat!"

"I never thought of it that way, but you're right!" David replied as he once again grabbed the ultrasound wand. "Now, let's make sure we've caught the lump inside this thing before we close the incision." Dr. Bradbury ran the wand over the mass. "Ah, there it is. Good work!" he said to his team. "All right, Miss Cat, time to close." He placed several sutures inside the wound. "In addition to the 3.0 Vicryl sutures inside the incision, we'll close the skin with subcuticular 4.0 PDS sutures and reinforce it with steristrips. Sound okay to you?" he asked.

"Poifect" Cat replied in her best 'Three Stooges' voice. "Couldn't have done better myself," she added.

"There. We're finished. As you know, the internal sutures will dissolve with time. You'll need to see your regular doctor to have the external sutures removed in about ten days," Dr. Bradbury instructed. "Right now, we'll send this mass of 'chicken fat' to the lab for a frozen section analysis. Hopefully, we'll have results in a day or two," he explained. "Any questions?"

Cat suddenly grew serious. "Yeah, can you tell me I'll be around to see my nine-year-old give me grandchildren?" she asked.

David walked over to Cat and brushed back her bangs. "I wish I could, Cat, but we both know better. All we can do is hope for the best. My thoughts will be with you."

Cat forced a grin to her face while fighting back the moisture that was filling her eyes. "Thanks, Doc," she replied and she watched him leave the room.

***

"Here, let me fluff the pillow for you," Billie said. She rearranged the pillow beneath Cat's head for the hundredth time that afternoon.

"Sweetie, I'm fine, really I am," Cat complained. "Look, you've been pampering me to death since we walked in the door this afternoon."

"Cat, you just had surgery," Billie reasoned.

"I had a *minor* procedure, Billie," Cat replied.

Just then, the phone rang.

Billie answered the phone, then handed it to Cat. "It's your dad."

"Hi, Daddy," Cat said into the phone.

"Hey, there kitten. How are you feeling?"

"A little sore, but okay, except Billie is driving me crazy with her fidgeting," Cat replied.

"Well, that's to be expected, little one," Doc said. "So, did they say when they'd have the test results?"

"Just the usual 'in a day or two'," Cat commented dryly.

"Well, that is unacceptable. Why, they should be able to have results within an hour," Doc exclaimed. "That is totally unacceptable. We'll just see about that," he huffed. "I'll call you later, daughter. My love to you all," he added and then hung up on Cat.

Cat raised her eyebrows to the phone.

"What?" Billie asked.

Cat reached over and placed the phone on its cradle. "Me thinks heads are about to roll," she exclaimed.

***

At eight the next morning, the shrill of the phone rang through the Charland household. Cat, having not slept well the night before, was up and sitting at the kitchen table. She was still clad in her night shirt and panties as she read the paper. As it turned out, she was alone in the house. The kids had spent the previous night at Jen and Fred's to give her some peace and quiet while recuperating from her surgery.

Billie was out on her morning run with Jen—a daily tradition they resumed within a week of Jen losing the baby. They both found the exercise to be cleansing and energizing, and, it was valuable medicine in treating Jen's broken heart over losing her child.

"Hello?" Cat said into the phone.

"Good morning, Cat. This is Dr. O'Brien."

Cat's knees turned to jelly. "Patty!" she said brightly into the phone. She hoped her tone of voice masked her nervousness.

"Cat, I have your test results," the doctor said.

"So soon? I didn't expect results until Monday," Cat commented.

"Well, your father being the Chief of Surgery has its benefits," she chuckled. "I understand he walked into the

Breast Center yesterday afternoon and turned the place upside down," Patty explained.

Cat reached out to the wall for support as she prepared to ask her next question.

Before the question came, Billie sprinted through the kitchen door. "Yes! I beat Jen home again!" She grabbed a paper towel to wipe the sweat from her face, and then bent over at the waist to catch her breath.

Billie stopped short when she saw Cat on the phone.

"So what do the results indicate?" she asked. She extended her free hand to Billie, who took it instantly and held it close to her heart.

Cat closed her eyes tightly as she listened to Patty relay the test results. Her body trembled uncontrollably as tears coursed down her face.

"Okay, okay. Thank you, Patty. Yes, I will. Okay. Thank you again. Bye," she said, barely able to talk through her tears.

At this point, Billie was a nervous wreck. "What did she say?" Billie watched Cat's trembling hand reach forward to hang up the phone.

Cat turned to her slowly and looked into her eyes. She looked so vulnerable it tore Billie's heart out.

Billie held her by the shoulders, lowered her forehead to Cat's and repeated the question. "What did she say, sweetheart?"

Cat took a great gulping breath. "Benign. It's benign," she replied. The damn suddenly broke, freeing the river of fear it had been holding back.

Billie could hardly see Cat through her own veil of tears. "Benign? Thank, God!" She pulled Cat into her embrace.

The two women held each other in desperate relief, as they released the penned up emotions they had been restraining for the last two weeks. Both sobbed uncontrollably and were unaware of a presence in the doorway between the kitchen and living room.

"Mom? Mama?"

Billie released Cat and they both turned toward the sound of the voice. Tara stood in the doorway…an expression of extreme anxiety on her face.

"Mama?" Tara said again.

Cat opened her arms to her daughter. "It's okay, baby. It's okay. It's not cancer."

Tara ran into her mother's arm and clung desperately to her. "Thank, God," she cried. "Thank, God."

Billie rubbed Tara's back for several moments while Cat held her. "Thank you for being there for Mama, Tare…and forgive us for not trusting you from the beginning. We love you so much, sweetie."

A sniffle drew Billie's attention to the kitchen door. She turned to see Jen standing there with her arms wrapped around her middle and tears streaming down her face.

"Jen, how long have you been standing here?" Billie asked.

"Long enough to hear the good news," Jen struggled to say between sobs.

Billie went to her, knelt on the floor in front of her and placed a gentle kiss on Jen's abdomen and then wrapped her arms around Jen. "Thank you little one. Thank you for your sacrifice. We will always love you."

Cat and Tara added their arms to the group hug as the love and warmth they all felt for each other permeated the room and they clung to one another in a bittersweet celebration of life.

Life would never be the same in the Charland and Swenson households. They were truly changed by all that transpired that summer. Unspeakable sorrow and sacrifice, maturation and a blossoming of womanhood, and realization that when all is said and done, what really matters is love of life, love of family and love of friends. All in all, they knew beyond doubt that they were truly blessed.

They had pulled out of the tailspin and landed safely.

They had made it through the storm.

Photo Credit: Song of Myself Photography

See Karen's author page at

www.karendbadger.com

About the Author

Karen D. Badger is the author of *On A Wing And A Prayer, Yesterday Once More* (a 2009 Golden Crown Literary Award winner for Speculative Fiction), *In A Family Way, Unchained Memories, Happy Campers, Collective Identity, Sweet Angel, and Relative-ly Speaking and Tailspin* (Books I, II, III, IV, V, VI and VII of the Commitment Series), *The Blue Feather, All My Tomorrows* (sequel to the 2009 award winning *Yesterday Once More*), and *1140 Rue Royale* (a 2017 Golden Crown Literary Award winner for Paranormal Fiction). All of these works have been released by Badger Bliss Books, which Karen co-owns with her wife Barbara Sawyer (aka "Bliss').

Born and raised in Vermont, Karen is the second of five children raised by a fiercely independent mother, who remains one of her best friends. Karen earned her B.A. in 1978 in Theater and in Elementary Education, and in 1994, earned a B.S. in mathematics. In addition to her novels, Karen is the author of many technical papers on photomask manufacturing, which she has presented at numerous semiconductor industry conferences, and is the holder if fourteen technical patents. Karen is currently in her 40th year as a Principal Member of the Technical Staff with a prominent semiconductor manufacturer in Vermont.

Karen and her wife, Barb (a retired Lt. Col., US Air Force) live in the beautiful state of Vermont—home of Ben and Jerry's. They spend their spare time with family as well as doing home improvement projects on both their homes in Vermont and New Mexico. They also enjoy camping, kayaking, motorcycling and singing Karaoke.

Please take a moment to visit Karen's author website at www.karendbadger.com, or the Badger Bliss Books website at www.badgerblissbooks.com. Also like us on Facebook!

TITLES BY KAREN D. BADGER

www.badgerblissbooks.com

<u>On A Wing and A Prayer</u>
First edition published by Blue Feather Books, Sept, 2005
Second edition published by Badger Bliss Books, Sept, 2014
Third edition published by Badger Bliss Books, August, 2016
ISBN 13: 978-1-945761-01-0, ISBN 10: 1-945761-01-6

<u>Yesterday Once More</u>
First edition published by Blue Feather Books, July, 2008
Second edition published by Badger Bliss Books, Sept, 2014
Third edition published by Badger Bliss Books, August, 2016
ISBN 13: 978-1-945761-02-7, ISBN 10: 1-945761-02-4
2009 Golden Crown Literary Society Award - Speculative Fiction

<u>In A Family Way – Book One of the Commitment Series</u>
First edition published by Blue Feather Books, March, 2010
Second edition published by Badger Bliss Books, Sept, 2014
Third edition published by Badger Bliss Books, August, 2016
ISBN 13: 978-1-945761-05-8, ISBN 10: 1-945761-05-9

<u>Unchained Memories – Book Two of the Commitment Series</u>
First edition published by Blue Feather Books, Oct, 2011
Second edition published by Badger Bliss Books, Sept, 2014
Third edition published by Badger Bliss Books, August, 2016
ISBN 13: 978-1-945761-06-5, ISBN 10: 1-945761-06-7

<u>Happy Campers - Book Three of the Commitment Series</u>
First edition published by Blue Feather Books, Sept, 2013
Second edition published by Badger Bliss Books, Sept, 2014
Third edition published by Badger Bliss Books, August, 2016
ISBN 13: 978-1-945761-07-2, ISBN 10: 1-945761-07-5

The Blue Feather
First edition published by Blue Feather Books, July, 2014
Second edition published by Badger Bliss Books, Sept, 2014
Third edition published by Badger Bliss Books, August, 2016
ISBN 13: 978-1-945761-04-1, ISBN 10: 1-945761-04-0

Collective Identity – Book Four of the Commitment Series
First edition published by Badger Bliss Books, January, 2015
Second edition published by Badger Bliss Books, August, 2016
ISBN 13: 978-1-945761-08-9, ISBN 10: 1-945761-08-3

All My Tomorrows – Sequel to Yesterday Once More
First edition published by Badger Bliss Books, May, 2015
Second edition published by Badger Bliss Books, August, 2016
ISBN 13: 978-1-945761-03-4, ISBN 10: 1-945761-03-2

Sweet Angel – Book Five of the Commitment Series
First edition published by Badger Bliss Books, June, 2015
Second edition published by Badger Bliss Books, August, 2016
ISBN 13: 978-1-945761-09-6, ISBN 10: 1-945-761-09-1

Relative-ly Speaking – Book Six of the Commitment Series
First edition published by Badger Bliss Books, March, 2016
Second edition published by Badger Bliss Books, August, 2016
ISBN 13: 978-1-945761-10-2, ISBN 10: 1-945-761-10-5

1140 Rue Royale
First edition published by Badger Bliss Books, September, 2016
ISBN 13: 978-1-945761-00-3, ISBN 10: 1-945761-00-8
2017 Golden Crown Literary Society Award – Paranormal Fiction

Tailspin – Book Seven of the Commitment Series
First edition published by Badger Bliss Books, December, 2017
ISBN 13: 978-1-945761-22-5, ISBN 10: 1-945761-22-9

COMING SOON FROM KAREN D. BADGER
AND
BADGER BLISS BOOKS

www.badgerblissbooks.com

Flashpoint – Book Eight of the Commitment Series
Expected release: 2018

Life at the Chraland's has been a challenge. All that had transpired over the past year transformed them in unimaginable ways. Between unspeakable sorrow and sacrifice, the maturation and a blossoming of their older daughter into womanhood, their son testing the limits of peer pressure and their friend's heartbreaking situation, they were ready for life to be easy again.

The Charlands plan a family vacation in beautiful Yellowstone National Park, but soon realize they are getting more adventure than they planned as Mother Nature decides to join them on their trip. They battle the odds against them and risk everything as they face the challenge of staying together as a family while their world falls apart around them. There is much at stake in this suspenseful and dramatic turn of events. Read this exciting seventh book in the Billie/Cat Commitment Series to see if they survive what Mother Nature has in store for them.

Book Eight
of
The Commitment Series

A BADGER BLISS BOOK

By

Karen D. Badger

CHAPTER 1

"My God, you're going to kill me one day," Billie struggled to regain her breath.

"Whaddaya mean?" Cat rolled onto her back and stretched her arms high above her head.

"Just when I think you've outdone yourself, you hit me with something like *that* and totally blow me away."

"I don't know what you're talking about." Cat acted coy.

Billie rolled over and pinned Cat to the bed. "Don't give me that innocent act, Red. I haven't experienced a climax like that since...since..." Billie struggled to remember the last time they had enjoyed such uninhibited love making.

Cat tucked a stray lock of hair behind Billie's ear. "Since before the breast cancer scare?" she suggested.

Billie's eyes softened and she recalled the past couple of weeks of anxiety and strife. She nodded slightly and smiled. "Yeah, since then." Billie rolled onto her back and thought for the billionth time about how lucky they were that the lump was benign.

During those tense two weeks, Billie spent countless agonizing hours fretting over what life would be like without Cat. Sure, she would go on. After all, the kids needed her, but without her soul...without her heart...without Cat's presence in her life, it would barely be worth the effort. Luckily the lump was not cancerous. She sighed deeply and thanked the heavens above once more for smiling down upon them and for giving them more time to live...and to love.

Cat watched a faraway expression cross Billie's face. She was convinced Billie was recalling the past two tumultuous weeks of waiting, wondering and agonizing as they lived through a crisis that could have changed their lives forever. For the first time, Cat noticed the worry lines around Billie's eyes. She leaned in to kiss them away and felt Billie's eye lashes flutter against her cheek as her lips made delicate contact.

"Hmmmm. That feels good," Billie murmured.

"I'm sorry," Cat whispered softly.

Billie's head snapped up. "For what?" she asked.

"For taking you to hell and back," Cat replied.

Billie rolled onto her side and ran the back of her fingers across Cat's cheek. "Kitten, that wasn't your fault. You have nothing to apologize for."

"I know, but still, it was a nightmare neither of us needed."

"Agreed. But it's over, and with a little luck, we'll never have to live through that again. One thing the experience taught me was to enjoy every moment we have together and not to fret about the future. Cat, we made it through...and we came out stronger in the end. Together we are invincible. Our love makes that possible. Promise me you'll let it go," Billie demanded passionately.

Cat closed her eyes and allowed a lone tear to escape and she silently nodded her promise. When she opened them again, her heart nearly stopped at the love she saw overflowing from cerulean eyes. A smile immediately graced her own china-doll features.

"There! That's my girl!" Billie said happily as the smile crossed Cat's face. "So, what would you like to do today?" she asked.

Cat's brow creased as she considered the possibilities. Suddenly a thought came to her. "I know! Let's plan a vacation."

Billie was a bit taken back by the suggestion. "A vacation?" she asked. "What did you have in mind?"

The excitement began to grow in Cat's chest as an idea took shape. She sat up and crossed her legs in front of her. "I'm not totally sure yet. Something fun. After all, we have my test results to celebrate. Let's do something that will make us appreciate life. Maybe something with a nature theme," she suggested.

Billie immediately scrambled off the bed and stood with her feet apart and hands on her hips. "No way am I doing the camping thing, Cat. Happy Trail Campgrounds is still pretty fresh in my mind. I will not live that nightmare again!"

Cat threw her head back and laughed.

"I fail to see what is so funny," Billie stated indignantly.

"You are just so damned cute!" Cat replied.

"Cute? Cute?" Billie exclaimed. "I wasn't so cute at Happy Trails when I was covered with poison ivy and mosquito bites! That camping trip with Jen, Fred and their kids was a total disaster."

"Billie, it won't be like that," Cat defended.

"You're damned right it won't, because I'm not going!" Billie paced back and forth across the room.

Cat tried hard not to smile. "Not even if we rent a fully furnished cabin?"

Billie stopped pacing. "Cabin?" she asked. "A cabin is good."

"Fully furnished cabin with running water, cooking facilities, a bathroom. You know... rain-proof, bear-proof and disaster-proof." Cat tried hard to entice Billie with the comforts they would enjoy.

"Disaster proof?" Billie's eyebrows were perched high on her forehead.

"Disaster proof. I guarantee it! So, how about it?" Cat asked.

"I'm listening." Billie sat on the edge of the bed to wait for the details. She looked at the blank expression on Cat's face for a moment or two before she became impatient. "Well?" she asked.

"Well what?" Cat replied.

"Details?" Billie waved her hands in front of her impatiently.

"I don't know. The thought just came to me a moment ago. I don't have it all planned out yet. We need to do research on-line before we settle on a destination."

"Okay." Billie rose to her feet once more and collected the clothes she had discarded around the room at the start of their lovemaking session earlier that morning. "I'll go power up the computer." She pulled a T-shirt over her head and headed for the bedroom door, only to stop in the doorway. "Oh, what time did Jen say she'd send the girls home?" she asked.

Cat looked at the clock on the bedside table. "Jen said yesterday that she was planning to take them to a movie and then out for ice cream this afternoon before she dropped them off at the mall, so it will be a few hours yet. Why?" she retorted with a question of her own.

"I want to get the kids' input on our trip. We'll talk to them about it when they come home from Doc and Ida's this afternoon," Billie replied and then disappeared through the doorway.

Cat grinned from ear to ear and leisurely climbed off the bed to collect her clothes. She wondered how Billie could go from stubborn and defensive one moment to excited and cooperative the next. "Don't ever change, Billie-girl. I love you just the way you are," she mumbled under her breath as she followed in the wake of her excited wife.

***

Billie made her way to the guestroom situated off the main living area which doubled as an office. She sat in front of the computer, pressed the power button and waited for the desktop unit to come alive. A few moments later, logged onto the Internet and opened her favorite search engine. "Okay," she said to herself. "What should I search for? Campgrounds? National parks? Cabins?"

She settled 'national parks and pressed the enter button. Within seconds, she was presented with a long list of websites.

"Damn! It'll take me all day to go through these," she mused out loud. "Maybe Cat can help me narrow down the search."

Billie made her way to the kitchen where cat stood at the counter with her back to her. Cat was obviously crying as she reached up to wipe her eyes. Billie stopped short at the sight, and gut-wrenching anxiety immediately gripped her stomach.

She approached Cat and placed her hands on Cat's shoulders. "Cat! Cat, honey, what's wrong?"

Cat turned around and sniffed loudly. "Onions!" she exclaimed. "I decided to start a spaghetti sauce for dinner. It will need to simmer for a few hours."

Billie raised one eyebrow to Cat. "Onions?"

Cat sniffed again. "Yeah. Wanna help?"

"You actually want *me* to help you cook?" Billie asked in disbelief.

Cat slapped her own forehead with the heel of her palm. "Jesus! What was I thinking?" she exclaimed in exaggeration. "You're right. We want this to be edible."

"Hey! Do you have to be so brutally honest? Can't you just humor me for once?" Billie asked.

Cat smiled and gently patted Billie on the face with an open palm. "Dear heart," she began, "Have you ever had food poisoning? Trust me, it's not fun. No, I think I've got this one covered."

"Good, because I'm actually in the middle of an Internet search for campgrounds and I need some advice," Billie explained.

Cat turned back to her cutting board and reached for a large clove of garlic. "Okay, shoot. What can I help you with?" She started to peel the skin from the fragrant clove.

Billie reached for the wooden spoon on the stove next to the frying pan where Cat had begun to brown the ground beef and onions, and absently stirred the mixture as she explained her dilemma to Cat. "Well, I entered national parks into the search engine and over 25,000 websites were returned. I need to narrow down the search. Got any suggestions?"

"Why did you choose national parks?" Cat asked as she chopped the garlic.

"I don't know. I guess it sounded like a good place to start. National parks are usually well maintained, and there are some really great parks to choose from...Acadia, Yosemite, the Grand Canyon, among others. I thought it might be good for the kids to see some of the national landmarks."

Cat scraped a large pile of chopped garlic into the pan and watched as Billie diligently stirred the small white slivers into the meat. "Sounds good to me," Cat commented. "Why don't you do a search within results using the word 'landmarks'?" she suggested.

Billie spooned a scoop of meat mixture into her mouth.

"You're gonna eat it all before I add the sauce if you keep that up," Cat exclaimed.

"I can't help it! It tastes so good!" Billie put the spoon down on the stove next to the pan. "So, narrow the search using 'landmarks', huh? Sounds good. Thanks." She stepped closer and placed a delicate kiss on Cat's mouth. "Hmm...I don't know what tastes better, you or the meat mixture." Billie scooted away just in time to avoid the rolled up towel that Cat snapped in the direction of her rear end.

"Gee thanks. It's not every day someone tells me I taste like ground meat," Cat exclaimed.

Billie ran from the kitchen before Cat could snap her with the towel a second time and returned to the office to continue her search. She typed in 'landmarks' and was able to narrow the field from more than 25,000 to just under 3,000 national parks.

"Ugh! Well, I guess I've got my work cut out for me," she murmured; still dismayed at the thousands of sites presented to her.

Billie sat back in her seat and stared at the screen for a few moments and then decided to make a list of all the amenities she thought would make their vacation comfortable. After a half hour, her list included the words landmarks, cabin, electricity, plumbing, swimming, hiking, horseback riding, kayaking, fishing, biking, and of course, for Cat's sake, shopping.

"Yes!" Billie shouted as the resulting search yielded just over two hundred sites. "*That* I can manage!"

Two hours later, Billie sat back and looked at the list of notes on the legal pad before her. A satisfied grin crossed her face. "Not bad, if I say so myself," she mused. Billie rolled her head around and then clasped her hands together and reached high above her head to stretch the stiffness from her shoulders. She closed her eyes and enjoyed the sense of relief that flooded her upper body. Seconds later, her eyes snapped open and her mind registered the enticing aroma wafting from the kitchen. "Damn, that smells good." Billie followed her nose straight to the pan of spaghetti sauce simmering on the stove. She lifted the cover and inhaled deeply, then lowered the spoon into the rich carmine sauce. A look of pure bliss graced her features as she brought the treasure to her lips.

"Caught you red handed!"

Billie jumped and dropped the spoon into the sauce. The cover of the sauce pan, which she still held hovering over the pan, fell to the floor with a loud clang. She turned to see Cat in the doorway to the basement.

"For crying out loud, Cat! You scared the shit out of me," Billie reached for a paper towel to clean the sauce from the floor that had from the inside of the lid.

Cat stood there with one hand over her mouth to hide a grin. "Serves you right," she said. "If you had your way, the sauce would be gone before dinner time."

Billie discarded the soiled paper towel and then looked at Cat with an exaggerated pout on her face.

Cat narrowed her eyes at Billie. "Don't you dare use that pout with me, Billie Jean Charland!"

Billie continued to pout and added puppy dog eyes to the fray.

Cat spared one glance at the pitiful look on Billie's face and then raised her arms into the air. "Okay. You win. Help yourself." she said.

Billie grinned broadly and then retrieved the spoon that had fallen into the pan. Within seconds, she stood there with a nearly-orgasmic look on her face as she savored tangy red sauce. "Damn, Cat. You're a good cook."

Cat wrapped her arms around Billie's waist. "That response is worth allowing you to cheat," she said. She planted a kiss in the 'vee' above Billie's breasts and then laid her head in the spot vacated by her lips.

Billie wrapped her arms around Cat's and held her in a firm hug for several moments before she remembered the progress she had made on her search. She took Cat's hand. "Come see what I've come up with for possible vacation destinations." She led Cat to the guestroom and gestured for her to sit on the bed while she retrieved her notes.

Instead of sitting, Cat climbed onto the bed and laid down with her head on one of the pillows. She pat the bed beside her when Billie returned with her notes. Billie lay down beside her and held the notepad above them.

"So, I've narrowed down the possible destinations to Acadia National Park in Maine, Yellowstone National Park in Wyoming, Redwood National Forest in California, Yosemite National Park in California and the Grand Canyon in Colorado," Billie began.

"That's a pretty diverse list. What made you choose those locations?" Cat asked.

"I was looking for places where there was enough to do to keep everyone busy. You know, hiking, kayaking, horseback riding, fishing, biking," Billie replied.

"And shopping!" Cat quickly added.

"And shopping," Billie confirmed. "In fact, one of the major attractions of Acadia in Maine was the Antique shops all along the east coast, oh, and the lighthouses. Apparently, there are dozens of them along the coast of Maine," she added.

Cat perused the list again. "So have you settled on any one of them?"

Billie laid the list of notes on her stomach and looked at Cat. "For starters, this needs to be a family decision. I have my preference, but I want to get everyone's input before we settle on one. I'm also open to other destinations that aren't on the list. Any thoughts?" she asked.

"Before I put my two-cents in, I'd like to see more information on each of these parks," Cat replied.

"Fair enough," Billie said. "I'll print out a package on each, then we can review it with the kids during dinner."

"Sounds like a plan." Cat rolled to her side to face Billie. She traced the side of Billie's face with her index finger and smiled broadly into her face.

"What's that smile for?" Billie asked.

"You're such a nerd," Cat commented teasingly.

Billie's eyebrows shot into her hairline. "Nerd?"

"Yes. I mean, look at your notes—so complete and orderly."

Billie looked at her notes and realized Cat was right. She grinned sheepishly. "Okay, I admit it. I'm a nerd. Got a problem with that?"

"Not at all. Nerds are good. Especially sexy nerds," Cat placed a kiss on the end of Billie's nose.

Billie rolled over to lie partially on top of Cat. "Sexy, huh?" She lowered her lips to Cat's mouth.

"Hello there!" A loud voice came from the kitchen.

Billie's head snapped up and she strained to look over her shoulder. "Great! That woman has remarkable timing."

Cat chuckled.

Billie rolled off her wife, and sat on the edge of the bed. "In the guest room, Jen!" she called loudly.

Seconds later, a curly blonde head appeared around the edge of the doorway. "Why is it every time I come over here, you two are in a bedroom?" Jen asked.

"Whatever do you mean?" Cat asked innocently.

"What do I mean?" Jen stepped fully into the room. "What do I mean? Does this sound familiar? 'Oh, my God, Cat. Harder! Harder!' 'Billie! Billie! Baby, more, please!'" Jen said in a loud and orgasmic voice as she ran her own hands up and down her body to exaggerate her point.

Billie and Cat's eyes met, each one's face beet red with embarrassment.

"Ah, I hope you're making that up, Jen," Billie said while avoiding Jen's gaze.

"Nope! On the way to the movies, I stopped in to see if you wanted to go with us, and when I came into the house, the two of you where nowhere in sight. I walked through the kitchen and living room looking for you, and by the time I reached the stairs to the second story, the sound of your little play time hit me square in the face. Thank God the kids waited in the car! Geesh! Is that ALL you two do when the kids aren't home?" she asked, teasingly.

Billie and Cat's discomfort increased tenfold when they realized their friend really did eavesdrop on their lovemaking earlier in the day.

Cat scurried off the bed and stood her ground in front of their friend. "You're just jealous," she said in their defense.

Jen threw her hands into the air. "You're damned right I am! How do you two do it? Tell me your secret! Please! I'll pay anything!" Jen fell to her knees and clasped her hands in front of her as though in prayer.

"Our secret? That's easy," Billie said. "Cat is a nymphomaniac."

Billie's comment drew a wide-eyed, shocked expression from Cat.

"Nymphomaniac?" repeated Jen. Disbelief tinged her voice.

Cat looked at Billie with a clearly mischievous expression on her face. "Oh yeah," Cat admitted. "I'm a big-time nympho. Gotta have it at least four or five times a day. Luckily, Billie is up for the challenge."

Jen looked back and forth between her friends. "So, is it contagious?" she asked hopefully.

"Unfortunately, no. You are born with it," Cat replied.

"Drats!" Jen exclaimed before another thought came to her. "Can it be learned?" she asked.

"That depends on who the student is—you or Fred," Cat answered.

"Fred. Definitely Fred," Jen quipped. "I have no problems in that arena. After all I'm approaching forty, and you know what they say about a woman's sex drive at forty. Fred, on the other hand, like most men, he reached his sexual peak in his twenties!" she explained.

Billie draped her arm around Jen's shoulders and led her toward the kitchen while Cat followed close behind. "Jen, my friend, you don't need nympho lessons...you need a woman," she said.

"Got anyone in mind?" Jen asked jokingly.

"Billie!" Cat scolded her wife for what seemed like the hundredth time for urging their *heterosexual* best friend into a lifestyle that didn't suit her.

"What's wrong with that suggestion? Think about it; two women approaching forty at the same time. Can't get any better than that." Billie cast a meaningful look at Cat and grinned as she watched a red hue rise to Cat's face.

"Sounds tempting," Jen said, "But to tell you the truth, Fred's kind of grown on me over the years, and as goofy and bumbling as he can be, I love him dearly."

"Yeah. He's a good guy. He's kind of grown on us too. We love him early," Cat added.

"He sure is fun to be with. Speaking of which, we are planning another camping vacation. Wanna come?" Billie pulled three mugs from the cupboard and filled the coffee machine with water while Cat stirred the spaghetti sauce. Jen made a move like she was going to sit at the table but at the last moment, followed Cat to the stove.

"Camping? I'm surprised you agreed to go, Billie. Especially after that disastrous trip to Happy Trails a few years back," Jen commented. She helped herself to a spoonful of Cat's spaghetti sauce. "Ummm, this is good, Cat," she added as an aside.

"Oh, I can assure you if there was any chance at all it would be like Happy Trails, I wouldn't be going. Cat promised me it would be disaster proof," Billie explained. "And by the way, why did you automatically assume Cat made the spaghetti sauce?"

Jen looked at Billie; a shocked expression on her face. "Yeah, right!" Jen sampled one more taste of the sauce. "Like I said, great sauce, Cat." She changed the subject back to the camping trip. "Disaster proof, huh? How so?"

Cat leaned her backside against the countertop and watched the interaction between her wife and friend.

Billie popped the first pod into the coffee machine and pressed 'brew' before answering her friend. "Picture this," she said, and made a picture frame with her hands. "Cabin, plumbing, electricity, rain-proof, bear-proof, swimming, hiking, kayaking, horseback riding..."

"Whoa, stop right there. Horseback riding? Count me out!" Jen exclaimed. "My ass *still* hurts from that god-awful ride I took at Happy Trails."

"Horseback riding is optional, my friend," Cat piped in. "We'd really like all of you to join us if you can."

"When are you planning this trip?" Jen asked.

"Billie starts a new case this week that should wrap up in early August. So we'd like to take the trip a week or two before school starts again," Cat replied.

Jen considered the timetable for the trip and then cursed. "Damn!"

"What is it?" Billie asked; a bit startled by the outburst.

"Well, you know I start my new teaching position when the school year begins, right?" Jen asked. "Unfortunately, I'm taking my final class this summer to be certified and it literally ends just days before school begins. Darn! I really would have loved to go, but I'm afraid we'll have to pass this time," she explained.

Cat hugged her friend. "That's all right. There'll be plenty of chances to vacation together during school breaks...or maybe next summer."

"Damn!" Jen said again. "I'm really sorry."

Billie placed three full cups of coffee on the table and retrieved the cheese cake and creamer from the refrigerator while Cat pulled plates and forks from the cupboard.

"No problem, Jen," Billie said. "Like Cat said, there'll be plenty of opportunities to vacation together later."

"So where are you going?" Jen asked as she accepted a plate of cheese cake from Cat, "Thanks, Cat."

"We're looking at several places..." Billie began as the ladies enjoyed the next two hours of dessert and lively conversation.

www.ingramcontent.com/pod-product-compliance
Lightning Source LLC
Chambersburg PA
CBHW070859250626
47159CB00003B/1128

* 9 7 8 1 9 4 5 7 6 1 2 2 5 *